T0110883

DANGER IN THE LAND OF GRANDEUR

BOOK I

ARLENE COTTERELL

authorHOUSE®

AuthorHouse™
1663 Liberty Drive
Bloomington, IN 47403
www.authorhouse.com
Phone: 833-262-8899

Published by AuthorHouse 10/06/2020

ISBN: 978-1-6655-0335-8 (sc)
ISBN: 978-1-6655-0334-1 (e)

Library of Congress Control Number: 2020919638

Print information available on the last page.

To my father, Christopher Scott Elrod, who recently passed (May 21, 1955–February 6, 2020)
I love you, Dad.

Your daughter,
Arlene Cotterell

PROLOGUE

The Land of Grandeur was like a second garden of Eden. It was cool and comfortably damp due to being underground. It was discovered by a child called Lloyd, who was the young son of a couple of scientists. The temperature was a steady seventy degrees and never changed. Light was provided compliments of the many lightning bugs that were there, so it was always daylight. There was a society of individuals called pale ones. They were originally descended from the few humans who had survived the worldwide nuclear war with their health intact because they had retreated to their safe houses in time. Those who were diseased by the radiation were called the walking dead. Two human scientists, Darren and Deanna, developed a vaccine to be injected into the thumbs of humans and the walking dead that would give them the ability to live for approximately two hundred years and to withstand the elevated levels of radiation on the earth's surface. Upon their passing, other scientists duplicated the formula to make enough of the vaccine for all surviving humans and the walking dead who were left, a few at a time.

The vaccine caused severe discomfort that quickly wore off during the rapid change, but in the end, it offered a new, productive life. Treated individuals turned a pale blue and developed telepathy and superspeed.

The commune they created was beautiful and surrounded by a great wall to keep the various wild animals out. Its structure resembled that of the lost city of Atlantis. The forest around them had every animal imaginable, including magical creatures, such as unicorns and Pegasus. There was even a beautiful lake with a great waterfall outside the commune that lay parallel to the forest's edge. There were mini-angels. They were like the pale ones' guardians. There was one mini-angel for each pale one. They visited their individual charges at the midnight hour nightly. The society could have been high-tech, but that was what got the humans in trouble, so the pale ones decided to keep their society simple. At that point, they were overseen by a king and queen, known as Andrew and Camillia. An older pale one had ruled from the time the society came alive until he decided to retire. Then he passed the responsibility down to his adopted children Camillia and Andrew.

The current king and queen had a daughter and son-in-law who would be taking over reign of the commune after finishing their lessons on the foundation of the commune and memorizing the community constitution. The daughter and son-in-law, Armellya and Jaden, had just had a daughter, who was to be called Jadellya. She would be queen of the mini-angels upon the age of accountability. Jadellya, like her parents and grandparents, had more abilities than regular pale ones, such as moving objects and warming or cooling things with her mind, flying, levitating, and entering others' dreams. It was prophesized that Armellya and Jaden would conceive a son, who would be of a demonic seed. Armellya and Jaden also knew their daughter, Jadellya, was an angelic child and would stand against her evil brother to save many innocent lives, starting with her mother and then herself. As it has been said before, without bad, good could not be recognized and appreciated. So the story of the Dinosaur Tail continues—not from Camillia's perspective but from that of her daughter, Armellya.

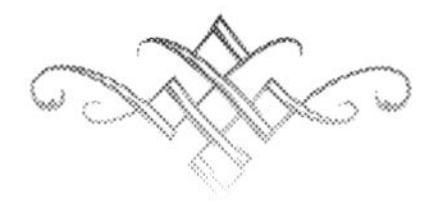

CHAPTER 1

ARMELLYA AND JADEN HAD JUST AWAKENED TWO hours earlier than the rest of the castle's occupants except for Andrew and Camillia. The four of them had scheduled a private two-hour meeting in the castle's family room before the rest woke up. The meeting was to be held every morning until the lessons were completed and Armellya and Jaden had memorized the community constitution. This morning's meeting was more of a discussion of the possibility of Jaden not being able to address the public at any given time with everything else he had going on. Additional lessons would also be held in the room of relaxation during the evening hours before dinner if the four of them had free time and it seemed that it would be necessary on the day.

Being head of the community was more than a full-time job because the king and queen had to be accessible for the land's individuals around the clock. With Jaden being a medical doctor during the day and an on-call veterinarian in the evening, along with being the head of the two medicine-making rooms at the hospital, he would have little time for himself and Armellya and much less time to being a king. That would essentially leave Armellya to stand as the sole ruler of the Land of Grandeur. It would not be impossible for Armellya to be the primary ruler; the chief was able to do it with ease. Jaden did not want to give up his medical license or his veterinary license, nor did he have any intention of doing so. Armellya and Jaden had already discussed the situation, and not having any choice in the matter, Armellya would do her best to continue the improvements to the commune without relying on technology, just as her parents and the chief had done.

Andrew, Camillia, Armellya, and Jaden could hear the kitchen staff walking the castle's hallways on their way to the kitchen, so they knew it was time to end the encounter for the time being. Because there was no time after the discussion to continue learning the law of the land, Andrew and Camillia advised Armellya and Jaden to plan for an evening of instruction, so they did. They stayed in the castle's family room and carried a light conversation about the joy of Jaden and Armellya making Andrew and Camillia grandparents with the birth of Jadellya while they waited for the rest of the family to get to the castle's family room. Little by little, family members started to trickle into the family room. Twenty minutes after the first family member arrived, the last one entered. With everyone present, Andrew led the way to the castle's private dining hall. They all found their places at the big round table and sat down. Melanie had the kitchen staff bring out breakfast.

Everyone ate in a leisurely way and shared what their day held in store for them before the lunch hour. Andrew had to go to the multiuse hall to see how the staff were getting along with the production of the gardening tools. Jaden had to go to the hospital to pull his eight-hour shift and oversee the medical and veterinary medicine-making rooms. Camillia and Armellya were going to go to the chief's private garden to practice flying, but they could not disclose that to most of the family members so they said they were going there to stroll. Bridgette needed to go to the room of relaxation to make the week's invitations for girls' day and get them disbursed so the women could reserve their spots. Melanie was going to supervise the kitchen staff with their duties and plan lunch. Everyone finished eating about the time they had all shared their plans for the first half of their day. Everyone wished one another a good day and then got up from the big round table and left the private dining hall in an organized fashion.

Camillia and Armellya got to the chief's private garden and dismissed the work crew. The women had levitation under control, so they worked on flying from a levitated position. Flying was not too difficult for them; it was the landing they really needed to get under control.

While Camillia and Armellya worked on their flying skills, Jaden was checking up on the two medicine-making rooms. Jaden checked for what they were making, how much of each drug they made, what chemicals were there, how much of each chemical was there, and the condition of the room. Jaden gave the medicine-making room a good report, and then he went to the veterinary medicine-making room. He did the same thing in this room that he had done in the medical medicine-making room and gave it a good report also.

As head of security, Matthew made his rounds inside

and outside of the castle to check on all the guards and ensure everything was going well, and so far, it was. One of the outside guards told Andrew the only action he saw was Lynndia's nanny taking her for an outing in her baby buggy around the castle's property.

Back inside the castle, Bridgette had completed the reservation cards for girls' day for that week and sent them to the distribution hall with one of the castle's runners. As planned, Andrew made it to the multiuse hall to check on how the workers were getting along with their many sets of gardening tools. The multiuse hall had completed fifty sets of gardening tools and had one hundred more to go. While Andrew was out in the community, the chief was spending the first part of his day inside the castle with relaxing activities. He spent the second part of his day setting his side of the castle up for a special pet; he wanted to raise a wolf pup.

Finally, there was Michelle, the head maid. Michelle was overseeing the many maids in the castle to ensure cleanliness.

Andrew was finished checking on the status of the gardening equipment and on his way back to his side of the castle to prepare for the lunch hour and family time. Matthew had made a full round of checks with all security inside and outside of the castle, so he was heading into the castle for one last round with the inside guards. Jaden was on his way to the castle from finishing his eight-hour hospital duties for the day so he could participate in the lunch hour and family time. Camillia and Armellya were heading to their side of the castle from the chief's private garden to meet the family. Since Bridgette had already finished with the girls' day cards, she finally left the room of relaxation to go to the castle's family room. Michelle let her workers go for the lunch hour so she also could head to the family room. After completing his tasks, the chief began to travel from his side of the castle to Andrew and Camillia's side of the castle. The last family member, Michelle, was getting the kitchen staff ready to serve everyone; then she would join the family for the lunch hour and family time.

Andrew finally made it to the castle and headed for the family room to greet family members as they arrived. He was the first to arrive. It only took fifteen minutes from the time Andrew got into the family room to when the last family member showed up for the lunch hour and family time. With everyone present, as usual, Andrew led them all to the castle's private dining hall where they all found their seats at the big round table. Melanie had the kitchen staff bring out lunch and serve everyone; then she sat down at the big round table. The lunch hour and family time had begun. They all took their turns sharing their day while they savored their lunch. From what everyone had said, they had all had a wonderful day and finished the demanding things on their list of things to do. The rest of the day up to the dinner hour, they all seemed to have tiny things to address so the day would likely end well.

When everyone was finished eating, the lunch hour was over, but there were a few individuals who had not gotten their chance to share their day so they remained in their seats until family time was over. The last few individuals shared their days, and it was time for them to go their separate ways to finish out the day before the dinner hour, so they fashionably dispersed.

Andrew and Camillia caught Armellya and Jaden before they could leave the castle's private dining hall to let them know they were requesting their presence in the room of relaxation for another lesson on ruling the commune and memorizing the community constitution. Before starting the lesson, Armellya and Jaden told Andrew and Camillia they had the community constitution memorized, so Andrew had them both recite it separately as he read along. After the recitals, Andrew confirmed to Camillia that Armellya and Jaden had the community constitution correctly word for word. Now that the young couple had the community constitution memorized, the majority of the lesson was completed. The final lesson was to understand the foundation on which the community was built and how to uphold those values. Half of the final lesson was detailed discussion, and the remaining half would be observation of the current king and queen, Andrew and Camillia. Andrew, Camillia, Armellya, and Jaden discussed the foundation that the community was built on, and the young couple fully understood what was being conveyed to them. Andrew and Camillia had asked Armellya and Jaden many questions. Their answers would show their level of understanding of the community's foundation, and it appeared they had a perfect understanding. At that point, there was nothing left to verbally teach. It was time to imprint their understanding through the observation of duties as they came. Andrew and Camillia had planned to test the couple when situations arose by getting their opinion on how to address the issue and then handling the event themselves and telling Armellya and Jaden what kind of result their solution had. Andrew and Camillia projected that Armellya and Jaden's responses would be much like their own, if not exactly the same.

During the teaching, Andrew, Camillia, Armellya, and Jaden were so enthralled in the lesson that it was near the dinner hour and the four of them had no clue. All the others had wound down their days and gone to the castle's family room. They were surprised that Andrew was not there already. Everyone waited for the four of them for fifteen minutes, and when they failed to show, the chief went looking for them. The chief knew Andrew and Camillia were grooming Armellya and Jaden to be the next king and queen, so the first place he looked for them was in the room of relaxation. When the chief knocked on the door, Andrew answered it. The chief told Andrew it was the dinner hour and everyone had been waiting for him. Andrew told Camillia, Armellya, and Jaden they were late for the dinner hour, so they followed the chief back to the castle's family room. When they got there, Andrew apologized for being late. Then he led the family to the castle's private dining hall.

Once in the castle's private dining hall, they all found their seats at the big round table. Melanie had the kitchen staff put the different meal components on the table, and they served themselves in an organized fashion. The family engaged in light conversation while they ate their dinner. In the middle of dinner, the butler retreated from the front door to the castle's private dining hall in search of Jaden. The butler told Jaden there was a veterinary emergency and the runner was at the front door. Jaden politely excused himself from the big round table, gave Armellya a kiss, and then rushed to the front door. The runner took Jaden practically across the commune to care for a sick and injured horse. The dinner hour ended before Jaden returned, so Armellya went to their home to wait for him.

The others all went to their quarters as well so they could wind down before going to bed. Armellya tried to stay awake for Jaden's return, but it was late and she was tired, so she lay down on her bed. Just like the rest of the individuals in the castle, Armellya fell asleep. She slept for an hour when suddenly she felt something touch her. She thought it was Jaden. When Armellya opened her eyes, she saw it was not Jaden but a large black angelic figure hovering above her. Armellya tried to move out of the way of the figure, but she could not. It was like there was a perfectly fitting invisible mold over her body holding her down. She wanted to scream for help, but her voice seemed to be muted as well. Armellya had never seen or heard of such a creature as that, and it filled her with fear. The dark figure went from hovering above her to lying upon her. She felt a strange yet familiar sensation flow through her body. It reminded her of when she had conceived Jadellya. Conceiving Jadellya had left a peaceful feeling. This sensation had a violent feel to it. After several minutes of the dark shadow lying upon her, it levitated above her once again. After another several minutes, Armellya realized she could move slightly so she struggled to get up from her bed. Suddenly, the mold was lifted, her voice returned, and the dark figure left in a puff of smoke. Armellya was so alarmed by what had happened that she felt she needed to see her mini-angel immediately.

Armellya got as comfortable as possible on her bed and then astroprojected to the Dinosaur Tail. Now at the Dinosaur Tail in spirit, Armellya found her mini-angel, and the mini-angel detected Armellya's panic. Armellya told her mini-angel what had happened with the dark figure and how it had lain upon her. The mini-angel became fearful for Armellya, and she picked up on that. The mini-angel explained to Armellya that she had encountered the fallen angel, and he was the source of evil. He was essentially powerless, but he created children with powerful mothers to wreak havoc on society. Armellya disclosed in detail the sensation that had come over her and how it was like the conception of Jadellya yet a bit different. The mini-angel told Armellya she had conceived a son from the seed of a demon, and he would grow to be evil. The mini-angel warned Armellya that the child would become more dangerous as he grew. Armellya, Jaden, and the mini-angels had foreseen the birth of a son to Armellya and Jaden who would be a serial killer by the age of accountability, and this was the pregnancy to deliver that child. Armellya was speechless and more frightened than she had ever been. She thanked her mini-angel for disclosing so much information and then left the Dinosaur Tail to go back into her body.

By the time Armellya got back to her body, Jaden was home. Because Jaden could tell Armellya had astroprojected somewhere, he did not disturb her body. Now that she was back in her body, he greeted her and tried to give her a kiss, but she jerked her body to move away. Armellya had never been distant and unaffectionate before, so Jaden asked her what was wrong. She started to sob as she tried to tell him what had happened with the fallen angel. Jaden felt Armellya's anguish, so he told her to slowly tell him all about what had her so disturbed and he would try to fix the problem. Armellya told Jaden about how the fallen angel had appeared, woke her with a touch, and then hovered over her. Jaden told Armellya that it sounded scary and then asked what happened next. Armellya told Jaden that the fallen angel had lain with her, and she had tried to fight it but was unable to move or yell for help at all. She said she was finally able to move after the dark figure hovered over her for a few seconds after lying with her.

Jaden asked Armellya if she knew the purpose of the passive assault. Then she said yes and turned her back to him. She told him she had conceived their evil son. Jaden asked if she was sure, and she told him she had already consulted with her mini-angel. Jaden asked what the mini-angel had to say about the situation, so Armellya told him what she had said. Jaden reminded Armellya that the event had been foreseen so they would get through it the best they could and hope to foresee something that would help. Armellya turned back toward Jaden then and apologized for not being able to fight for her innocence. Jaden told her that he still loved her just the same. Then he asked her for a hug, and she said she was not the same individual she used to be so she could not be close to him for his protection. Jaden asked why she felt that way. Armellya told Jaden she had been raped by a demonic force and conceived an evil and dangerous child. She was no longer pure and innocent. Jaden grabbed Armellya by the upper arms and firmly told her she was still his wife and he was still gladly responsible for her. Jaden told Armellya he loved her and always would, no matter what happened to her or around her, because she was his life. Armellya responded that she loved him dearly and he was her life also, but at the same time, she had to protect him where she could when danger presented itself. Jaden told Armellya to let him worry about himself and for her to turn to him with her concerns. She said she would.

The two hugged and kissed passionately. Then Jaden said they would do their best to save their child from himself. It was past the time for them to go to bed for the night, so the couple changed from their day clothes into their bedclothes and then got into their bed for the night. Armellya and Jaden held each other in their arms and fell asleep that way. When the midnight hour came, two mini-angels arrived; one was Armellya's angel and the other Jaden's angel. Usually, when a pale one was pregnant, the child's mini-angel visited also, but this child did not have one. Armellya asked her mini-angel why the boy child had no mini-angel, and the mini-angel told her the entity that sired the child prohibited that and they could not break through the bond between the child and its father. The mini-angel went on to tell Armellya that the child would have no maternal bond with her, but she would still have the strong telepathic link with him. Jaden asked his mini-angel if there had been other cases of women delivering soulless children, and she told Jaden not within the pale ones' existence, but many humans had succumbed to that fate. Armellya asked the mini-angels what happened to those children after their birth. They told Armellya that those children grew to be well known throughout history to be influential and dangerous, for instance, the leader of a country that participated in the mass murders of certain races. Armellya and Jaden said they remembered encountering many historical events in history books when they went to Dobbins Memorial as humans. Armellya commented that those individuals had reigned over many people for a time before their demise and took many lives before then.

Armellya's mini-angel told her and Jaden that the Dinosaur Tail already knew what would happen to the child she carried as well as what he was capable of and because of some weaknesses, he could be easily stopped by the right individual. Armellya's mini-angel told her and Jaden she could not say much about the future that far in advance but not to worry about the damage he would be responsible for.

Jaden told the mini-angels he knew Jadellya was an angelic child and would have a standoff with the child considered to be her brother, and she would rise above the challenge, but he wondered how many pale ones would die before the standoff was over. The mini-angels told Armellya and Jaden no pale ones would die, but the community would feel the essence of the good versus evil because of their telepathy and the ability to be one with the land. The mini-angels said as far as the telepathy, others would get the silent words from the young couple, and those words would transfer from individual to individual with simple interaction.

Through the intense encounter with the mini-angels, Armellya was somewhat relieved over being the mother of death and worried less over how it was to play out before serenity returned to the commune. Now that Armellya and Jaden had a better view of the events to come, the mini-angels said they had exceeded their time to be away from their bodies and they must leave. The new parents expressed their love for the mini-angels, and they returned the expressions of love and then went back to the Dinosaur Tail. Armellya and Jaden were both quite relieved after their mini-angels had shared some of what they knew about the intrauterine child's future and the safety of the community.

It seemed that Armellya was back to her bubbly self and that in turn allowed Jaden to handle her softly because he did not like that he had to grab her earlier and speak firmly to her. Jaden considered Armellya as his equal always, so her state of mind was extremely important at this point. Up to then, it had always been strong and sound. Armellya advised Jaden that because of the circumstances, she believed it would be beneficial to spend as much time with Jadellya as possible to allow a better bond with them and the child who was to be her brother. Armellya said they could put Jadellya's nanny on a temporary leave with pay and let her know it was because of family dynamics. He said the less anyone knew about the male child's disposition, the better off they and the community would be. Armellya thought about what Jaden had said and agreed. She asked him what his thoughts were on giving the nanny a leave of absence anyway.

Jaden told Armellya he thought they should keep the nanny on active duty and take Jadellya every moment possible; if work of some sort arose, the nanny would be readily available. Armellya confessed that Jaden was correct and a compromise with work and family was in order. With the time Armellya and Jaden had spent with their mini-angels and talking after they left, the couple realized there were only a few hours left to get some rest before it would be time to wake for the new day. They scrunched down in their bed, cuddled, and then tried to go to sleep.

After the event with the dark shadow and time spent with the mini-angels, Armellya and Jaden found it difficult to fall back to sleep, so they decided to get up early. Normally, this would be the time to wake for the meeting with Andrew and Camillia for their lesson, but they had finished their memory and verbal portions of the lesson the day before. All the couple had left to learn was purely observatory with a possible proposal of their ideal way of handling what may be encountered, if anything. The community contained very little drama, and when it did come about, it was dramatically obvious to the whole community, such as the situation with the scientists. However, the incident with the scientists was the first of its kind since the pale ones had come into existence.

Armellya and Jaden went ahead and changed from their bedclothes into their day clothes and then washed their faces, brushed their teeth, and combed their hair. The young couple felt a stroll in the chief's private garden would be a delightful way to start the day, so they left their side of the castle to go to the chief's. When they got there, Jaden knocked on his front door. The butler was still in his quarters, but the chief awoke and heard Jaden knock on the front door so he went to answer it himself. The chief was a bit surprised to see Jaden and Armellya there so early, and he could see in their eyes they had not gotten much sleep. The chief asked the couple how their night was, and they told him it was restless. He offered to talk to them about what had them up all night besides their mini-angels' visits. Jaden told the chief they were asleep when their mini-angels arrived and sang their beautiful wake up song, but they could not get back to sleep after they left. Then the chief asked Jaden if they wanted to talk about how the visit went.

Armellya and Jaden told the chief they could enlighten him on their current predicament only if he never spoke of it to anyone else except maybe his mini-angel. The chief agreed to never speak of what the couple was about to share, not even with Andrew and Camillia.

Armellya, Jaden, and the chief went to the private garden, where the environment would be fresh and relaxing. The three of them sat on a beautiful stone bench, and then Jaden and Armellya began to reveal the night's events. Armellya told the chief about the fallen angel who visited her while Jaden was across the commune taking care of an emergency veterinary call. She explained how the dark figure had lain with her and she had conceived a son. The chief said that her experience with the dark angelic figure must have been frightening, and she agreed. The chief was concerned about Armellya and Jaden because of the association of the dark figure with the depths of hell.

Armellya continued talking about the child she now carried and how he would detrimentally affect the community if he were not stopped. Jaden then told the chief that Jadellya was an angelic child, and her purpose in the world was to oppose her deadly brother and bring salvation to the commune. Jaden also told the chief that it had been prophesied that Jadellya would become queen of the mini-angels upon the age of accountability. Armellya added that Jadellya's age of accountability would come as she passed toddlerhood. Instead of waiting until she reached the approximate age of eight, she would reach her accountability at the age of five. The chief asked the couple if their unborn son had to reach the age of accountability before the terror began, and Jaden told the chief the child would have more and more ways to spread his malice as he reached each growth milestone. Jaden told the chief that the mini-angels made it clear that Jadellya would be able to conquer the male child as he grew because she would always stay stronger than he. Armellya said that she had seen the future to some point, but the mini-angels had seen further, and they guaranteed a positive outcome. The chief was relieved to hear about the guarantee of a positive outcome, but he knew the battle would be a difficult one. The chief thanked Armellya and Jaden for confiding in him. Then he told the couple that he was there to talk any time they needed him, no matter what time it should be.

They thanked the chief and told him they would take him

up on his offer to talk if the need should arise. Now that the chief had been caught up on the latest events and there was not much else to discuss, the trio decided to go to the couple's side of the castle for a cup of Melanie's specially brewed coffee before the breakfast hour. At the last minute, Armellya asked the guys if they could go down the long hallway that connected the two sides of the castle to get to their side so she could look in on Jadellya. The chief and Jaden did not mind going through the long hallway. It was a more direct route to the other side of the castle. Jaden told Armellya he would take the chief directly to the castle's private dining hall while she made her stop in Jadellya's nursery.

Armellya did not mind. She said she would catch up to them. When Armellya got to Jadellya's nursery, the child was awake, so Armellya picked her up out of her bassinet. She immediately nestled into her mother, and they cuddled. They shared a loving mother-and-daughter moment. Armellya told Jadellya she loved her and how special she was. Then Armellya laid Jadellya back in her bassinet. She left the nursery and headed for the castle's private dining hall to meet up with Jaden and the chief for coffee.

Upon approaching the dining hall, Armellya could hear several voices, and she wondered if she was late to breakfast, so she checked the time and realized it was still early. Armellya wondered who else was already up and having coffee with the chief and Jaden. She walked a bit faster, eager to cure her curiosity. When she got to the dining hall, she saw that Camillia and Andrew were at the big round table with the chief and Jaden. Armellya went on in and sat by Jaden. Then Melanie brought her coffee.

Everyone was engaged in light conversation when

Camillia broke the mood by asking Armellya if she was okay. Armellya told Camillia she was great. Then Camillia told Armellya it looked like she had not slept a wink. Jaden cut in and told Camillia he and Armellya were spending some quality time together and were up very late. Then they spent some time with their mini-angels. Camillia asked Armellya what she was not telling her, because she could sense secrecy through telepathy. Camillia knew Armellya was blocking her thoughts and she only did that when she had a grave concern over something out of her control. Armellya asked her mother to please not try to read her mind. If she wanted her to know something, she would freely speak to her. Camillia apologized for the intrusion and then told Armellya she worried about her little girl. Armellya told Camillia she was not so little anymore, and Camillia said she would always be her little girl.

Jaden tried to take the focus off Armellya and lighten the subject matter by starting some casual talk. The chief knew what Jaden was trying to do, so he supported him and followed his lead. Andrew stayed out of the conversation even though he too noticed it appeared that Armellya had not slept, but he was sensitive to her hesitation to discuss the night hours. Andrew knew Armellya would talk to him and Camillia when she felt the time was appropriate. He did not even get into the small talk that the chief and Jaden were trying to start because of the conflict between his wife and daughter.

Camillia pushed Armellya for reasonable answers once more. Armellya looked to Jaden for his opinion on whether to tell Andrew and Camillia about their latest occurrences. The chief saw the nonverbal communication going on between Armellya and Jaden. He verbally told Armellya and Jaden to enlighten them also because they may need the support of their parents at some time. Armellya told Andrew and Camillia of the black angelic figure that lay upon her and how she was with its child. She continued by telling them the unborn child was of demonic seed and would be an evil child; it was his destiny. Jaden told them Jadellya was an angelic child and would be queen of the mini-angels by age five. She would also defend the commune by defeating her black-hearted brother.

Andrew and Camillia told the couple they would be there for them anytime and to just come to them if they needed anything. Armellya and Jaden thanked them saying they would keep them and the chief informed of the latest developments. The conversation ended, and they changed the topic to a lighter matter as they enjoyed their coffee.

Melanie returned to the big round table to see if the group wanted more coffee, and everyone declined because it was so close to the breakfast hour. They all felt it was good timing that they changed the conversation subject when they did, or Melanie would have heard about the near future situation to come between their children. The last thing they needed was an unnecessary scare spreading throughout the community. Armellya and Jaden did not want anyone other than Andrew, Camillia, and the chief to know about their children's dynamic contrasts.

Everyone was starting to show up for the breakfast hour, and once they were all seated at the big round table Melanie could have the kitchen crew serve the food. When they were all at the big round table, the kitchen staff had their breakfasts in front of them in no time. Everyone participated in casual conversation while eating, which made the meal seem to go by quickly. Those who had immediate things to do left the castle promptly, and the rest went about their own ways to engage in relaxing behaviors. Melanie supervised the kitchen crew in cleaning and starting the lunch meal. Andrew needed to go to the multiuse hall to see how much further the workers had gotten on the gardening tools.

When Andrew got inside the multiuse hall, the lead worker approached Andrew with a large smile on his face. He told him there were only fifty more sets to be made. Andrew was pleased with the multiuse hall's progress and their productivity. The multiuse hall seemed to be the best way to utilize the old science hall. Andrew left the individuals to their work and headed back to the castle. On his way back home, he ran into Jaden, who had gotten a late start and was in a hurry to get to the hospital for his eight-hour shift. When Andrew got to the castle, he walked into the family room, where Camillia and Armellya were having an obviously heated conversation. Andrew made a quick turn to walk out of the family room, but Camillia saw him and called him into the family room. Armellya told Camillia not to involve Andrew in the conversation, but she said it would be beneficial to get his opinion.

Andrew said he had no idea what they were talking about. Camillia interrupted him in midsentence. She told Andrew they were discussing prenatal care for the child she was carrying. Andrew told Camillia that was a woman thing, and he did not want to take part in the conversation. Camillia said it was a parental thing and that the father should be just as involved as the mother. Andrew reminded Camillia that the child had a donor not a father. Camillia told Andrew they had a difference of opinion over getting prenatal care and who the doctor should be. Armellya told Andrew if she needed any prenatal intervention, she would go to Jaden because of the nature of the conception. Camillia was not happy about Armellya's decision to forego prenatal care. Armellya told Camillia that the child had a destiny to fulfill, and because it would come to pass, he did not need contact with any more individuals than she could absolutely help. Camillia told Andrew to talk some sense into Armellya, and Andrew told Camillia that he could see Armellya's point of view, but it would be good to make sure the pregnancy was not harming Armellya in any way. Armellya told Camillia she would see Jaden for any prenatal needs and that was all there was to it, so Camillia dropped the matter for the time being.

Camillia decided to leave Armellya alone about consistent prenatal care with a hospital doctor instead of Jaden. Andrew knew Camillia was finished with the conversation, so he asked her to go to the chief's private garden for a romantic walk. Camillia accepted, and off they went.

Armellya was expecting Jaden to get home soon so she went to her home to catch a short nap before the lunch hour. Armellya noticed this pregnancy was already different than her pregnancy with Jadellya. She did not know if the differences were from the child being the prince of darkness or if it was just because each pregnancy could be different. As Armellya was falling asleep, she heard a knock on her front door. It was unusual for anyone to seek her out when she was home, so she quickly answered the front door. It was Jadellya's nanny in a slight state of panic. The nanny told Armellya that Jadellya was crying and would not stop. It was not a normal cry.

Armellya stepped out of her home to follow the nanny to

the nursery. As they were walking, the nanny told Armellya that Jadellya never cried. When they got to the nursery, Armellya went to the baby and instinctively picked her up and held her close to her chest. Jadellya settled right down, but Armellya's stomach started to cramp the instant she picked her up. Armellya impulsively believed that the cramping was due to the boy child not liking Jadellya so close to him. With that belief, she wanted to do a little experiment. Armellya put Jadellya down in her bassinet, and the cramping stopped, but Jadellya started to cry again. Armellya picked her up again, and she stopped crying, but the stomach cramping started again. She repeated this routine six times and had the exact same results. Armellya thought the struggle between good and evil had already begun.

The nanny could not understand what was going on with Jadellya. She was such a quiet baby, and now suddenly she would not stop crying. Until this incident, the nanny had never heard Jadellya cry, and neither had anyone else. Armellya told the nanny that she was going to keep Jadellya close to her but to stay on duty, and the nanny acknowledged Armellya and took a seat in the rocking chair. The longer Armellya held Jadellya, the worse the cramping got, so she went back to her home to lie down in her bed with Jadellya right next to her. There was still quite a bit of time before the lunch hour to get some quality rest, if the children would let her.

Jadellya seemed to know the boy child had been conceived; she lay next to Armellya with her hands on her stomach. Even though the cramping had stopped, there was an indescribable sensation between the boy child and Jadellya. Armellya felt that the two babies sensed each other.

Armellya finally fell asleep and got forty-five minutes of rest before Jaden woke her gently. He was trying not to wake Jadellya, but when Armellya woke up, so did the boy child, which woke Jadellya.

Jaden finished his long day at the hospital and was getting Armellya for the lunch hour and family time. Everyone was already in the family room waiting for her. Because he was late getting off work, they were going to start without him since there was no way of knowing how late he might be. When Jaden did get to the castle, it was a unanimous decision to send him after his wife. Armellya took a few minutes to tell Jaden about the heated discussion with Camillia over prenatal care. Jaden agreed with Armellya to keep the boy child from being exposed to others he would care for her prenatal needs. Armellya also took time to explain the odd occurrence between the two children. Jaden was concerned about the cramping but not surprised by Jadellya's possessiveness of her mommy. Jaden could see that until the boy child was birthed, Armellya would be caught in the middle of the children's war. It was obvious to Jaden that Jadellya knew her destiny better than they, and she was aware that immorality had come to pass.

Jaden told Armellya they could discuss the day's events and any concerns after the lunch hour and family time because they were already late and everyone was waiting for them. Armellya told Jaden she had to keep Jadellya close so she was taking her to the castle's private dining hall with them. She got off the bed and then turned to pick up Jadellya.

Then Armellya, Jaden, and Jadellya headed for the

castle's family room. Right when Jaden and his immediate family got near the family room, Andrew started everyone headed to the castle's private dining hall. Jaden, Armellya, and Jadellya could bring up the rear. They all found their seats at the big round table and quickly sat down so Melanie could get the kitchen staff to bring out lunch. They went around the table and shared their day, hopes, prayers, and upcoming events that involved the whole family. With all the communication, eating was a slow process and kept everyone at the big round table past the time when the lunch hour and family time should have been over. No one really had much to do the rest of the day, so no one was really concerned about running over time.

Thirty minutes late, the lunch hour and family time did end, and Armellya, Jaden, and Jadellya went to their home to relax and converse. Right after the small family got inside their home and shut the door, someone knocked on the front door. Jaden was still close to the door, so he answered it, and there was Camillia. She said she wanted to talk to Jaden privately but did not mind Armellya being there, so he invited Camillia inside. Camillia told Jaden that she had spoken to Armellya earlier about consistent prenatal care. Jaden stopped Camillia in her tracks and told her he and Armellya already had it planned. He told Camillia that he would see Armellya when it was necessary and that was it until it was time to birth the child. Then he would do that too. Camillia told Jaden that was unethical. Jaden told her a demon child was unethical and then showed her to the front door.

Camillia got puffed up and left abruptly. Jaden told Armellya Camillia would get over herself.

Armellya handed Jadellya to Jaden, and she started to

cry again. Jaden gave Jadellya back to Armellya and told her that she wanted her mommy. The young parents agreed that Jadellya wanted Armellya because she knew of the boy child's existence. With the few contemporary issues that had come about, the couple could not wait to see their mini-angels to get their advice on the best way to address them. Armellya suggested that Jaden astroproject to the Dinosaur Tail and see if he could get their mini-angels to visit early and let them know Jadellya was with them so maybe her mini-angel would come also. Jaden said he would go and see what he could do.

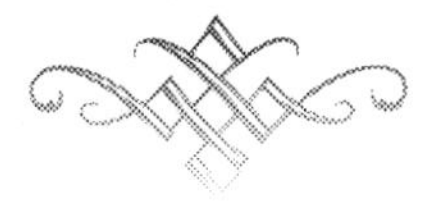

CHAPTER 2

JADEN GOT COMFORTABLE ON THE BED AND astroprojected right away. He found their mini-angels and asked if they could visit right away because there was a new development. The mini-angels said they would be there shortly and then told Jaden to go back to his body right away, and he did. Jaden got off the bed and went to the family room, where Armellya and Jadellya were. He told Armellya the mini-angels would be with them soon. Right after Jaden told Armellya the mini-angels were on their way, they appeared.

Armellya told the mini-angels that Jadellya would not stop crying unless she was with her mommy. Jadellya did not even want her daddy. This was abnormal. The child had never cried until this day. Armellya told the mini-angel that it appeared Jadellya knew the boy child existed and about his destiny and her own for that matter. The mini-angels said that Jadellya did know her purpose and was aware of the boy child and his destiny, and until he was birthed, Armellya would be caught in the middle. It was likely that Jadellya would want to stay with her mommy to ensure her safety.

Jaden asked the mini-angels how aware of things the boy child would be while intrauterine. The mini-angels told the couple he was very aware of his purpose, and the closer to his due date, the more he would be able to endanger to Armellya's health. The mini-angels told Armellya to keep Jadellya with her always, even in bed during the sleeping hours because that was Armellya's most vulnerable time. Armellya said she would do that and ask about when it was time to deliver the boy child. She could not hold her then. The mini-angels told Armellya just to keep her close, and once the umbilical cord was cut, she would no longer be caught in the middle of the children's battle. The mini-angels said they would be watching over them and would help where they could. The couple thanked the mini-angels, and then they suddenly disappeared. Armellya was exhausted because of the pregnancy so she decided to take Jadellya and lie down.

Jaden and Armellya had planned to stay in their home the rest of the afternoon until the dinner hour. Jaden was going to relax and keep an eye on Armellya and Jadellya. No sooner had Armellya gotten to sleep than there was a knock at the front door, which woke her. She thought the mini-angels probably left so quickly because they knew there was company coming. It was the chief. He had come to their side of the castle to check on Jaden and Armellya. He did not know Jadellya was with them. Jaden took the chief to their bedroom to talk to Armellya and say hello to Jadellya.

Armellya told the chief how Jadellya's behavior had changed and what the mini-angels had to say about it. The chief was stunned at how much Jadellya was aware of at her immature age. The chief asked Armellya if Andrew and Camillia knew about the new development with Jadellya yet, and she said no because it was only discovered a brief time ago. Armellya explained to the chief that Camillia was upset with her over her choice for prenatal care, so they had not seen them since then. The chief asked what there was to be upset over, so Armellya told the chief their prenatal care plans. The chief understood Armellya's views, but he also understood Camillia's. The chief told Armellya that Camillia only wanted what was best for her in her opinion but to do what made her comfortable. The chief commented that the pregnancy was an unusual one so the care and delivery may be unusual also. The chief said it was a shame that the battle between good and evil had already begun, but it was bound to start some time. He continued and told Armellya she would be just fine. She was strong mentally and physically and she had Andrew, Camillia, Jaden, himself, the mini-angels, and Jadellya watching over her. Armellya said she was more worried about Jadellya's safety than her own, and the chief told Armellya that Jadellya had everything under control and to keep the prophesies in mind because they suggested Jadellya would overcome her brother.

Armellya was so sleepy that she started to doze off while speaking to the chief so he left the bedroom to let her rest and asked Jaden if he would mind having company. Jaden welcomed the chief. The two men sat in the family room and discussed many different things and even laughed a little. After about an hour, there was another knock at the front door, so Jaden answered it. It was Andrew and Camillia coming to check on Armellya. Jaden told them she was asleep with Jadellya, and they asked why Jadellya was not with her nanny.

Jaden asked Andrew and Camillia to take a seat and said he would fill them in on the latest development. He told them how Jadellya's behavior had changed and why, which was why Jadellya was with Armellya and not the nanny. When Andrew and Camillia found out that the battle between siblings was underway, they were shocked that the children were aware of so much. They were really concerned for Armellya's health, so much that they asked Jaden if he could get the boy child to deliver a little early without harming him. Jaden told everyone he was prepared to take the boy child if it became too much for Armellya to handle, but she did not know that. Now that Andrew and Camillia were caught up on the latest news, they were ready to leave, but Jaden invited them to stay for a while. They decided to stay and converse with him and the chief. Once again, they were laughing and enjoying themselves while discussing funny things that had occurred in the past. It was finally getting close to the dinner hour, so Andrew and Camillia left to go to the castle's family room to wait on family to arrive. The chief was going to wait for Armellya, Jadellya, and Jaden. Jaden went to his bedroom to gently wake Armellya and get her ready to go to the castle's private dining hall.

Armellya got out of bed and picked up Jadellya. Then they went out to the family room with Jaden and the chief. When they got close to the family room, Andrew announced it was time to go to the castle's private dining hall and then led the way. Jaden, Armellya, Jadellya, and the chief would bring up the rear on the way to the castle's private dining hall. When they got there, they sat in their seats at the big round table. Then Melanie had the kitchen staff bring out dinner and serve everyone. Andrew, Camillia, Jaden, Armellya, and the chief did not have much to say because their minds were on the volatile situation between the two children with Armellya caught in the middle. Everyone else was having a cheerful conversation and had not noticed their silence at first. Eventually, they noticed the five of them being extremely quiet and asked the reason for the silent treatment.

Andrew told them he had a lot on his mind and that as king, he could not reveal his thoughts. They all excused Andrew, Camillia, Jaden, Armellya, and the chief from the conversation and then innocently went on to finish wrapping up the subject until a later time. They finished their dinner and their business and withdrew to their quarters for the night.

Camillia and Andrew were talking with each other about the situation Armellya was in with her children and how they could be of help. The chief was contemplating the situation also; he was extremely concerned for Armellya's and Jadellya's safety, so he too was trying to find a way to be of help. Andrew, Camillia, and the chief intended to ask their mini-angels if there was anything they could do to help Armellya and Jadellya through their crusade. They wanted to be there for Jaden, because like them, he could only watch as the encounters occurred.

Meanwhile, Jaden and Armellya were sorting out the facts to expose what he could do to help support her and Jadellya through the altercation with the boy child. Armellya and Jaden wanted to give the boy child a name but were not sure what would be appropriate for him. Jaden suggested giving it a little more time to see if it would come to them from another source, as Jadellya's name had. Jaden and Armellya, like everyone else, got ready for the night hours by changing from their day clothes into their bedclothes.

Right after the couple changed their clothing, Armellya picked up Jadellya, and she began to gaze at empty space and babble strange words. She was acting differently than she had ever acted before. It was as though she saw something that the couple could not see, which alarmed them. Suddenly, the large black figure showed itself, even though Jaden was there. Jadellya put a bubble of protection around her mother and herself promptly. That was a gift no one knew about because no one else had it. For the first time in several visits, the dark figure not only appeared before Jaden but spoke. It said the boy child was to be called Santuvious and then disappeared in a cloud of dark-gray smoke.

After the dark figure left, Jadellya took down the bubble of protection. Armellya got close to Jaden and hugged him tightly out of fear. He hugged her back and asked her if she was okay. Jadellya giggled as she sent a joyous sensation through their bodies to let them know they were okay. The young parents knew the sensation of elation was coming from their daughter which was another gift they did not know she—or any other pale one—had.

Now that Armellya and Jaden were feeling secure, they lay down in their bed with Jadellya between them. The young parents kissed Jadellya's head and told her they loved her. At the midnight hour, their mini-angels arrived, and Jadellya woke instantly and giggled, which woke Armellya and Jaden. The couple saw their mini-angels and were glad they were there. Jadellya was reaching out to her mini-angel. The mini-angel went to her and got situated on her hand. Jaden and

Armellya were dumbfounded at how alert Jadellya was to her surroundings and how she always seemed to be a step ahead of everyone and everything.

The mini-angels greeted them, and they sent greetings back. Armellya and Jaden told their mini-angels they had a few questions for them. The most important question was what Jaden could do to help Armellya and Jadellya during their challenging time with the boy child and the fallen angel. The mini-angels told them that they had already touched on that, but they would clarify their previous explanation. They told Armellya and Jaden that he was clear of any involvement in the situation unless he were to find a way to make alterations to something the evil pair were to be doing at that moment. The mini-angels then told Jaden that if it were to occur, Jadellya would protect him as she had been herself and her mother.

Armellya asked the mini-angels what gifts Jadellya had that no other pale one had, including the royal family, because they had just found out about two of them as she used them. The mini-angels told the couple they were finding out about her advanced skills at the same time as they were. They did not know she had accelerated abilities. The mini-angels mentioned that she was more powerful than they were and had far more talent. That was why she was to be their queen.

The last thing Armellya and Jaden needed to talk to their mini-angels about was that the fallen angel had returned and named the boy child. The parents-to-be again asked their mini-angels if they had to give the boy child the name they were given by the fallen angel or if they could find a name from another source. The mini-angels told Armellya and Jaden no other source would come forward to name the child in question because he was from a demon seed. The mini-angel added that they had two options, the first was to accept the name already given and the second was to name the child themselves. It did not seem that the mini-angels had been with them very long, but they said they needed to return to the Dinosaur Tail. They said their farewells, and the mini-angels departed.

❧

While Jaden, Armellya, and Jadellya were visiting with their mini-angels, Andrew and Camillia were visiting with theirs as well. Andrew and Camillia wanted to know if there was anything they could do to help Armellya, Jadellya, and Jaden with the struggle between them and the evil forces that were attacking them. The mini-angels told them that it was a situation between light and dark that did not involve them, so there would be no harm to them. The mini-angels went on to say that all they could really do was to be there for them to talk to and to lend moral support. The mini-angels reminded Andrew and Camillia that only Jadellya could oppose the forces at play because of their significant strengths and abilities.

Andrew and Camillia had been hoping there would be more they could do, but they were willing to do anything, no matter how insignificant.

❧

While Andrew and Camillia were speaking with their mini-angels, the chief's mini-angel was visiting him. Like everyone else who knew of the frightful encounters with the dark side of life, the chief was asking how he could help Armellya, Jadellya, and Jaden. His mini-angel told him, just as the other mini-angels told their pale ones, he was in no danger, so his position would be to provide moral support and lend an ear.

Finally, everyone's mini-angel left to return to the Dinosaur Tail, and the castle's occupants were back to sleep.

The morning hour was upon the community, so everyone was rising to a new day. Armellya and Jaden could not wait to tell Andrew, Camillia, and the chief about their visit from the fallen angel. Before getting day clothes on, Jaden summoned one of the castle's runners to bring the chief for breakfast and conversation. The runner got dressed quickly and then ran to the other side of the castle.

When the runner knocked on the chief's front door, the butler answered it in his bedclothes. The runner told the butler he needed the chief for Jaden, so the butler invited the runner inside to sit in the family room and wait for the chief. When the chief got to the family room, the runner told him Jaden wanted him for breakfast and conversation. The chief knew when the runner mentioned conversation that was a code for the latest information on the war between good and bad. The chief left with the runner.

Andrew, Camillia, Armellya, and Jaden were already in the castle's private dining hall waiting for him. When the chief got to the other side of the castle, he went straight to the private dining hall and took his seat at the big round table. They told the chief he had not missed anything; they had just greeted one another.

With the pleasantries over, Armellya and Jaden announced that they had some new developments. Everyone leaned into the table as though not wanting to miss out on anything. Armellya told the small group that the fallen angel had come again and showed himself in front of Jaden. She also told them that for the first time, the fallen angel had spoken, and he had said that the boy child was to be called Santuvious.

Jaden finally got a chance to speak and said something wonderful had happened during the encounter. He told the group that Jadellya had exposed two more gifts that no other pale one had. She had sent a sensation of joy and contentment throughout their bodies after everything was over to assure them that everything was okay, and when the fallen angel was there, she had enclosed Armellya and herself in a bubble of protection, which she dropped when the dark shadow left. Everyone was amazed by Jadellya's talents and how she seemed to know everything before it came to pass.

Armellya looked down at Jadellya, smiled at her, and then gave her a kiss on the cheek and told her she loved her. Jadellya giggled and reached her hand up to touch her mother's cheek. Everyone saw the interaction between Armellya and Jadellya and was sentimentally touched by it.

Melanie had just arrived at the kitchen area and brewed some of her special coffee. She asked the group if they would like to enjoy some coffee while waiting for the breakfast hour to arrive, and everyone said yes. It was no time at all before the kitchen staff brought out the coffee cups and coffee. They served everyone and then went back to making breakfast.

Andrew and Camillia told Armellya and Jaden they had asked their mini-angels about how they could help them. They told the couple that their mini-angels said they could only be there for them and offer moral support. The chief butted into the conversation and told Jaden and Armellya that was also what his mini-angel had told him when he asked what he could do to help. The three of them told Armellya and Jaden that was what they were going to do, and if anything else came up to enable them to help, they would take full advantage of it. Armellya and Jaden thanked Andrew, Camillia, and the chief, and then they told them that they loved them and were lucky to have them in their lives. It was getting close to the breakfast hour, so everyone got up from the big round table and transferred to the family room to wait for the rest of the family to show up.

As soon as they got into the family room, they all hugged and verbally expressed their love for each other. While they were waiting, Andrew joked with Armellya and Jaden about them being late and being on time this day. Armellya and Jaden just laughed. Family started to show up, and within a few minutes, they were all there, so Andrew led everyone to the castle's private dining hall.

The kitchen staff had breakfast waiting on the big round table for everyone. All they had to do was sit and eat. They all sat in their spots at the big round table and started to eat as they went around telling what their day held for them. No one had very much to do, and what there was to be done would be completed before the lunch hour and family time. For the first time, they finished going around the big round table sharing their daily business with each other before finishing breakfast. They finished eating their breakfast in silence then went to start their day.

Andrew needed to go to the multiuse hall to check on the

farming tool production. Jaden had to go to the hospital for his eight-hour shift. Armellya was going to stay home with Jadellya and enjoy the experience of motherhood. Camillia was going to go to the chief's private garden to practice flying without levitation first. The chief was going to finish preparing his home for the new wolf pup he was going to get, and he would be checking on Armellya periodically while Jaden was at work.

Now that everyone was done eating, they all went their separate ways. Jaden rode casually to the hospital since he was leaving a bit early, which was unusual. When Jaden got to the hospital, he decided at the last minute to check the medical medicine and the veterinary medicine rooms that day since things were slow in the hospital.

Jaden started with the veterinary medicine room first this time to switch things up. He had a list of medicines, chemicals, the number of vials of each medicine they were supposed to have, and a logbook of who was checking out what medicine and how much at a time. Jaden also took note of the cleanliness, organization, and dress-code compliance. After checking everything, Jaden gave the veterinary medicine room a perfect report. Now it was time to check the medical medicine room, and Jaden did the exact same thing there. They also got a perfect report. Now that Jaden had thoroughly checked both medicine rooms, he needed to go to his office to write up the reports.

While Jaden was in his office, Andrew was on his way to the multiuse hall. When Andrew got there, he noticed the woodworkers and the ironworkers were all gone. The only individuals left were the few workers who supervised all projects and stayed at the multiuse hall. That had to mean good news, and when Andrew looked at the men's faces, he saw happiness. As Andrew looked around the hall, he noticed up against the wall in the corner near the back of the hall were many gardening tools. The multiuse hall workers told Andrew they had finished the job. Andrew told them they had done excellent work and then asked them to disburse one set of tools to every residence. The men were happy to do that and said they would start the next day and finish that evening. Andrew told the men that was acceptable and to remember that they could look for work prospects while out in the community. The men said they would, and if anything looked like it had potential, they would bring it to his attention. Andrew said, "Very well," and then left the multiuse hall to go back to the castle. Andrew planned to join Camillia in the chief's private garden to practice flying also.

Camillia had gone to the chief's private garden from the breakfast table and had been practicing flying all that time. She finally got the hang of lifting off the ground and assuming a parallel position with the ground without levitating first. She was shaky with the actual flying and not good at all with the landing, but she would be practicing those things in due time. The chief knew Camillia was in his private garden because he gave her permission, so he stayed clear of the garden area to keep from distracting her.

During the time that Andrew was at the multiuse hall and Jaden was at the hospital, so far, he had checked on Armellya and Jadellya twice. They were doing just fine, and Armellya was loving motherhood. In the meantime, Andrew made it to his side of the castle and used the adjoining hallway to go to the chief's without anyone seeing him so he would be left alone for a while.

Andrew announced his presence as he entered the private garden so he would not disturb Camillia's concentration. When Andrew found Camillia, she was completely on the ground, and that eased his mind because he was concerned about his arrival creating an accident for her. Andrew told Camillia that no one knew he was there, and Camillia told him it might be a clever idea to at least let the chief and Armellya know. Andrew agreed that would be good in case Armellya needed him and the chief could let Armellya know since he was keeping an eye on her. Andrew went to the chief's butler to find out where he was in his castle, and the butler told him the chief was in his new dog grooming room. Andrew did not know where that was, so he waited in the family room, and the butler went to get the chief.

When the chief arrived, Andrew told him that he was back from the multiuse hall and would be in the private garden with Camillia practicing his flying skills. The chief told Andrew he did not have to report to him. Then Andrew told him he was letting him know in case he was needed. On second thought, the chief said it was an excellent idea. Then the chief wished Andrew good luck with flying and said to be careful. It was getting close to the time for Jaden to get home, so the chief felt he had better do one more check on Armellya and Jadellya.

The chief got to Armellya and Jaden's house and knocked on the front door as he had done before. There was no answer at the door like before. The chief knocked harder and longer, but there was still no answer. The chief assumed Armellya and Jadellya were sleeping in the bedroom and just did not hear the door. The chief knew Armellya was leaving the front door unlocked just for him, so he entered and quietly crept through the house, looking for them. The chief did not find them in any of the communal areas of the house, so he headed for the bedroom. When the chief got to the bedroom, he was slow to peek around the halfway closed door. When he looked at the bed, he did not see Armellya, but Jadellya was on the bed, alone. That alarmed the chief because he knew Armellya would never leave Jadellya unattended on the bed to possibly roll off and get hurt.

Jadellya was awake and eerily gazing into nothingness. The chief went to the bed and tried to get her attention, but nothing was working to break her gaze. When the chief walked up to Jadellya and touched the child, she was cold to the touch and visually appeared to be close to unresponsiveness. The chief hollered for the castle's runner, and surprisingly, the runner heard him and responded. The chief told the runner to get Jaden from the hospital; it was urgent. The runner ran to his horse and had the horse running as fast as it would go.

Once at the hospital, the runner ran into the hospital toward Jaden's office.

As Jaden was leaving his office, he ran into the runner, who grabbed him by the arm and started to forcefully drag him to the hospital's exit as he told Jaden the chief had sent him for an urgent response.

While the chief was waiting for Jaden to get there, he picked Jadellya up in his arms and found her to be limp. The chief turned about to finish searching the bedroom for Armellya. The chief noticed he got a strange response out of Jadellya. While he turned about, Jadellya appeared to continue gazing at some sort of focal point by turning her head to keep it in view. The chief had looked almost everywhere for Armellya. The only place left was the view of the four walls of the room from midlevel wall height to the ceiling. Not knowing what else to do, the chief tried to get a glimpse of what Jadellya was concentrating so hard on. He figured out Jadellya's focal point was on the wall behind him, so he turned to see if he could narrow down what she seemed to be watching, though he was not sure what to expect.

Right as the chief turned to what he felt would be the correct wall, he automatically looked above eye level and found Armellya. The distress from what he saw dropped the chief to his knees. Armellya was floating above eye level up against the wall, and she appeared to be frozen. Her eyes were stuck open, and she was not moving. There was no explanation as to how she was being held up there.

Right after the chief made the discovery, Jaden walked into the house and called out to Armellya. He heard Jaden and called to him saying they were in the bedroom. Then he went into a state of shock. When Jaden got to the door of the bedroom, he observed the chief on his knees, holding Jadellya tight.

Jaden noticed that Jadellya did not look right, so he walked the rest of the way into the bedroom to take her from the chief. Then he saw Armellya. Now that Jaden understood why the chief was on his knees, he had to overcome the disbelief of seeing Armellya up against the wall above eye level with nothing apparent holding her there so he could care for Jadellya.

Jaden tried to get Jadellya from the chief's arms, but he was holding her tightly. With the chief being in some sort of state of shock, it was not going to be easy to get her loose. Jaden tried to get the chief to respond to him by talking to him and shaking him, but it did not work. The only other thing Jaden could think to use to get the chief to respond was painful stimuli. Jaden squeezed his fist between Jadellya and the chief's arms, though he was barely able to. Jaden unforgivingly rubbed his knuckles into the chief's sternum as hard as he could. Then the chief sort of shook his head and looked up at Jaden with a blank stare. Jaden was happy that he had gotten some sort of response from the chief, so before the chief could slip further into a state of shock, Jaden shook him and told him to talk to him. The chief mumbled some incoherent words, and Jaden told the chief to give him the baby.

The chief's grip on Jadellya loosened, so Jaden rapidly grabbed her out of the chief's arms. He found that she was cold and limp, so he wrapped her in a heavy blanket to warm her up. After about fifteen minutes, Jadellya started moving a little bit, but she kept her eyes on Armellya. Jaden walked to the wall where Armellya was and tried to pull her down. When Jaden touched her, he got a jolt of electricity that threw him across the room. He knew Jadellya understood what was going on, so he got the idea of taking her close to Armellya and observing her actions. Jaden was amazed when he got Jadellya close to her mother because the child reached out to touch her. Jaden was uncertain whether he should let Jadellya touch Armellya, but he moved closer to Armellya to see if Jadellya was going to follow through, and if so, he would let her do it. When Jadellya touched Armellya, there was a bright electrical spark, and then Armellya went limp and fell to the floor with her eyes closed.

Jaden looked back at the chief to see how alert he was, and he appeared to be fully recovered. Jaden asked him if he could safely hold Jadellya, and the chief told Jaden he was now okay. Jaden gave Jadellya to the chief and told him to make sure she stayed alert. Then he turned his attention to Armellya. He did a primary and secondary exam on her and found her body temperature was low, like Jadellya's was, so he wrapped Armellya in the bed comforter. After fifteen minutes, just like Jadellya had done, Armellya started to move slightly. Jaden tried to talk to Armellya to find out what had happened, but all she did was mutter bits and pieces of words. She made no sense. Jaden took Jadellya from the chief and then laid her in Armellya's arms to see if mother and child could join forces and recover easier.

After ten minutes, Armellya responded to Jadellya and vice versa. Jaden moved Jadellya to being under the comforter with Armellya at a level that she could touch her mother's face. Jaden's theory came to play out. Jadellya placed her hand on her mother's face and kept it there. Then Jadellya's hand started to glow brightly. As her daughter's hand glowed on her face, Armellya became more alert. Her body temperature returned to normal, and she could communicate. Once Armellya returned to normal, so did Jadellya. Armellya sat up, took the comforter off, and picked up Jadellya. Armellya checked Jadellya to make sure she was okay and was satisfied with how she found her. Armellya stood up and then pulled

Jadellya close to her chest and gave her a big hug with a kiss to top off the feelings of joy that they were still alive and well. Jaden asked Armellya what had happened, so Armellya told him and the chief to sit in the family room and she would explain as best she could.

When everyone was seated in the family room, Armellya told them the angel of death had showed up and was draining their essence, and he separated mother from child to do it. Armellya explained that with the two of them together, they were too strong for him to affect. However, she did not remember how he got them apart or anything else until she saw Jaden putting Jadellya in her comforter. Jaden asked if the angel of death was the same as the black angel figure. Armellya told Jaden they were two separate entities. Jaden suggested they talk to their mini-angels and see what they could find out, and Armellya agreed. Then she told Jaden to astroproject to the Dinosaur Tail.

The chief said it was close to the lunch hour and family time and suggested that he astroproject afterward. Jaden asked Armellya if she was up to going to the castle's private dining hall or if she wanted to eat at home. Armellya said she would rather eat at home, but she had better go to the castle's private dining hall to keep up appearances. With Armellya's response, Jaden took charge and told Armellya he was more concerned for her and Jadellya than appearances, so for that night, they would eat at the house. The chief said he would stay there with them if they did not mind, and Jaden spoke up before Armellya, telling the chief he was welcome at their home anytime. Then Armellya asked the chief to please stay. Jaden sent one of the castle's runners to the kitchen to let Melanie know Armellya, Jaden, and the chief would be eating at Jaden's house. Then the runner was to go and let Andrew know they would not be eating in the castle's private dining hall that night.

The castle's runner was to return with confirmation. The runner left to do as he was asked. Armellya set the house's round table out for the three of them to eat together. She also wanted the round table ready when Michelle showed up with lunch. It was not long before the castle's runner returned with confirmation that Melanie would bring their lunch to their house and a message from Andrew to feel better. Andrew also said he and Camillia would stop by after the lunch hour and family time to see how everyone there was doing.

Andrew and Camillia were in the family room waiting for the family members to get there, and they were all there in a brief time. Andrew led everyone to the castle's private dining room, and they sat in their seats. Then Melanie had the kitchen staff serve their lunch. While the kitchen staff served lunch for the individuals at the big round table, Melanie took lunch to Armellya and Jaden's house. After Melanie gave the three adults at the house lunch, she told them she hoped they felt better soon and then left.

In the castle's private dining hall, they all ate as they went around the big round table sharing their day. They finished eating about the time they were done sharing.

Armellya, Jaden, and the chief had a quiet lunch because they already knew how one another's day had gone. Just as they finished their lunch hour, Melanie returned for the dirty dishes. She was in and out promptly.

Now that the lunch hour was officially over, Jaden was

going to astroproject to the Dinosaur Tail to speak to their mini-angels about what role the angel of death had in the clash between the children. Jaden went to the bedroom, lay on the bed, and got comfortable. Then he astroprojected. The next thing he knew he was at the Dinosaur Tail. Jaden found his and Armellya's mini-angels fast, but before he could say anything to them, they told Jaden they knew why he was there. His mini-angel told him to go back to his body, and everyone's mini-angel would be there shortly. Jaden left the Dinosaur Tail with an expression of love and returned to his body.

Armellya went into their bedroom to watch over Jaden's body and to get some answers to her questions more rapidly. When Jaden returned, Armellya knew he had no answers for her because he had not been gone long enough. Armellya's heart sank. Then Jaden told her their mini-angels were on their way, and she regained some hope. Jaden told the chief that his mini-angel was coming also because she was concerned for his mental status from the shock and terror he had experienced. The chief said he was fine, but he would never forget the horror. He saw death coming for him, Armellya, and Jadellya. Jaden told the chief he had seen it also, but with his extra abilities, he was able to look away and do what he could to break them out of their deadly trance. Jaden told the chief that was why death showed its horrid face, to rid the community of special pale ones who posed a challenge to him and the fallen angel. Jaden and the chief did not have a chance to speak any more of the experience before their mini-angels arrived.

The chief was glad to see his mini-angel so he could put a friendly face in his mind's eye. His mini-angel told him he was not supposed to have seen the deadly incident, but the angel of death felt he needed to get to Armellya and Jadellya right then. The chief was just collateral damage. It was the angel of death's first chance to get Armellya and Jadellya apart, and he could not resist the opportunity. The mini-angel told the chief that Jadellya had become stronger and was developing more and more skills that were beyond those of the royal family. The mini-angel told Armellya, Jaden, and the chief that Jadellya had skills that superseded those of the angel of death and the fallen angel. The fallen angel could not do much damage with Jadellya around, so he summoned the angel of death for her. The mini-angel said that even Armellya was a guarantee to damage Jadellya beyond salvage.

The chief's mini-angel told him she could remove those images from his memory if he wanted, but he declined. The chief was not going to abandon his daughter and granddaughter. The chief's mini-angel assured him he would have nightmares over the incident, and if it became a problem for him, he should send Jaden or Armellya to the Dinosaur Tail to retrieve her, and she would take it all away. The chief said he would remember the proposition and take full advantage of it if the night terrors become too much to handle.

Jaden told the chief he would be the one to go to the Dinosaur Tail and to come to him any time and not to be afraid to wake him during the night hours. The chief thanked Jaden for his understanding and cooperation and then told him he would do whatever was necessary. Now that the chief had been addressed, it was time to attend to Armellya and Jaden. Armellya's mini-angel spoke first, telling her the angel of death was just that: an angel who came for souls, leaving the body lifeless. Armellya asked her mini-angel if she knew how the angel of death had separated her and Jadellya. She said it was not hard. While sleeping, Armellya had gotten far enough away from Jadellya for the angel of death to swoop Jadellya up into his arms without disturbing Armellya. Just before flying down upon Jadellya, the angel of death muted her voice so she could not cry out and alert her mother.

Jaden's mini-angel cautioned him that because he had the rare ability to look beyond death and function normally, he would most likely be the next target and would stay that way until he was no longer in the picture to save his wife and daughter. Jaden told the mini-angel that his professions had allowed him to handle death. Then the mini-angel revealed that when anyone or anything passed away, the angel of death would be there to fight for the soul, but he mostly lost. The mini-angel declared that they could defeat the angel of death, but it would take some precision on their part.

Jaden said he could take an unspecified leave of absence from his eight-hour shifts at the hospital, but he would still have to do checks on the two medicine rooms. He decided he could just take his family with him. Jaden's mini-angel said that would be fine if the hospital had no problems with that arrangement.

Then, right in the middle of the conversation, the mini-angels left without warning of any kind. They did not even leave their affections, which was highly abnormal.

Suddenly, there was a knock on the front door. Everyone then knew why the mini-angels had left so abruptly. Jaden got up and went to answer the front door. It was Andrew and Camillia. They were stopping by to see how everyone there was doing. They had also assumed more issues had occurred and were probably more serious than anything they had had so far.

Jaden hesitantly invited Andrew and Camillia inside the house and told them to sit in the family room where everyone else was, and they did. Andrew and Camillia greeted Armellya and the chief and then told them they had been missed at the castle's private dining hall that afternoon. Jaden told Andrew and Camillia there had been a new event that nearly took the lives of Armellya, Jadellya, and the chief.

Andrew and Camillia froze in their seats, speechless, until Armellya asked them if they were okay. They said they were and then asked if everyone else was. Jaden told them fortunately the chief had walked in as the angel of death was attacking Armellya and Jadellya, and before he could get the chief subdued, he got help. Jaden explained to Andrew and Camillia that the angel of death was different than the fallen angel. The angel of death came for souls. All that would be left would be a dead body. The fallen angel produced life by impregnating women with his spawn. Then the evil child would create havoc in the world somewhere, usually through diplomacy. Andrew asked Jaden if they were strong enough to ward off the angel of death, and Jaden told him Jadellya could do it, but it would take him and Armellya together to render him ineffective for an abbreviated time. Jaden said it might be a possibility for them to get rid of the angel of death for good if he, Armellya, and Jadellya went against him together with complete exactitude. Jaden told Andrew and Camillia that the mini-angels would not get involved in the war of good and evil because they were no match for the two corrupt angels. The mini-angels could give valuable information, and if they did not have it, destroying the two angels in question would be a guessing game. With the mini-angels' input, Jadellya, Armellya, and he himself would know what their weak points were and how to confront them. Armellya told Andrew and Camillia there was going to be a true war of the worlds that existed in a parallel formation—the pale ones, who were the last of humanity, against the forces of evil, which would live freely on earth if Jadellya were to fail in her destiny.

Andrew and Camillia asked how they could help Jadellya's chances of overcoming the two angels, and Armellya said to stay away from them so they did not become a security deposit for the angels. Armellya told them that they had already gotten ahold of the chief, and he would have lifelong consequences for being at the wrong place at the wrong time. Jaden told Andrew and Camillia that he, Armellya, and Jadellya were going to isolate in their home to prevent any other simple pale one from being affected and becoming an insurance policy for the two angels. The two angels had figured out that they would not leave a pale one behind to die, and that was how the angels were trying to weaken them. The two angels were trying to use distraction as a tactic. Andrew asked if the chief would stay with them or go back to his side of the castle. Jaden told Andrew it would ultimately be up to the chief if he stayed there or went home, but he recommended that the chief stay with them because of his fragile involvement.

The chief spoke up and told everyone he would be staying with Armellya and Jaden if Armellya was okay with it also. Armellya told the chief she had the same recommendation as Jaden because he was now a target.

Armellya was holding Jadellya, and she started to get fidgety and babble, which was definitely a sign that something was not right, so Armellya told Andrew and Camillia that they must leave immediately. Andrew and Camillia practically ran for the front door as they called out that they loved them. Then without looking back, they shut the door behind themselves. Camillia and Andrew understood that getting thrown out hastily was for their protection, so they did not take it personally. Once Andrew and Camillia were out of the house, Jadellya calmed down. It was Armellya's guess that the angel of death was going to target Andrew and Camillia to distract Jadellya so he could attack her more easily while subduing Jaden and Armellya. Armellya and Jaden found that the angel of death was very good at multitasking. The one thing that would help Armellya and Jaden contribute to the triumph over the angel of death was to know what his abilities were. It would help establish how much of a match they were to him. Armellya asked Jaden if it would be possible for their mini-angels to know that information and maybe even more. Jaden said it may be possible because the mini-angels said they had been around since the dawn of time, and he was guessing that with their presence came the angel of death and the fallen angel. The chief said it made sense to have both; it would create a balance in the world and would account for having good people who gave back to their world in some way and the destructive people who took from the world. There had been dramatic accounts of both throughout history.

Jaden and Armellya wholeheartedly agreed. Then Armellya asked Jaden if he was up to going back to the Dinosaur Tail to bring their mini-angels back so they could finish their conversation and get the additional information they had just discussed. Jaden told Armellya he would go on one condition: that she watch over his body in his absence because that would be a prime time for the angel of death to take his life without them knowing until it was too late. Armellya said that she and Jadellya would watch over him but to make it brief, and he said he would.

Jaden and Armellya went into their bedroom, and Jaden lay on the bed. Once Jaden was comfortable, he astroprojected and promptly found himself at the Dinosaur Tail, where his, Armellya's, Jadellya's, and the chief's mini-angels were waiting for him. The mini-angel told Jaden it was too dangerous to leave his body because it left him more vulnerable than anything else he could do and something could happen to his body. His mini-angel told him to get back to his body at once and they would be at his home by the time he got there. Without a word, he left the Dinosaur Tail. As Jaden opened his eyes, the mini-angels appeared and greeted everyone. Jaden, Armellya, the chief, and even Jadellya greeted the mini-angels back.

Jadellya's mini-angel went to her. She lay on Armellya's arm next to Jadellya's face and loved on her. Jadellya was smiling and joyfully cooing. Her mini-angel understood her words even though the adults around her did not. The mini-angel told the adults there that she understood Jadellya's communication and that Jadellya understood the adults'. Jadellya's mini-angel asked Armellya, Jaden, and the chief if they had any questions for Jadellya. She would interpret Jadellya's answers or comments, but at the same time, if Jadellya had any questions for them, she would ask them so they could respond to her. The adults felt that was fair. They were thankful that the mini-angel could understand her baby talk and grateful that she was willing to interpret for them.

Armellya asked Jadellya how they could best help her to be triumphant in the hostilities between virtue and iniquity.

The mini-angel told Armellya that Jadellya said to worry about protecting themselves, and she would help watch over their safety, but there was nothing other than that they could do besides stay together and keep her close. Jaden asked if she knew the two angels' weaknesses and strengths. The mini-angel said Jadellya knew their strengths because they had some of the same as hers but not as strong as hers and she had not learned of their weaknesses yet. The mini-angel said she knew of only one weakness for the angel of death and that was that he had a heart and could be extinguished by piercing the center of his heart or ripping it from his body. The mini-angel said the angel of death had no other organs, so piercing his heart required getting close enough to do it and exactness to get its center, not around it. The mini-angel said it would be better to get close enough to reach into his chest and rip it out. Then there would be no guessing if the center was pierced or not. The mini-angel told the adults that was why the angel of death always kept a certain distance from his prey.

Jaden asked Jadellya if she could occupy the angel of death long enough for him to get behind him and grab his heart out of him. Jadellya said she would have to try to physically subdue him because he was very observant and aware of what and who was where. Jaden asked Jadellya if they could try to do that. Then Armellya offered to be bait so he would be busy with her because she did not believe he would want to kill Santuvious. Jadellya was conceived for a purpose with a destiny. Santuvious was also conceived for a purpose and a destiny. They opposed each other. Jadellya said they would try that, but they had to discuss a plan in the smallest of details because enticing the angel of death was an extremely dangerous thing to do. The mini-angel told

Armellya that the demise of the angel of death and the fallen angel might give a chance for Santuvious to have a normal life without insanity. The mini-angels, Jaden, Armellya, Jadellya, and the chief came up with a detailed plot to destroy the angel of death. It had taken four hours of debating, and it was now the dinner hour.

Melanie would be at their front door soon, so the mini-angels expressed their love and left. Sure enough, soon after the mini-angels left, there was a knock at Jaden and Armellya's front door.

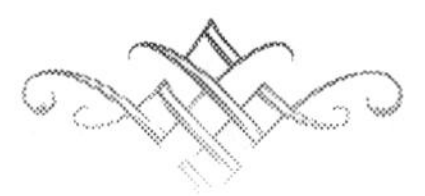

CHAPTER 3

JADEN GOT UP TO ANSWER THE FRONT DOOR, AND IT was Melanie with their dinner. She set it on the round table and left in a hurry as she was instructed to do at all meals. Armellya straightened up the round table, and everyone sat down to begin eating.

As they were eating, Armellya, Jaden, and the chief were comparing some personal observations involving the angel of death. The only thing their observations had in common was the angel of death's efforts specifically to stay away from Jadellya, as far as he physically could. That meant Armellya could not have Jadellya near her while she was being used as bait, which would leave her completely defenseless. It was a chance Armellya felt she had to take. She figured she would be the safest individual out of the three of them to be bait because she had something the fallen angel wanted, and that was Santuvious.

There was so much negativity surrounding the ambiance of the house that no one could get comfortable enough to eat dinner. They were not sure they would be able to sleep very well either. Everyone, including Jadellya, was on edge. It was tough not knowing when the next faceoff with the angel of death and the fallen angel would be. The anticipation made the dinner hour seem to last forever, but they realized it was finally over when they heard a knock at the door. It was Melanie coming for the dirty dishes. She was in and out in a flash.

As Melanie was shutting the front door, she told everyone she loved them, missed them, and hoped they would be back soon. Now that the chief knew he would be staying with Armellya and Jaden, he realized he needed items from home. He told Jaden he needed some things from his house, like clothing and grooming items. Before Jaden could say anything, Armellya said she had an idea on how to get the things that the chief needed from his home to theirs. She told the chief to make a detailed list of the things he wanted and send it by runner for the personal maid to put together. Once the items were all there, the castle's runner could bring it to the front door. The chief liked the idea. It saved all of them from having to go so they could stay together and avoid exposing who knew how many others to the forces of evil. The chief made up his list. Then Jaden called one of the castle's runners to take it to the other side of the castle and deliver it to the chief's personal maid.

Twenty minutes later, the castle's runner had returned with a big bag containing everything the chief asked for. The chief's maid had slipped some of his favorite goodies into the bag for him and his hosts. When the chief went to put his belongings in the spare bedroom, he happened to see them on top of the bag and took them out to Armellya and Jaden. He suggested they play a game and eat some treats to try to relax a little bit. Armellya and Jaden thought it was an excellent idea, so Armellya brought out a board game, and the men sat on the floor to set it up while Armellya and Jadellya went to get some plates to put their goodies on.

Armellya and Jadellya came out of the kitchen, and before getting to the family room, Jadellya got fussy. Armellya knew that meant danger was near. She hurriedly walked into the family room, and as she got to the threshold, Jaden and the chief looked up at her because they heard Jadellya fussing. They also knew what that meant. Before Armellya could cross the threshold, Jadellya threw her tiny hands in the air above her head and babbled, causing Armellya to stop dead in her tracks.

Jaden and the chief saw a dark figure directly behind Armellya. In fact, it was so perfectly placed that it looked more like a silhouette. Jaden and the chief swiftly bounced to their feet and slowly walked toward Armellya. The men could not determine which corrupt angel was behind her because of how close it was and the fact that it was centered behind her. Armellya knew one of the dark angels was behind her, so she used her senses to determine where he was. She realized the non-life-threatening angel was directly behind her. Armellya took a bet that it was the fallen angel because the angel of death would not get that close to her or Jadellya. She turned about and discovered she was correct. Armellya instinctively shoved Jadellya into the dark shadow, and it crumpled to its knees. Then she stepped into the figure so she and Jadellya were in direct contact with it. Armellya firmly called for Jaden to join her and Jadellya, and he responded. The chief stayed where he was. Suddenly, there was a shrill scream of pain. The fallen angel was trying to move away from them. Then Jadellya instantly put a protective bubble around herself, Armellya, Jaden, and the fallen angel. The fallen angel could not penetrate the protective bubble, even though he was intuitively trying. Jaden's, Armellya's, and Jadellya's hands began to glow. Then the glow started to spread throughout their whole bodies, and the fallen angel continued to screech in pain.

As the family's glowing got brighter, the dark angel's shriek got quieter. The fallen angel exploded abruptly in a puff of black smoke. The smell of death spread throughout the bubble. Jadellya kept the protective bubble around her mother, her father, and herself for fifteen minutes past the annihilation of the fallen angel. The smell of death wore off, and that was when Jadellya let the protective bubble down.

The chief watched this all happen and could not believe what he saw. The chief told Armellya and Jaden that when he was a human, he used to hear stories of ghosts, exorcisms, and the supernatural, but he never believed any of it. The chief said he was recanting his beliefs after having the experiences with the fallen angel and the angel of death. Armellya said that whatever was done to terminate the black angel's reign was done by Jadellya. She and Jaden only offered strength to what Jadellya was doing. Jaden said the real work would come when the angel of death emanated again. Out of curiosity, Jaden checked the time to see how long it took Jadellya to eradicate the fallen angel. From the time that Jadellya started to fuss to when they were released from the protective bubble was an hour and a half. Jaden told Armellya how long they contested the black angel, and she said it did not seem that long. The chief told Armellya and Jaden it was about bedtime. Then he asked where they wanted him to sleep. Armellya reminded Jaden and the chief that they needed to stay close together, so it would not be wise to put the chief in the spare bedroom by himself. Jaden said there were two options: one was to put a cot in their bedroom and the other was just to have him sleep in their bed with them because it was large enough.

It turned out that Armellya, Jaden, Jadellya, and the chief were all going to sleep in the one enormous bed. Having everyone in the same bed put the adults at ease a bit. They were hoping it would lead to a good night's sleep. Everyone knew if the angel of death were on his way, Jadellya would know before he got to them and alert everyone. The adults were so exhausted that they fell asleep right away. They did not even say good night to one another.

A few hours passed by, and all was well. Then without warning, Armellya was awakened by sharp abdominal pains. Even though the severe pains were in Armellya's abdomen, they stretched out around to her back. Armellya was silently suffering, but Jadellya must have known her mother was not well because she woke up, shimmied closer to her mother's stomach, and buried her tiny hands into her mother's body. The pain eventually got more intense, and Armellya became concerned so she woke Jaden. Jaden asked if everything was okay, and she told him it was Santuvious, that something must be wrong. Jaden asked Armellya to describe what she felt. Armellya told him she was having fierce pains in the abdomen that shot around to her back.

Armellya and Jaden were whispering to avoid waking the chief, but he was a light sleeper and had heard everything the couple had said. The chief asked Jaden if there was something wrong with the pregnancy or if it was something paranormal.

Jaden said he was not sure, but according to Jadellya, the angel of death was not the problem. Jaden told Armellya that he was going to give her a prenatal exam to rule out anything they may be able to fix.

The chief got out of bed and took Jadellya while Jaden did the exam. The first thing Jaden wanted to do was an ultrasound, and the chief wanted to watch over Jaden's shoulder because he had never seen one done before. When Jaden saw Santuvious, he was very active and had the umbilical cord wrapped around his neck more than once, but Jaden could not tell how many times. Jaden told Armellya that Santuvious was in the process of turning head down, but she should not experience pain from that. Jaden was trying to determine how many times the umbilical cord was wrapped around the baby's neck. Then, finally head down, he unexpectedly stopped moving. That was when Jaden saw an oddity. Santuvious was putting off a shadow as though there was something in there with him. This was the first time Jaden had seen anything like this for any pregnancy, human or animal. Jaden went ahead and did the physical exam and found that Armellya was dilated to four centimeters. She still had several weeks to go before her due date, although Jaden knew if Armellya gave birth right then, the baby would easily survive. Jaden got an abrupt instinctual concern that delivering Santuvious would take Armellya's life because of his mischievous disposition and breeding. If that proved to be the case, Jadellya may not be able to save her mother's life.

Jaden was unusually silent, so Armellya asked him what he had found out. Jaden was always honest with her, and this was the first instance where he wished he could lie to her, but it was not in him to lie to anyone. Jaden told Armellya it was slightly possible that she was in labor and that the delivery of the baby may take her life for reasons he could not explain. Jaden went on to tell Armellya that there appeared to be something unnatural in the womb with Santuvious. Jaden finished giving her a report on his findings by telling her it appeared that the umbilical cord was around the baby's neck more than once. He asked her how she felt now since it had been fifteen minutes since he had checked her, and she said the pain was still there and just as forceful. Jaden asked to check her cervix one last time for the night, and she agreed. It appeared Armellya was in labor because she had dilated another centimeter in that short amount of time. The night was going to be a prolonged, intense one with the delivery of a dark-sided child. Jaden knew he was going to have to keep a close eye on his wife and their children. Armellya was dilating fast like she did with Jadellya, but this delivery was far more agonizing for her.

Jaden wanted to do another ultrasound just to see the baby's neck and to look at the shadowy figure. Jaden got the ultrasound on Armellya, and he saw the baby as it should be with nothing around his neck. Then he saw another figure that looked like a second baby, and he could not explain his findings. The second baby appeared as a dark angelic shadow still, but it was very defined and separate from Santuvious. The chief placed Jadellya next to Armellya on the bed, and she fussed a bit. That told the adults something was near, but they did not know what. It could be Santuvious, or the shadow with him, or the angel of death. As fast as Armellya delivered babies, Jaden could not worry about danger until it was to present itself. In the meantime, he decided to check

Armellya for any progress. Sure enough, there was a crowning baby.

As the baby was being born and showing great strength, Armellya was becoming weak and barely conscious. Jaden told the chief to talk to Armellya and try to keep her alert, and the chief gladly did as he was asked. Unfortunately, talking to Armellya was not helping her in any way, for she was fully unconscious. Finally, Santuvious was born, and Jaden handed him to the chief to hold. Then, when Jaden was waiting for the afterbirth, there seemed to be something else crowning. At that point, Jadellya was fussing and could not get close enough to her mother. Jaden started to realize he was birthing an entity, so he got Jadellya over to her mother's groin so she could do her miracle of overcoming evil.

Jadellya started to glow, and just as before, there was a horrible noise coming from the half-birthed entity. It sounded like fingernails on a chalkboard. Jaden placed both of his hands on Jadellya for a stronger and hopefully faster obliteration of that monstrosity. It was not long before Jadellya abolished the shadow child that Armellya had in her womb with Santuvious. Just like the fallen angel, it burst into a puff of black smoke and gave off the scent of death. Jaden moved Jadellya to her mother's side and then went on to check on Armellya's status. As Jaden was checking on Armellya, without warning, she started to seize. It lasted for four minutes. Now Armellya was breathing only five times a minute, and Jaden could not find a pulse because it was so slow and weak. It appeared her heart was barely beating. Jaden did not want anyone else involved in the whole dark-side-of-the-world thing. The chief was enough, but Jaden had to involve the other doctor at the hospital in Armellya's care.

If Jaden did not get some equipment to his house, he would surely lose Armellya.

Jaden wrote a list of all the things he would need for Armellya plus some extra supplies and then got the castle's runner out of bed to go to the hospital and give the note to the doctor on call. He demanded that he made it speedy. By the time the runner got back with the on-call doctor and all the equipment, he requested, Jaden was performing cardiopulmonary resuscitation on Armellya. The doctor got everything set up as he was asking what happened to Armellya. Jaden told the doctor Armellya had a tough delivery, but the infant was all right. Together, Jaden and the doctor got Armellya on life support, but being as Jaden was a doctor and knew exactly what happened, he knew her chances of pulling through were slim to none.

Jaden thanked the doctor for his help and for bringing the medical equipment without question. Then he escorted the doctor to the front door and said goodbye. Once the doctor was gone, Jaden and the chief were glad there was no incident with the angel of death. Jaden and the chief were expecting the angel of death to arrive any time for Armellya's soul since her condition was grim and there was no bond for survival between Armellya and Santuvious. Jaden was curious if the infant dark shadow had been a part of Santuvious that was demonic and somehow had separated from him. To test his theory, Jaden brought the newborn over to Armellya and Jadellya. When the children were side by side, Jadellya cooed, and Santuvious smiled. There were no signs of agony or peril between the two children, so Jaden figured it was true that somehow Santuvious was separated from his evil spirit and that may have accounted for the agony Armellya was in. Jaden wondered how Santuvious was alive. If his soul was overpowered by Jadellya, where did he get a soul from to continue to live since the soul was the essence of life? Then it occurred to Jaden that he must be surviving off Armellya's soul, which would account for her state of being. It was said that once the umbilical cord was cut, there would be no more reliability of survival for Santuvious from Armellya.

Jaden was at a loss; he had a thriving son and a dying wife. The only thing he could think to do was to use his healing ability to try to bring Armellya back to her lively self. Jaden told the chief to stay back and no matter what should happen not to call on anyone. The chief agreed. Jaden put his hands on Armellya and started to try to heal her. His hands lit up. Then the bright yellow light spread throughout his body. Shortly after the healing started, a vision of a large and a miniature soul were entangled and appeared to be struggling with each other. It was obvious that Armellya's and Santuvious's souls were intertwined, but why was Santuvious still thriving? Jaden took one hand off Armellya to touch the souls, but there was a protective shield around them, possibly done by Jadellya. Jaden realized he could do nothing with his healing ability, so he decided to consult with their mini-angels. Jaden took his hands away from Armellya as he told the chief to watch over everything because he was going to astroproject to the Dinosaur Tail.

Jaden lay on the bed next to Armellya, and as soon as he got comfortable, he was at the Dinosaur Tail. Jaden called for his mini-angel. Then she went to him. Jaden explained to the mini-angel the condition Armellya was in and the birth events and then asked the mini-angel what could be done to save Armellya. The mini-angel told Jaden they could pierce the protective shield and try to untwine the souls and guide them to their proper individuals. Jaden asked the mini-angel if she would at least try, and she said yes, they would get there right away. He left the Dinosaur Tail and went back to his body. By the time he opened his eyes, all the mini-angels were surrounding Armellya.

As the mini-angels started to glow, Jaden saw the intertwined souls in the protective bubble. While the mini-angels got brighter, the protective bubble started to disappear. The mini-angels started to move to the two souls. During that time, Armellya's vital signs began to rise, and she quit unintentionally fighting the ventilator. The mini-angels were struggling hard to untwine the two souls, and after ten minutes of trying, they did it. The larger of the two souls soared to Armellya and immersed itself in her. The smaller of the two souls fluttered about in an obvious state of confusion. The mini-angels tried to guide the small soul to Santuvious, but it would not go near him. That told the mini-angels his state of existence was of a wraithlike nature. The only way the infant soul was going to go into Santuvious was if they could lure the malevolent soul out of him first. Jadellya spoke to the mini-angels and told them she could subdue the dark soul in Santuvious. Jadellya told the mini-angels to have her brother brought to her, so they told Jaden to place Santuvious up against her on the family room chair. Jadellya did not want her mother near in the event Santuvious should try to assault her soul again. Jaden wasted no time. He grabbed Armellya and Santuvious and placed them on the chair in the family room. The mini-angels stood by waiting for Jadellya to give them their instructions. Jadellya started to glow slightly, and Santuvious began screaming like he was in agony. Jadellya went from a slight glow to an all-out glow within two seconds. Santuvious had no defense for Jadellya's strategic action of attacking him before he could become aware of it. Santuvious's heart stopped from shock. It was like literally being scared to death. Jadellya ordered the mini-angels to herd the soul to Santuvious's lifeless body, and they did. Jaden and the chief watched the soul switching occur, and even though they witnessed it, they had a tough time believing it could occur. The dispossessed soul lay in Santuvious's body as though it was meant to be there. Now hovering above Santuvious was the dark shadow of the soul they had just displaced. Jadellya placed a protective bubble around it and easily eradicated it. That black soul, like the others, gave a shrill scream and released a foul smell of death.

When the soul switching was complete, Jaden called the chief over to pick up Jadellya while he went to pick up Santuvious. When the two men approached the chair, the chief got Jadellya, while Jaden just observed Santuvious. Jaden's heart descended from his chest when he realized Santuvious was not breathing and had no pulse.

Out of the instinct of being a doctor, Jaden swiped Santuvious off the chair and was ready to do cardiopulmonary resuscitation on him, but the mini-angels stopped him and told him to lay him on the floor. Jaden laid the newborn on the floor and moved away with tears in his eyes. Even though Jaden did not sire the child, he still considered the child as his son, and he was a part of Armellya, so there had to be some good in him somewhere. The mini-angels swarmed around Santuvious like bees and held the appearance of lightning bugs; they did not get brighter as usual. The mini-angels seemed to be around the child for a long time when it was only a couple of minutes. At that moment in time, all Jaden wanted was to hear Santuvious cry out. Finally, another minute went by. Then Santuvious cried, and it was music to Jaden's ears. The mini-angels ceased glowing and took their places around Armellya. Before the mini-angels could channel their abilities onto Armellya, Jaden asked them how Santuvious was. His mini-angel told him the infant was now 100 percent pale one but to still watch for signs of being a serial killer because that and other behavioral abnormalities seemed to be instilled in a certain part of the brain and had various triggers—in other words, it may be genetic, and he was conceived of a demon. It was not a part of the soul.

Now that both children were settled down and safe from anything subhuman or health related, Jaden asked the chief to watch over Jadellya and Santuvious so he could focus on what the mini-angels were doing with Armellya. The chief said, "Sure," and went to the children. Right at that moment, Armellya was doing somewhat better since the soul that was probably hers descended into her. Now it was just a matter of getting her body to bounce back from being soulless for so long. Jaden observed the mini-angels as they stayed around her. It was not clear to Jaden what they were doing, and he dared not interrupt them to ask. It did not appear that the mini-angels were doing anything. Then, without warning, one of the mini-angels directed Jaden to take the life support away. Jaden was hesitant because from a medical doctor's point of view, she still was not doing well enough to remain existent without the life support.

Jaden told the mini-angels that he did not believe Armellya would survive without medical intervention, and the mini-angels' response to that was that Armellya had to make the decision on her own whether to live or die. Jaden started sobbing. Then the mini-angel told him not to fret; Armellya had it in her to prevail over death. The mini-angel told Jaden and the chief that Armellya could hear them while Jaden was doing as the mini-angels asked, so she hoped she heard him because she was now on her own.

Jaden bent over her and kissed her. Then he told Armellya he loved her and wanted her to come back to him. He told the chief if Armellya passed away, he would never forgive himself for not doing everything medically possible for her, and he would turn in his medical license. The chief reminded Jaden that the mini-angels had always been honest and pulled through for them, so they must know something they did not.

The mini-angels continued to surround Armellya, and the chief still had the children. Jaden was standing between the chief and the mini-angels, trying to observe Armellya. He was waiting on some type of response from her, but it was difficult to see her through all the mini-angels surrounding her. One of the mini-angels told the chief to place the children alongside their mother. The chief did as he was told and put one child on each side. Then he moved away from them. As soon as the children were with Armellya, Jadellya started crying worse than Jaden or the chief had ever heard her cry. At the same time, the mini-angels disappeared into thin air.

Jaden and the chief were alarmed but left the children with Armellya. The two of them walked to one side of the bed and stayed there. Out of nowhere, the angel of death was at Armellya's side on the other side of the bed. It did not appear that Jadellya was doing anything to protect anyone yet. The angel of death leaned over Armellya to suck the life out of her so he could take her soul. The chief was so fearful of the angel of death that he froze where he was and could not even move his head away as to avoid seeing any more dreadful things. Jaden was going to try to get close to the angel of death to tear his heart out of his chest. Before Jaden could move at all, Armellya harshly sat straight up, thrust her hand into the angel of death's chest, and plucked his heart out. While Armellya sat there with the angel of death's heart still beating in her hand, the angel of death staggered. There were no screams, just silence. Then the black figure converted into a black puff of smoke and gave off the robust stench of death. The angel of death's heart that Armellya held quit beating and converted into dust.

The chief finally regained his composure and then fainted. Jaden left the chief on the floor, and instead of checking him out, he grabbed Armellya and gave her a big bear hug. Jaden told Armellya he loved her and was overjoyed that she was back. Armellya told Jaden she could hear everything that was going on; she just could not get her body to comply with attempts at functioning. Jaden asked Armellya how she could get her body to comply with the will to pluck the heart out of the angel of death. She told him it was not a matter of asking her body to comply; it was a forced attempt that she was not certain would be followed up with any action. Armellya told Jaden she was fine, but she was not so sure about the chief. Jaden chuckled and then knelt beside the chief to check him out. The chief was out cold, so Jaden went to get an ammonia inhalant from his black bag. Jaden cracked it open and then waved it under the chief's nose.

The chief woke up moving his head away from the ammonia while telling Jaden to get that stuff away from him. He gently sat up and then asked what happened, so Jaden told him he fainted, probably from the shock and fright. It gave a surge of adrenalin that raised his blood pressure. Then there was a sudden drop in the blood pressure. Jaden helped the chief off the floor as he told him to get up gradually. Once the chief was up, Jaden had him sit on the edge of the bed. The chief did not realize Armellya was alert and oriented until she asked him if he was okay. The chief stood up, turned toward the bed, and hugged Armellya while asking her if she was okay. Armellya said she was fine, and then the chief giggled and said he was fine also.

Armellya told Jaden she wanted to go sit in the family room with the children. Armellya said she had not really seen Santuvious. Then she asked how he was. Jaden proudly told Armellya that Santuvious was 100 percent pale one with a heavenly soul thanks to Jadellya and the mini-angels. Together, the chief and Jaden helped Armellya to the family room and had her sit on the couch so there was enough room for her and both children. Jaden asked Armellya not to be offended, but he needed to know if she had the strength in her arms to hold the children safely. Armellya told Jaden that she honestly did not know and then asked him to stand by until they found out. Jaden told Armellya it would not be a problem to stay close. Then he asked the chief to get one of the children.

While the chief was getting Santuvious, Jaden went to get Jadellya. The two men brought the children to Armellya, and then the chief handed Santuvious to Armellya. The chief stayed right beside her in case she needed help holding her son. Armellya's arms were doing just fine, so she asked for Jadellya. Jaden gave Jadellya to her, carefully placing her daughter in her arm, and then he stayed close. The children seemed to like each other, and Jadellya was playing with her brother's hand while cooing. Although Santuvious had had a rough start, he seemed to be a happy baby just as Jadellya was. After a few minutes, Jaden and the chief both sat down in chairs, and they started to discuss the recent events and how they were ecstatic that it was all over.

In the middle of complimenting one another over how well everyone stuck together and incapacitated the forces of evil, there was a knock on their front door. None of them could guess who was at their door, but Jaden went to the front door and cautiously answered it. It was Melanie with breakfast. So much had happened over the night hours that they had lost track of time. Jaden told Armellya that before breakfast and while they were discussing the end of their terror, he needed to tell her something. Armellya felt the seriousness of his upcoming words through vibes, so she gave him her unbroken attention. Jaden told Armellya that the mini-angels told him that even though Santuvious now had a heavenly soul, they still needed to keep an eye on him to keep him from becoming a serial killer because it had to do with the brain not the soul. Jaden told Armellya it was in the genetics, and he was conceived by evil. The mini-angels had warned him that something could trigger the corrupt behavior. Armellya was saddened, but she told Jaden maybe they could heal the malformed part of the brain before it got triggered. Jaden said he would have to check with the mini-angels.

With that, Jaden went to the dining room to set the round table and put the food where it needed to be. Then he went back to the family room to help Armellya to the dining room. When Jaden got to the threshold of the family room, Armellya was there and walking normally. He asked her how she felt. Armellya said she had her strength back. Then Jaden told her to take it easy for a couple days to make sure she not only had the strength to function but also the endurance for repetitive actions and lengthy activities.

Armellya, Jaden, and the chief sat at the round table and ate their breakfast. While they were eating, the chief asked if it was safe to go back to his side of the castle and be a part of society again. Jaden suggested that they summon the mini-angels to find out if they had truly ended the wicked reign of terror, and while doing that, they could ask them about healing Santuvious's brain. Armellya and the chief agreed with Jaden. Then Jaden said he would go to the Dinosaur Tail right after Melanie retrieved the breakfast dishes. Everyone finished eating and much faster than usual. They did not realize how hungry they were until they started to eat. Melanie finally arrived to gather all the dirty dishes and, not knowing any different, left in a hurry.

Now that Melanie had been there, Jaden went to the bedroom, lay on the bed, and got comfortable. Seconds later, Jaden found himself in the Dinosaur Tail, looking for his mini-angel. Jaden found his mini-angel and then asked her if she and Armellya's, the chief's, and the children's mini-angels could visit again. She told Jaden to return home, and they would be there right behind him. When Jaden opened his eyes back at home, the mini-angels were with them. Jaden's and Armellya's mini-angels told them to tell them why they needed them, so Jaden asked the mini-angel if it was safe to be back in society and let the chief go home. Then before the mini-angel could respond, Armellya asked the mini-angel if there was any way that Santuvious's brain could be healed so he would not become a serial killer.

The mini-angel said she was happy to report that they could join society again and the chief could go home. The things of the dark side were gone. The mini-angel told Armellya there was no healing that would change Santuvious's genetics. Then she apologized for the grave news. The mini-angels said they would resume their midnight visits, and if they were needed outside of that they should feel free to visit the Dinosaur Tail. The mini-angels expressed their love, and Jaden, Armellya, the chief, Santuvious, and Jadellya expressed theirs. Then the mini-angels returned to the Dinosaur Tail. Jaden told the chief he would help pack his things when he was ready, but the chief said he had an idea of how to get back into society.

Jaden and Armellya were both interested in hearing his idea, so they all sat at the round table in the dining room. The chief said to summon Melanie to have a small reintegration party.

Once everyone was at the castle's private dining hall sitting at the big round table, the five of them could walk in together and surprise everyone. The chief pointed out that no one knew Armellya had the baby, so they would take both children to the party. After the lunch hour and family time, they could give the children to their nannies. Armellya said she liked that idea, and Jaden said it was an innovative idea. Jaden sent for the castle's runner. Then when he got to the couple's house, Jaden told him to bring Melanie and make sure she had paper and pencil. The runner left right away and returned with Melanie five minutes later. Jaden thanked the runner and then grabbed Melanie's hand and dragged her into the house, shutting the front door behind her. While Melanie was there, the children were in their bedrooms sleeping, and that pleased Armellya because she did not want Melanie to know she had the baby until everyone else found out.

Jaden, Armellya, the chief, and Melanie sat at the round table in the dining room and had a discussion. Jaden told Melanie that they were free to be in public again, but they were going to hide out until the lunch hour and family time. Jaden asked Melanie if she could put together a small party on such short notice to celebrate success and being back. Melanie said, "Absolutely."

Melanie was so excited to hear the good news that she was ready to get back to the kitchen and start working. She loved throwing parties, and there were not many that came up. Melanie changed the subject and asked Jaden what had them so isolated for so long. Jaden told her she would find out during the lunch hour and family time. Armellya told Melanie that they also had a blessed surprise to reveal when they saw everyone. Melanie was anxious to know what the surprise was so she asked to see it and promised not to tell anyone, but Armellya stood her ground and told Melanie she would see the surprise when everyone else saw it.

Jaden was finished speaking with Melanie so she left promptly to get started with the lunch hour and family time preparations. Melanie was going to put the prepared lunch food on hold for the dinner hour and start a whole new lunch menu. Once Melanie left, the chief said it was going to be a short amount of time before the lunch hour and family time, so he suggested playing that game they did not get to play the night before. Armellya was too fatigued, so she suggested they all take a nap because it was going to get busy after their isolation period ended. The chief agreed that was an excellent idea. He confessed he was exhausted, so Armellya, Jaden, and the chief went to the couple's giant bed and lay down. They were all sleeping as soon as their heads hit the pillows.

A few hours later, Armellya woke up because she had gotten enough sleep, but Jaden and the chief were still trying to catch up on theirs. Armellya had some downtime while she was on life support so she did not need as much rest. Armellya happened to notice what time it was and realized it was close to the lunch hour and family time. She woke Jaden and the chief, telling them the time for the party in their honor was there. Jaden and the chief jumped out of the bed and then went to the bathroom to freshen up, and when they were done, Armellya would go and freshen up. In the meantime, Armellya was getting the children ready to go see the whole family. Armellya finished with the children at the same time Jaden and the chief finished in the bathroom, so she went into the bathroom to freshen up. By the time everyone in the house was ready to go to the castle's private dining room, they could hear the rest of the family in the family room. Eventually, it got quiet, so Jaden, Armellya, the chief, and the children went to the castle's family room to listen for the best time to pop in on everyone.

Once all those in the dining hall were seated at the big round table, they noticed the party setup and then asked Melanie what the party was for. That was when Jaden, Armellya, the children, and the chief walked in. Everyone stood up and clapped, saying, "Congratulations!" Then they realized the last time they had seen Armellya, she was still pregnant. Now she held the infant in her arms. Everyone could not wait to see the new child. Armellya, Jaden, and the chief sat down at the big round table. Then they introduced the new addition to their little family as they passed Santuvious around. Everyone adored him. He was a beautiful baby and so tiny. Jaden was holding Jadellya, and when Santuvious made it around the big round table, Armellya would have him back. Then everyone could start to eat. They were all curious about what had Armellya, Jaden, the chief, and the children isolated for so long. Armellya told everyone there were two dark spirits after them, and they could not be around anyone because the dark spirits would have killed them also. Jaden told them there was no need to worry now because Jadellya and Armellya had vanquished them. Everyone was shocked that evil even existed in their realm, and Jaden told them where there was good, there had been evil at some point.

Now that Armellya, Jaden, and the chief were finished recounting the story of their ordeal in detail and had shared the birth of Santuvious, it was time for the others to share the events of their day. They all finished sharing their day and expressing how much Armellya, Jaden, and the chief were missed. They did not see Jadellya much because she was always with her nanny, but they were delighted to see her as well, and Santuvious, he was a great surprise.

Next, Melanie brought out a colossal cake and some homemade ice cream. Everyone agreed that Melanie should cut the cake because there was more than one guest of honor, so she did. Melanie served everyone, starting with the guests of honor.

They all enjoyed the treat as they held light conversations during the cake and ice cream time. It was a pleasant change from the somber lunch-hour conversation. It was also a relief to have Armellya, Jaden, and the chief back because everyone was so worried about them and had no information about their condition. They just knew Jaden, Armellya, and the chief were in a severe position. If they had known the circumstances were life-or-death, they may not have stayed away because they would have wanted to help them endure the challenges that they were going through.

The lunch hour and family time had run into overtime, so once everyone was finished with their cake and homemade ice cream, they got up from the castle's big round table and lined up to give hugs and kisses on the cheek to Armellya, Jaden, the chief, Jadellya, and Santuvious. Before leaving the castle's private dining hall, Jaden told Armellya he was going to take the rest of the day and spend it with her and the children. He would go back to work at the hospital and on call for the veterinary hospital the next day. Armellya did not mind because she wanted to spend some peaceful time with her husband. Still in the castle's private dining hall, the chief told Armellya and Jaden he was going to go get his new wolf puppy because he had his side of the castle prepared for the pup right before the seclusion period that just ended for them. The chief was supposed to already have picked up his puppy, but he had to be segregated the same day because of the angel of death and the fallen angel. Jaden and Armellya told the chief they were happy for him and maybe later they would go over to his side of the castle to meet his new wolf puppy. The chief told them they were more than welcome to his side of the castle anytime. Jaden and Armellya found their home staff and told them they could return to work, so all the staff went back with Jaden and Armellya and got started on their work without hesitation.

At this point in time, the chief was mounting his horse to go get his wolf puppy. The chief was so electrified about his wolf pup that he hurried to get to the animal shop. At the animal shop, the chief went inside and proceeded to go straight to where the puppies were. The worker at the animal shop remembered which pup the chief had taken a liking to so he kept the pup on hold. The rest of the litter were already in their new homes. When the shop worker saw the chief, he ran to him at the front door and greeted him, telling him he had some good news for him. The chief got to the puppy kennels and did not see any puppies left. His heart sank. That was when the shop worker went to the back room of the kennel area. He was gone for three minutes. When the shop worker came back out of the kennel room, the chief had just turned around to leave. Then the shop worker called out. The chief turned toward the shop worker to find out what he had to say. Then the chief noticed a wolf pup in his hands. The chief walked fast toward the shop worker. The shop worker told the chief it was the male wolf pup he had wanted. They had held on to the pup for him.

The chief thanked the worker. Then he took the pup from his hands and started to love on him. The chief told the shop worker that evening he was to come to the castle and help him get the pup settled in and have dinner with him. They could discuss a good name for the wolf pup. The shop worker accepted the invitation. The pet shop worker was eager to have dinner at the royal castle and with the chief. It was a real honor to be in his presence with his full attention all to himself.

The chief left the pet shop to take his wolf pup home and introduce him to his new home. When the chief got back to his side of the castle and took his wolf puppy inside, he let the pup down on the floor. The pup automatically started to sniff things out. The chief figured it would be best to leave the puppy be for a while so he could adapt to his new surroundings. While the puppy was doing his own thing, the chief went to his bedroom to take a nap for a short while. The chief was still overtired from being up for two days and one night.

Meanwhile, Armellya and Jaden's house staff had just finished with their duties, so Jaden gave them the rest of the day off and advised them that starting the next day they would return full-time. Armellya and Jaden were mentally exhausted from the confrontation with the fallen angel and the angel of death. They told each other they would not use their abilities for a couple of days so they could get their strength back. Armellya and Jaden were getting ready to lie down in their oversized bed, but they were delayed when someone knocked on their front door. Armellya told Jaden to go ahead and lie down; she would take care of whoever was at the door and join him soon.

Armellya opened the front door. It was Andrew in a state of distress. Andrew said Camillia was in their bedroom lying down, but something was wrong with her. Armellya asked Andrew if they needed Jaden, and he said, "Please send him over." Then he ran off.

Armellya hollered for Jaden as she grabbed his black bag. Jaden raced into their family room and asked who was in need. Armellya told Jaden they were going to Camillia's bedroom. Then they ran to Camillia's room. When they got there, Camillia was on her bed appearing to be in agony, and Andrew was there holding her hand. Jaden asked Camillia to describe what was going on.

Camillia looked up at Jaden, and with tears in her eyes, she said she was having some terrible cramping in her lower abdomen that made it virtually impossible to move at all. Jaden asked Camillia when her last menses was, and she told him she was three months late. Jaden asked her if there was a possibility that she could be pregnant, and she told him she did not know. Jaden repeated the question in a distinct way. He asked her if she and Andrew were planning for another baby. Camillia said they never really did plan their children. She knew when she was ready to conceive and would ask Andrew if he was ready for another child. He always said yes, so they made love and conceived.

Jaden asked Camillia if she had felt the ability to conceive recently, and she said no but she and Andrew had been making love regularly. Jaden told Armellya to give him the handheld ultrasound machine from his black bag, and she did. Jaden did the ultrasound on Camillia's entire abdomen and saw that all her organs looked normal, but there was a baby in her uterus, so he looked at everything else around the baby that mattered, and it all looked normal.

Jaden asked for Armellya to hand him his black bag. After she did, Jaden gathered the things he needed to get blood samples for all the tests he wanted to know about. Instead of waiting for a runner, Armellya ran the blood to the hospital herself, and when she got there, she told the charge nurse that Jaden needed the results stat. The charge nurse took the vials of blood to the laboratory and told the technician to drop what he was doing and run the blood tests immediately.

Armellya waited at the nurses' desk for the paper results while the charge nurse waited in the laboratory. Fifteen minutes went by. Then the charge nurse came running down the hallway with the test results in her hand. She passed them off to Armellya, and Armellya ran them back to the castle.

Twenty-five minutes later, Armellya gave the test results to Jaden so he could read them, and he was not happy with the results. Camillia had a lot of low values. Jaden asked Camillia if she had any vaginal bleeding, and she denied it, but according to a couple of the blood values, there was bleeding somewhere. Jaden spoke to Camillia in simple terms and told her that her pregnancy hormones were too low for the number of weeks the embryo appeared to be, which meant she would most likely lose the baby if something was not done. That would account for the abdominal cramping. Camillia appeared to be twelve weeks along, so Jaden told Camillia and Andrew he could give her medicine to stop the muscles in her abdomen from contracting, which would relieve the majority of the pain. Jaden said the next thing he could do was to give Camillia another medicine and supplement to increase the pregnancy hormone and iron level. Jaden added that Camillia would have to be on strict bed rest for sixteen weeks. Jaden also made sure to warn Camillia and Andrew that the actions they would be taking to save the pregnancy might not work, but it would give them higher chances than if they did nothing.

Jaden did assure Camillia and Andrew that he would do everything possible to try to save the baby. Andrew thanked Jaden for figuring out what was wrong with Camillia. Then he told him that they could not afford to lose the baby. Andrew said Camillia would not be the same if she lost the baby. She would blame herself. Armellya asked Jaden to step outside of the door with her for a few minutes.

When Jaden and Armellya were alone, Armellya asked if

their healing ability would allow Camillia to have a healthy full-term pregnancy. Jaden said it would, but he was warned by his mini-angel about combining healing abilities with traditional medicine.

Armellya could not understand why Jaden would not use his healing abilities. What could it harm? Armellya was going to ask their mini-angels about that to better understand the conflict, if there was one. She was just about to speak to Jaden when Jadellya's nanny came barreling up the hallway with Jadellya. She was fussing boisterously, and the nanny told Armellya she believed Jadellya wanted her mother. Armellya said that was fine and took Jadellya from the nanny, but Jadellya continued to be troubled about something. Camillia heard little Jadellya carrying on so she called out to Armellya to let her see the child. Armellya was willing to try to see if Jadellya would settle down for Camillia, so she took her into the bedroom. Armellya laid Jadellya on the bed next to Camillia, and sure enough, that was what Jadellya wanted. She started to coo and smile. Jadellya babbled. Then her body lit up, and she shot a stream of light from her body to Camillia's belly. Camillia's stomach started to glow slightly, and everyone in the room saw an outline of Camillia's baby.

A few minutes later, all the lights and glowing Jadellya created were gone, and Camillia said the pain was gone also. Armellya told Jaden that the mini-angel may have scolded him on medical practices, but she obviously did not scold Jadellya. Camillia got Jadellya in her arms. Then she sat up, kissed the child's cheek, and thanked her. Jadellya giggled. Camillia looked up at Jaden and asked him if he could take her on as his patient for the pregnancy, and he said yes. Jaden told Camillia although it was not highly looked upon to take family as patients, it did happen, and he would always be available for family.

Camillia was delighted, and she thanked Jaden. Then he told Camillia he wanted to see her again in two weeks unless she felt she needed to be seen earlier. Camillia agreed. Then she asked if it was still mandatory to have bed rest. Jaden said Jadellya had healed her and the baby so no bed rest was necessary, but he still wanted her to take it easy. Camillia asked Armellya if it would be okay to keep Jadellya until the dinner hour so she could spend some time spoiling her with her favorite things, and Armellya said it was fine. Armellya reminded Camillia that she was Jadellya's grandmother and joked with her that spoiling the grandchildren was her job. Then Camillia and Armellya laughed together.

Armellya bent over Jadellya and kissed her forehead. Then she told her what a wonderful thing she had done. Jadellya giggled again, and everyone laughed. Andrew commented that he was relieved to see things work out for everyone. Jaden, Armellya, Camillia, and Andrew hugged one another. Then Jaden and Armellya left Camillia and Andrew's home. As Armellya and Jaden went back into their house, they both felt it was not worth going to bed for a nap because they had spent a considerable amount of time with the emergency. Armellya had the idea to go visit the chief and see how he was getting along now that he had peace and quiet again.

Jaden thought that visiting the chief was a great idea to let him know he was missed already. Armellya and Jaden dropped of Jaden's black bag and then went down the elongated hall that connected the chief's side of the castle to theirs. Jaden knocked on the chief's back door, and he answered it. The chief had the back door barely cracked and was speaking through. Jaden asked the chief if everything was okay, and the chief said yes. The chief told Armellya and Jaden that he got his wolf puppy earlier that day and did not want him getting out. Jaden asked the chief if he and Armellya could visit, and he told them to let him pick up the pup. Then they could let themselves in. When the chief finally caught the wild wolf pup, he called out to Jaden and Armellya to come in. The couple went into the chief's side of the castle to the family room. When they saw the pup, they just adored him. They asked what he was to be called. The chief said he did not have a name for him yet, but he was going to have some help later that evening. The chief told the couple that the pet shop had saved that pup for him during the time they were on sequestration. The shop person knew how much the chief wanted that pup, so when he went to the shop earlier and spoke to him, he invited him over for the dinner hour.

Armellya and Jaden were very happy for the chief. The chief said he wanted to talk to the couple along with Andrew and Camillia about putting a doggy door in the adjoining hallway door so the pup could protect both sides of the castle when he got older. The chief also said the children could play with him. Armellya and Jaden told the chief that was a grand idea. The chief said now that he had their approval, he would go to Camillia and Andrew for their thoughts on the matter. Armellya said she had a name for the wolf pup. The chief inquired as to what she had in mind. Armellya told the chief to call him Deuteronomy, and when Armellya said the name, the wolf pup ran to her feet. The chief walked across the family room. Then he said, "Deuteronomy," and the wolf pup ran to him. The chief said the pup seemed to like that name so Deuteronomy was what it would be.

Armellya and Jaden spent an hour with the chief and Deuteronomy. Then it was getting close to the dinner hour, so the chief called Deuteronomy, and he went directly to him. The chief picked him up, and then the couple slipped out the back door and went through the adjoining hallway again. Armellya and Jaden agreed that they would not tell anyone about Deuteronomy because that was to be the chief's excitement for the lunch hour and family time on the next day. As Armellya and Jaden walked up the hallway, they passed Jadellya and her nanny on their way back to the nursery for her dinner. Armellya told Jaden she doubted Jadellya would want dinner after being with her grandmother. Jaden laughed and agreed. The couple went on and made it to the family room to meet up with Camillia and Andrew.

Andrew led the way to the castle's private dining hall. Then everyone sat at the big round table. They were still talking about how enjoyable it was to have Armellya and Jaden back, and the couple was flattered. Melanie joined everyone at the big round table. Then she had the kitchen staff bring out dinner and serve everyone. They carried on a tranquil conversation while eating. It was a relaxed atmosphere. When everyone was finished eating, they wound everything down to turn in for the night. Everyone in the land looked forward to seeing their mini-angels, especially Camillia, Andrew, Armellya, and Jaden. The four of them were in their homes as the rest of the castle had just wound everything up and were headed for their own. Armellya, Jaden, Andrew, and Camillia were changing from their day clothes to their night clothes as the castle finally got still.

All were in their quarters, so the two couples got into their beds to get as much sleep as possible before their visit with their mini-angels. Everyone in the land had gotten several hours of sleep at least when all the mini-angels arrived to see their pale ones. Armellya told her and Jaden's mini-angels she had a question for them, and they said to ask it. Armellya told Jaden's mini-angel that she had given him a word of caution about using his healing gift during a medical situation. Then she asked why. Jaden's mini-angel said it did not matter now that the angel of death was abolished. The mini-angel said by healing everyone, there would be no deaths and that would offset the balance of life. The angel of death would come and barter for souls but would not win the souls. The only souls the angel of death could get were the dark souls, and no pale one had one since the time they were created. The pale ones were a peaceful people who balanced the taking and giving of the land. Humans were incapable of that because of their greed and reliance upon technology. Jaden's mini-angel told him he was free to use his healing ability at his discretion and that was why Jadellya healed Camillia and her baby. Jadellya understood the fight between the angel of death and God's angels over every soul that was released upon the passing of a pale one, and to date, there had only been near a dozen deaths among the pale ones. Even though those pale ones had ulterior motives in the community, their souls still went with God's angels.

Armellya and Jaden were thankful to hear that all the souls were with God and Jaden could heal freely when he needed to. It was time for the mini-angels to return to the Dinosaur Tail because they had been with Armellya and Jaden for quite some time. The mini-angels expressed their love to the couple, and the couple returned the expression of love. Then the mini-angels returned to the Dinosaur Tail.

Armellya and Jaden were thrilled to be able to use their healing ability freely again. Armellya's ploy of pretending to be unconscious to lure the angel of death close was clever. Because of that, the angel of death got close enough that she could penetrate his chest with her bare hand and uproot his heart.

Jaden and Armellya got comfortable in their bed and held each other. Then they fell asleep in each other's arms. The couple got another five hours of sleep before it was time to wake up for the new day. Jaden and Armellya woke up and greeted each other with love. Then they got out of bed to get themselves ready for their new day. The couple changed from bedclothes into day clothes. Then they did their grooming routine and headed for the castle's family room. Camillia and Andrew arrived after Jaden and Armellya. They all chirpily greeted one another. Then Jaden said he was looking forward to a fresh day. He said he was itching to get back to work. He loved his jobs. Armellya pointed out that it was girls' day, and she could not wait to get pampered. She could certainly use the massage after braving the time they had just gotten over.

Camillia said she was looking forward to the shopping spree. She had some gifts to purchase, and she already knew what she wanted to astound the recipients with. Andrew said he needed to go to the multiuse hall to see if they had anything to propose as a project. If not, it was up to him to facilitate that. They were all enthusiastic about starting their day. While they were examining how they could not wait to go to work, the chief came into the castle's private dining hall. Everyone welcomed the chief. Then Melanie offered the chief some coffee and breakfast. The chief told Melanie a cup of her special coffee would be a real treat. Then he told Camillia and Andrew he needed to ask them about something. Andrew asked the chief to have a seat at the big round table, and he did. Then Melanie got back with the cup of her special coffee. The chief thanked Melanie for his coffee and then told Andrew and Camillia he needed their authorization for a project. Andrew told the chief to tell them about the project, so he started to talk. The chief told them that he had just gotten his wild wolf pup the day before, and he was to be called Deuteronomy. The chief was going to train the pup to be a guard dog and friend to the castle's residents. The chief told them he had his side of the castle set up for the pup's needs, but he was thinking about putting a doggy door in the door down the conjoining hallway for the pup to be able to have access to both sides of the castle. The chief pointed out that it would give the pup more room to wander and allow enough contact with everyone to grow a friendship with all the castle's occupants.

Andrew cut the chief off and told him it was a marvelous idea and they would be honored to share Deuteronomy and the responsibilities that came with him. Armellya and Jaden told Andrew and Camillia they had already told the chief they would love to share the pleasure and labor of having a wolf. Andrew and Jaden told the chief if he needed to make any adjustments to their side of the castle to go ahead and have them done. The chief was thrilled. He thanked the two couples and then finished his coffee and scuttled off to his side of the castle to plan for the alterations on the other side and the doggy door. On the way up the elongated hallway going to his side of the castle, the chief got the notion to take the door down and turn the threshold into an arched walk-through.

While the chief was on his way back to his side of the castle, Andrew, Camillia, Armellya, and Jaden had finished their breakfast and coffee. Jaden passionately kissed Armellya and told her he would see her in eight hours if everything went well at the hospital. Armellya told Jaden she loved him and to have a magnificent day at the hospital. Then Jaden left the castle's private dining hall. Andrew tenderly kissed Camillia and told her he would see her when he was finished with the multiuse hall, and she told him to have an exhilarating time. Then Andrew left the castle's private dining hall also. Armellya and Camillia sat at the big round table for a bit longer, having some of Melanie's specially brewed coffee and talking about girls' day.

Melanie joined Armellya and Camillia at the big round table while the kitchen staff were following through with her orders. Halfway through the coffee break, Michelle and Bridgette got to the castle's private dining hall and joined the rest of the women at the big round table. Camillia, Melanie, Michelle, Armellya, and Bridgette were examining their girls' day arrangements. None of them had anything to do before the lunch hour and family time, so they pondered starting girls' day without delay. They were all for the idea so that was what they were going to do.

The women left the castle's private dining hall to get the new stable boy to hitch Armellya's horse and buggy so they could start their special weekly day. The stable boy brought the horse and buggy. Then the women loaded on the buggy and left at once. They went to the beauty shop to get their massages, pedicures, manicures, and facials. When they were finished there, they would go on their shopping spree. For them, it was time to enjoy being pampered and feeling temporarily notable. The women elected to get matching pedicures and manicures. They got the pink and white natural-looking style for their manicures and a medium-brown earth-tone color with their pedicures. Their faces felt rejuvenated after their facials. Now for their massages. They each went into a private room and took off their day clothes. Then they got onto the massaging tables. The masseuses gave the women their massages with coconut oil, and their skin felt so soft afterward. When the one-hour massage was over, the women got off the massage tables to put their day clothes back on. All the women met in the lobby of the beauty hall and then paid their bill and loaded back on the buggy.

The women were heading to Jaden's parents' shop to hold their shopping spree, and Camillia had planned to get some unique gifts. Camillia would not tell anyone whom the gifts were for, so she was not so apprehensive about any of the women seeing what she would purchase. The women had decided this shopping spree would be to buy gifts for the special men in their lives. On the next girls' day, they would pick another theme to shop for. Armellya and Camillia were buying for their husbands. Melanie and Bridgette had their eyes on single men so they bought for them and included a special card with the gifts. The women were at the beauty shop for two and a half hours total. Then they shopped for three and a half hours so they got finished just on time to restfully return to the castle for the lunch hour and family time.

Back at the castle, the new stable boy took Armellya's horse and buggy so he could put the buggy away and care for the horse before the lunch hour started. The women left their treasures in the buggy so after the lunch hour and family time, the butler could bring them into the castle's family room. Once the butler got his job done with their packages, they would separate them and go to their quarters to fix them up for giving. Bridgette and Michelle would have to deliver theirs, but the rest of the women would present theirs after the dinner hour. The women elected to present their gifts outside of a major gathering hour so anyone who did not get a gift would not feel out of place.

While the women were waiting on the rest of the family to arrive at the castle's family room, the butler went ahead and brought their packages into the family room and set them on the couch. Since no one had shown up yet, the women divided their purchases and quickly ran them to their quarters.

Andrew and Jaden made it to the castle's family room about the time the women returned. The family was only waiting for a couple of individuals who were running a bit late. Finally, after a few minutes, everyone was at the castle's family room, so Andrew led them to the private dining hall. They all sat at the big round table. Then Melanie had the kitchen staff serve lunch. They enjoyed the meal while sharing their day with one another. The women were saying how much more they relished that day's beauty treatments and how the shopping was relaxing and fun. Before the shopping had just been fun. Jaden said things at the hospital were slow so he could catch up on some paperwork and what had been happening in his absence. He did not get a chance to inspect the medicine rooms though. Andrew reported that the multiuse hall was not working on anything and had not found anything to propose as a project so he was asking that anyone with an idea please see him directly. The chief was proud to proclaim that Deuteronomy was adjusting to his new home well. He said he was going to make some small adjustments to the castle for Deuteronomy in relation to them, and it was going to be a sensation. He spent fifteen minutes telling everyone how he was starting to train Deuteronomy and the pup was responding faithfully. The lunch hour and family time ended when the chief was finished sharing.

They all left the big round table to go take care of the rest of their day, relaxation for those who had completed their daily tasks and work for those who had unfinished responsibilities. Andrew had completed his tasks for the day and could spend the rest of the day with Camillia and their children, but he could not get the hopelessness of the multiuse hall's employees out of his mind. Andrew asked Camillia if she wanted to go for a ride through the land, and she asked if it was for work purposes or just to enjoy being out of the castle. Andrew told Camillia it was his responsibility to help the multiuse hall find work in the community, and he would welcome her help. Andrew told Camillia she had an eye for special things that would be nicer with some redecorating and possibly making new things from scratch. Camillia knew there was a compliment to what Andrew had said somewhere, but she decided to go just to be with her husband.

As they were getting ready to leave, Camillia recommended they take Armellya and Jaden with them since they would be the next rulers and very soon. Andrew told Camillia to sit in the family room, and he would go get their children for the community look-around project. Andrew went to Armellya and Jaden's home and knocked on their front door. Jaden answered the door. Then Andrew asked if he could come in for a few minutes, so Jaden moved aside and motioned for Andrew to enter. Andrew asked the couple if they would help them find something for the multiuse hall to do from out in the community. Jaden checked with Armellya, and she was up for the challenge, so he took her by the hand and told Andrew they were ready to go. Andrew, Armellya, and Jaden went through the castle's family room and got Camillia. Then they went out the front door. Jaden and Andrew told the new stable boy to saddle two more horses, so he went immediately to do as he was asked. He was back promptly with the four horses. Then Andrew, Camillia, Armellya, and Jaden mounted their horses, and off they went. The four of them had planned to ride from one end of the town to the other looking at everything visible to the naked eye from outside.

As they started out, Armellya asked Andrew about adding some things to the pale ones' homes to make them more self-sufficient. Andrew asked Armellya what she was referring to. Then she said, "Better kitchens, for starters." Armellya pointed out that the royal family was self-sufficient in a lot of ways that the community was not. The public had to eat in the public dining hall, while the royal family got to eat in the castle's private dining hall. Armellya suggested making simple kitchens in every home. That would get the construction workers, the castle's decorator, and the multiuse hall busy for a long time. Armellya told Andrew it would mean more responsibilities for the families, but if they had the money, they could employ some of the public dining hall's workers. Camillia asked what would become of the workers who were not hired by the public. Armellya suggested they could be trained in another position where they would be needed. Andrew told everyone to start riding, and they could discuss some home-changing options along the way. Everyone complied.

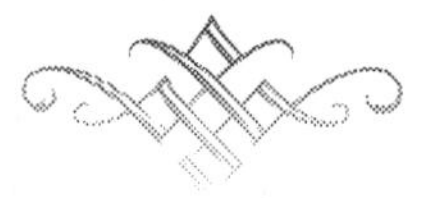

CHAPTER 4

JADEN KNEW THERE WAS NO COMMUNITY PLAY HALL for the children that they had helped to create, and it would be needed soon. The castle had an oversized private play room, but the public homes did not have anything of that nature. Jaden went on to say that the multiuse hall could make the big and small toys for the children. Andrew, Camillia, and Armellya liked that idea, so Andrew said they would get the right individuals on it right away. Andrew told Armellya and Jaden to visit the construction crew to get them to build the outsized building. Andrew and Camillia were going to the multiuse hall to give them the good news about producing the toys for the community play hall.

Armellya and Jaden got to the home of the head construction worker and told him of the project. The building would need to have a lot to offer so the children would not get bored with it, and there needed to be enough room to hold all the children at once. Armellya and Jaden knew all the children would never be there at the same time, but there would be a lot of them, plus one or both parents. Armellya added that she was going to speak to Andrew about a swimming pool being around the back of it. The head construction worker told the couple to let him know what the start date was going to be, and they would be there. The head construction worker was going to start working on blueprints to be ready to build when they got the go-ahead. Jaden told the head construction worker someone would be in touch with him soon. Then they said their farewells.

Meanwhile, Andrew and Camillia were at the multiuse hall giving them the good news about working. Andrew declared they were going to be doing a large project for the community, for all the children, from toddlers to teenagers, and the multiuse hall became ecstatic. Andrew said they could start with the small toys that would not be mounted down. Then by the time they were done with that, the construction of the building should be finished. Once the building was finished, they could work on the big toys that would be mounted to the floor, ceiling, and walls. Camillia told the multiuse hall to make every toy that they had on the earth's surface, whether it was an outside toy or inside toy. She said if the toy must be outside, check with her or Andrew. The use of outside land was not a problem. Andrew and Camillia said their farewells and rode back to the castle for the evening.

When they got there, Armellya and Jaden were arriving also. The four of them dismounted and gave their horses to the new stable boy. Then, they went to the castle's family room to tell what each one of their individuals had to say. Andrew told Armellya and Jaden that the multiuse hall was eager to do the community play hall. He said the multiuse hall was already starting to make things to go into the community play hall. Jaden told Andrew and Camillia that the head construction worker said to let him know when to start, and the crew would be there. Andrew told Jaden they could start on the blueprints immediately. Then Jaden said he would make a quick ride over to tell him. Andrew told Jaden to just send a castle runner, so Jaden summoned one of the runners. When the runner got to Jaden, he told the runner what he wanted done, and the runner was right out the door.

Fifteen minutes later, the runner was back to report to Jaden, telling him the head construction worker would be working on the blueprints that night and would bring them over for Jaden's approval when he completed them. Jaden thanked the runner and then discharged him from his presence.

Andrew told Camillia, Armellya, and Jaden it was close to the dinner hour, so they might as well stay in the family room. Everyone there stayed. They were talking about how wonderful the community play hall would be for the children in the community. Then Jaden asked Andrew about putting a swimming pool in the back of the community play hall. Andrew said he told the multiuse hall to produce all the toys that children's playgrounds above ground had, and he said pools were a famous gathering spot, so he did approve the pool. Jaden said someone needed to let the multiuse hall know to go forward with the pool. Andrew told Jaden he had to ride out to the multiuse hall the next day so he could let them know, and Jaden acknowledged Andrew.

Bridgette was the first individual to arrive at the castle's family room with the two couples. Bridgette knew they were discussing something important, so she asked if there was anything she could do to contribute to what they were talking about. Andrew told Bridgette they were talking about making a community play hall for the children in the community to have a place to burn off some energy and have fun. Bridgette thought that was simply wonderful. She asked Andrew if there was anything they could use her for because she would love to contribute. Armellya said Bridgette was great with making announcement cards and maybe she should make some to send out to every household. Jaden liked the idea because she could put a clause in the cards that any suggestions were welcome; they just needed to find Jaden or Andrew to speak with. Andrew liked the idea so he asked Bridgette if she was up to the task, and she said, "Certainly."

Andrew said the construction was to start the next day. Then he asked her how soon she could get those announcements out. Bridgette said the cards would be on their doors when they got home for the lunch hour. She would make one up right after the dinner hour and then get it to the copy hall first thing in the morning. Then when they were copied, she would have them sent from the copy hall directly to the distribution hall with a rush on them. Andrew said Bridgette did some magnificent work. He did wonder if she should start them that night instead of spending time with Matthew, but that was between them.

Right then, Matthew showed up in heroic spirits, and Bridgette told him about the cards she was going to work on that evening. He was accommodating, saying he would help if he could. Everyone else was slowly showing up for the dinner hour. Then after a short while, they were all there. Andrew led everyone to the castle's private dining hall, and they all sat in their places at the big round table. Melanie helped the kitchen staff bring out dinner, and then she sat at the big round table. For the first time, everyone ate in silence, finished their dinner, and then went to their quarters.

Bridgette and Armellya had gifts to give to their husbands. Melanie and Michelle had to deliver theirs to the men who had caught their eyes and return before the street curfew was up. Armellya gave Jaden a pocket watch made of gold so he would have the time of day with him always instead of having to use whatever clock may be around, if any. Bridgette gave Matthew some of the security items he should be carrying on his belt but was not. His security crew carried the items Bridgette got him. His crew would be disciplined if they did not have those items for whatever reason. Bridgette told Matthew he was to set an example, and if he did not have all his equipment, he was in the wrong to correct his crew for the same thing.

Matthew agreed and thanked Bridgette for the gifts. He told her she was very fair-minded and such an understanding wife.

Melanie and Michelle saddled their own horses because the new stable boy was already at home. The two women rode hard to get to their destinations. Melanie gave her gift to the man she secretly admired, and after opening the gift, he told her he was her secret admirer also. Right at that moment, Melanie and Michael decided to get serious and start courting. She invited him to breakfast at the castle's private dining hall, and he said he would be there. Melanie quickly mounted her horse and returned to the castle, beating the curfew.

Michelle gave her gift to the one she admired, Allen, and before opening it, he took her into his arms and adoringly kissed her. Then said he was in love with her and wanted to sire her children. Michelle and Allen were now courting, and she too invited him to join her for the breakfast hour at the castle's private dining hall. He accepted. Allen knew all about Michelle. He had been observing her and learning about her since she became a pale one. It was love at first sight for both Michelle and Allen. Michelle mounted her horse and rode hard to beat the street curfew. She made it back to the castle, just making curfew.

While Melanie and Michelle were gone, after Bridgette had presented Matthew with his gift, she started the card for the community play hall. Matthew helped her make the card by offering design recommendations. It only took an hour to perfect the card. Matthew and Bridgette then had an hour to spend together before it was vital that they go to bed for their mini-angels to appear. Everyone else in the castle was in bed readily awaiting their mini-angels.

The castle was tranquil with everyone sleeping, including Deuteronomy. The tranquility throughout the castle was abruptly disturbed by an ear-piercing uproar coming from the chief's side of the castle. In fact, it sounded like the chief. Andrew, Camillia, Armellya, and Jaden were stirred by the cries of distress, so they rushed to the chief's side of the castle.

When they got to the chief, he was in a state of being dead to the world and still crying out. The chief was writhing about in his bed like he was trying to wrestle with something. Armellya and Jaden had the ability to enter others' dreams so Andrew and Camillia stood by while Armellya and Jaden went into the chief's dream. It did not take long before the young couple encountered the chief dreaming about the angel of death and being murdered by him. The couple woke the chief from inside the dream, and when he awoke, he saw Andrew, Camillia, Armellya, and Jaden standing before him. Armellya and Jaden were alarmed by the dream and had to remind themselves that the angel of death could not harm them anymore because he no longer existed. However, he could still kill the chief out of panic from within the dream world. Jaden and Armellya advised the chief that he have the mini-angel take the threat of the angel of death from his memory. The ability to erase something from another's mind was a gift that Armellya and Jaden did not possess. Jaden told Andrew and Camillia they would stay with the chief until his mini-angel arrived; they could go back to sleep.

Camillia and Andrew left the chief's side of the castle and went to their own. As soon as Andrew and Camillia got back into bed, they fell asleep right away. Once Andrew and Camillia were asleep, the chief's mini-angel appeared, and she was aware of the nightmare. Armellya and Jaden revealed to the mini-angel what they had seen in the chief's dream. The chief told his mini-angel what he saw and how he felt in the nightmare. The chief's mini-angel told him she had offered to take the risk of those nightmares from him, but he declined. Now she was asking again if he wanted the peril taken away.

The chief apologized to Armellya and Jaden and then told his mini-angel to please take the danger from him. Armellya and Jaden told the chief he did not have to apologize; there was no purposeful reason to have the life-threatening memory. The chief's mini-angel fluttered around his forehead. Then she shot rays of light from her body into the chief's brow. After a few minutes of the light shining brightly, it started to gradually dim. Once the rays of light were gone, the chief had no recollection of the nightmare he had just experienced. His mini-angel told them that he had some recall of the true experience with the angel of death and the fallen angel, but it could not penetrate his subconscious mind anymore. With that issue being resolved, Armellya and Jaden went back to their side of the castle to go to their bedroom and leave the chief to visit with his mini-angel in private.

As soon as Armellya and Jaden reclined on their bed, their mini-angels materialized before them. The mini-angels asked Armellya and Jaden how they would feel having Jadellya take her position as queen of the mini-angels soon. Armellya asked the mini-angels how soon was soon. The mini-angels told Armellya and Jaden as soon as the next day. Armellya told the mini-angels that Jadellya was still so young. The mini-angels told Armellya that the child might be young, but she had a mature spirit. Jaden asked what the mini-angel meant by Jadellya having a mature spirit. The mini-angel said they had been waiting on the spirit to govern them, but there was no human or pale one deserving of the soul. The soul stayed in the utopia waiting for a very long time for a body that was virtuous, and until Jadellya, there was no body that was unadulterated. The mini-angel told Jaden and Armellya that Jadellya was handpicked by God to house the superior and prevailing soul. Armellya and Jaden agreed that they could not contest God. Whatever God wanted of them was what God would get. Not only were pale ones a peaceful people; they were a God-fearing people.

Armellya and Jaden offered Jadellya to be what God wanted of her. Then the mini-angel told the couple that

Jadellya's responsibilities would start on the morrow. Armellya and Jaden told the mini-angels, "Very well."

Just as the chief's mini-angel told him, Armellya's and Jaden's mini-angels told them that there was to be a double wedding as soon as they could be arranged. Then the mini-angels told the chief, Armellya, and Jaden there was to be a healing for the ability to conceive for the two married couples. The chief, Armellya, and Jaden asked their mini-angels which pale ones were to be married. Then the mini-angels revealed it was to be Melanie to Michael and Michelle to Allen. The mini-angels told the chief, Armellya, and Jaden that on this night, their mini-angels were telling them to marry as soon as they could and to reproduce. Armellya knew how the two women felt about the men they had their eyes on but had no clue if the two men had a mutual liking.

Armellya was not even sure that the women were to marry the men they had their eyes on. The mini-angels told Armellya and Jaden both couples experienced love at first sight and were more than compatible. That confirmed to Armellya that the men the women were to marry were the men they had their eyes on. Armellya, Jaden, and the chief told their mini-angels they would make it happen. Armellya was ecstatic for the women. The chief, Armellya, and Jaden had to say good night to their mini-angels because the mini-angels had to get back to the Dinosaur Tail. They were the last to get back. Now the community was back in a slumber, and the mini-angels got to take care of their affairs with the pale ones that they had dealings with.

A few hours had passed, and it was now time for the castle to rouse. Michelle was first to leave her quarters so she could let Melanie know there was going to be an extra guest for breakfast. Melanie was already in the kitchen brewing some of her special coffee for everyone. She was motivated to get this day started because of what her mini-angel had told her.

Melanie and Michelle sat at the big round table informing each other about what had happened when they delivered their gifts to their secret loves. They also shared what their mini-angels had told them about getting married. They could not wait for their steadies to get there for the breakfast hour because they knew that the men's mini-angels had told them about matrimony also. Once they passed on good wishes to each other, they could hear the other members of the castle stirring in the hallway.

Armellya and Jaden were on their way to the castle's private dining room when they heard a knock on the front door. Jaden answered it. It was the chief. Jaden and Armellya told the chief they knew why he was there. Armellya told the chief to come to the private dining hall for breakfast, and they could talk during that time. The chief entered and shut the front door, and then there was another knock on the front door. The chief opened the door and saw two men he was not familiar with standing there. He asked them if he could help them with something. One of them introduced himself as Michael and then said Melanie had invited him for the breakfast hour. The other man introduced himself as Allen and said Michelle had invited him for the breakfast hour. The chief let them in and told the men to follow him to the private dining hall, and they did. Armellya and Jaden introduced themselves and welcomed the two men. When the chief, Armellya, Jaden, Michael, and Allen got to the private dining hall, Melanie and Michelle were energized and welcomed their new fiancés. They told them they were delighted that they had made it over. Both men launched themselves at their women and in their own ways asked them to marry them. Both women accepted without hesitation.

The chief, Armellya, and Jaden were not taken by surprise because their mini-angels had told them this was to occur. The chief asked both couples when the weddings were to be, and they both said on the next day. They needed this day to prepare the ceremony and reception. Allen and Michael told Michelle and Melanie they would get their wedding ring sets as soon as the shops opened after the breakfast hour. Armellya and Jaden told Melanie and Michelle to take the entire day off to do what they needed to do. One of them was to take her buggy and the other Jaden's, so they had somewhere to put their merchandise. The women thanked Armellya and Jaden for their help. Armellya told the women that their mini-angels had told them about them getting married so if they needed any help, she and Bridgette could split up and help. Michelle and Melanie thanked Armellya again.

Now Camillia and Andrew entered the private dining hall and noticed Michael and Allen right away. They instantly introduced themselves to the men. Camillia and Andrew had heard most of the conversation in the hallway so they were prepared to meet the men. Camillia and Andrew welcomed the men to the family and told them if they needed anything to just let them know. The men thanked Andrew and Camillia. Camillia said she was going to get the castle's decorator after the breakfast hour to do the wedding and party arrangements. She told the women the castle's decorator could hitch her horse to Andrew's buggy to transport her purchases. Andrew said while everyone was busy with the weddings, he had to go by the multiuse hall to let them know to put a swimming pool in the back of the community play hall. Andrew also had to tell the head construction worker about the swimming pool in the back of the building. Bridgette and Matthew finally got to the private dining hall, and Michelle and Melanie told them there was going to be a double wedding that day. They were thrilled for Michelle and Melanie. The women introduced their men to Bridgette and Matthew. Armellya told Bridgette that she offered her assistance for the weddings. Then Bridgette said she would love to help. While most everyone would be busy with preparing for the double wedding, Jaden had to go to the hospital for his eight-hour shift. Andrew had to work also, as he was the head of security for the castle and its occupants.

It was now the breakfast hour so Melanie had the kitchen staff serve breakfast to everyone. As they ate, they talked about the weddings. Andrew changed the subject of conversation slightly by mentioning housing. Now there were two houses to build onto the castle. Andrew told Melanie and Michelle to get with him to make home specification requests. The women said they would at the first chance they got. With that request from Andrew, the breakfast hour was over. It was time for everyone to start the busy day. Jaden went to the hospital. Andrew went to the multiuse hall. Melanie, Michelle, Michael, and Allen left for wedding and reception shopping. Bridgette called for a runner to get the community play hall card over to the copy hall. She was just waiting on the runner to get to her.

Andrew got to the multiuse hall and told them the swimming pool at the back of the building was a great idea, and they had his consent. The employees of the multiuse hall were pleased to hear the swimming pool was approved. They believed it would attract just as much attention as the inside toys. Andrew did not stay any longer than necessary because he wanted to get back to the castle to help with the double wedding arrangements. When Andrew left the multiuse hall, he went to go see the head construction worker. When Andrew got to the home of the head construction worker, he told the worker that the swimming pool was to be built around the back of the hall. The head construction worker told Andrew he would get it done. Andrew had just finished with his errands so now he could go back to the castle.

Jaden had to work at the hospital and do his checks of the medical medicine-making room and the veterinary medicine-making room. Jaden had told the other doctor at the hospital about the family's double wedding. He told Jaden to take care of his room checks and go home with the family. Jaden said okay, but if the hospital got busy, he was to send the hospital's runner for him to come back. The doctor said okay.

Jaden did his thorough checks of both medicine-making rooms and then left the hospital. He would write his reports on another day. The castle's runner finally got to Bridgette, and she gave him the card with instruction to take it to the copy hall and tell the copy hall to send them to the distribution hall. They needed to be delivered by the lunch hour. The runner said he would take care of it and then left speedily.

Both Andrew and Jaden were back at the castle looking for their wives. Andrew found Camillia. She was talking to the castle's decorator about the wedding decor. Jaden found Armellya. She was in their quarters relaxing. Melanie was with Michael shopping, and Michelle was with Allen shopping. The chief was on his side of the castle supervising the stone workers doing the archway between his side of the castle and the kids'. There was no longer a door separating the two sides of the castle in the adjoining hallway. Once the archway was completed, all the chief had left to do was delicately modify the kids' side of the castle for Deuteronomy.

Time was going by quickly. It was nearing the lunch hour, and Andrew was beginning to wonder if Michelle, Melanie, Allen, and Michael were going to make it back in time for the lunch hour and family time. Jaden sat in the castle's family room waiting for the rest of the family to filter in. Right on time, Jaden and Armellya got to the castle's family room. Then Bridgette and Matthew arrived. After everyone in the castle's family room had conversed for fifteen minutes, Camillia and the chief arrived. The chief was telling everyone all he had left to do for the modification of the castle for Deuteronomy was minor changes to their side of the castle, and he was so thrilled. They all said they were elated for the chief and could not wait for the modifications to be done so they could share Deuteronomy. With that, Michelle, Melanie, Michael, and Allen came through the castle's front door.

With the whole family in the family room, it was time for Andrew to lead them to the private dining hall. When they got to the private dining hall, there were some changes made to the seating arrangement so Melanie and Michael and Michelle and Allen could sit together without displacing other couples. Once everyone was finally seated, the kitchen crew brought lunch out to everyone and served them. As they were relishing their lunch, they talked about the double wedding. All the shopping had been done, so after the lunch hour, the castle's decorator would be given the items she needed to decorate the private dining hall on the next day. The decorator did some shopping of her own for the double wedding, and she completed her shopping on that day.

While they were eating and conferring on the double wedding, there was a knock at the front door. The butler answered it, and it was the runner from the distribution hall. The distribution hall sent their runner to see Bridgette to let her know the community play hall cards had been delivered on time. Bridgette thanked the runner and then excused him to go about his way. Usually they went around the big round table and all shared their day, but everyone was helping with the double wedding, so having everyone examining the double wedding, they did not need to go around the big round table. Andrew told Michelle and Melanie to go pack their bedrooms as soon as they left the big round table, because he was going to take half of the construction crew to build their housing additions to the castle. They would place their items in the storage show room for the time being, and their men could help them. They were to sleep in the chief's extra rooms on the far side of Lynndia's nursery starting that evening.

Armellya offered to let Michelle and Melanie walk through her home to see if they wanted the same model. If not, it would still give them something to work with. Andrew called for a runner to send to the head construction worker. The castle's runner arrived, and Andrew told him to fetch the head construction worker. The runner departed right away. Armellya, Michelle, and Melanie excused themselves from the big round table to go consider Armellya's home plan.

While the women were looking at Armellya's home, they were in awe. It was organized, spacious, beautiful, and functional. Michelle and Melanie liked the layout of the house and determined right then and there that they wanted the exact same floorplan. Armellya was pleased to be of help. She told the women if they needed to see it again to let her know. It would be her pleasure. Going back to the castle's private dining hall, the women thanked Armellya for her help with the housing plans, and she told them that was what sisters were for and much more.

Back at the castle's private dining hall, Melanie and Michelle told Andrew they would like to have the same floorplan as Armellya. Andrew asked the women if they wanted to check with their men. Then the men spoke up. They agreed the home was the woman's castle; the workforce was the man's responsibility, so whatever they chose was more than acceptable. Everyone thought that was sweet of the men to say, and the men stood by their word.

Finally, the runner Andrew sent out returned with the head construction worker. Andrew told him he wanted half of his men on the community play hall to work on a double housing project, a quarter on Michelle's house and a quarter on Melanie's house. The head construction worker told Andrew that was fine. Then Andrew asked if he could start the houses this day and work some overtime. They were looking to have the homes done without delay.

The head construction worker said they could work around the clock if they delayed the starting date of the community play hall until the homes were finished. Andrew told him to do the round-the-clock work and worry about the community play hall when the homes were built. The head construction worker said he would be back in two hours. The women said they would be packed and out of their rooms by then. Andrew and the head construction worker agreed on two hours and then thanked each other. The head construction worker excused himself to gather his men and pull the blueprints of Armellya's house.

Speaking to the head construction worker at the big round table had the lunch hour and family time run over a bit, but that was not a problem. Everyone agreed that they needed to stay at the big round table to compare who was doing what so nothing was left out and everyone had a different responsibility. They were going to work on the preparations some that day and then finish them up by the lunch hour the next day. The ceremony would be conducted during the lunch hour, and the reception meal and gift opening would be during the family time. The next day was going to be all about the two sets of newlyweds. Michelle, Melanie, Michael, and Allen were thrilled about the double wedding and starting their lives over, so to say. It only took an hour to ensure everyone had their responsibilities understood and everything for the preparations were covered. Now everyone got up from the big round table and scattered to start on their given tasks for the double wedding. The two couples went unswervingly to the women's quarters to pack and move everything out for the construction crew to start working. Their men were an immeasurable help. The couples had to work extra swiftly because they spent one of the two hours at the big round table. The newlyweds-to-be worked persistently on packing up the women's quarters on time so the construction crew would not have to wait on them to finish moving things. They finished right on time. The men were taking the last box out of the rooms as the construction crew arrived.

Melanie and Jaden were stupefied that the four of them got done emptying two quarters so quickly. It took them half of the day to move out of Armellya's quarters for the construction crew to work on her house. The head of the construction crew told Andrew the homes should be finished by the end of the next day, and Andrew was astonished. He said that would be a great wedding present. The head construction worker told Andrew he was aiming for the completion of the homes just for that reason. Andrew shook his hand and thanked him. Andrew went to Michelle and Melanie to ask them if they wanted the castle's decorator's help with their home decor. They both told Andrew they wanted to decorate their individual rooms but wanted the castle's decorator to make the rooms merge effortlessly. Andrew told the women he would relay the message, and when they were ready for her to send for her. The women thanked Andrew and then went on to take care of their marital duties.

The castle's decorator was putting up decorations in the private dining hall and setting up the extra table for the gifts. Melanie's mother was working on two wedding cakes, so each couple could have their own top cake to store away for their one-year anniversary. Melanie's father oversaw the luncheon for after the ceremonies. The chief's only responsibility was to perform the ceremonies, as the only patriarch of the pale ones. The Land of Grandeur had no matriarch, and everyone hoped that the chief would take a bride. There was someone for everyone in the Land of Grandeur, including the chief; they just had to find her.

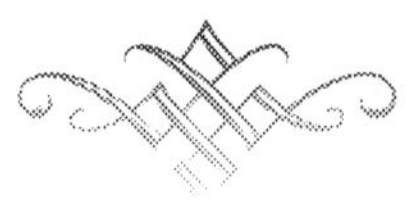

CHAPTER 5

TIME WAS GOING BY RAPIDLY WITH EVERYONE scuttling to get things prepared for the double wedding. It was already nearing the dinner hour, but they all agreed to finish their projects before sitting at the big round table to eat because things were so close to being completed ahead of schedule. While everyone was dashing about, there was a knock at the front door of the castle. The chief answered the door, and there was an older woman standing at the door with many oversized flower arrangements. She started to speak, but the chief was not able to hear a word she said. He was memorized by her. Whatever she said, she was waiting on a response from him, so she called out his name several times, trying to get his attention. Because the chief never responded and everyone could hear what was going on, they all looked toward the front door. They agreed the chief was smitten by the woman. They had to find out who she was. It appeared they had found the one for the chief to possibly take as a bride.

Andrew stepped forward and asked who she was. The

woman said she was called Sharonna. She was the owner of the flower shop. She said her purpose there was to contribute some flower arrangements to the royal house because she had heard of the double wedding. Andrew told Sharonna how much they appreciated the flowers and that they were beautiful. He asked her to join them for the dinner hour as their special guest as a token of appreciation. Sharonna said she had no one at home so it would be nice to eat with someone. Andrew commented that she had no one at home, and she replied that she never married and had children before becoming a pale one. Sharonna did admit that since she had become a pale one, she had her eyes on the chief but figured he had no time for a wife and family.

Andrew told Sharonna that now that the chief had retired, he had time for all the activities the community had to offer, including a wife and children. Andrew brought Sharonna into the private dining hall and introduced her to everyone. Sharonna felt privileged to be inside the royal castle and among the royal family. Andrew told Sharonna that the commune was one big family made up of smaller family units. Sharonna liked how the royal family viewed their community.

The chief finally got over being lovestruck and asked Sharonna for a date. Sharonna accepted the date with the chief, and they planned to go on their date the day after the double wedding. Everyone was very joyful for the chief, but what they did not know was he had had his eye on Sharonna since she became a pale one many years ago. The chief and Sharonna sat in the family room on the couch together getting acquainted. Sharonna asked the chief if she could be forward with him, and the chief told Sharonna she could tell him anything. The chief told Sharonna he would even keep her secrets to himself. She shifted closer to the chief and took one of his hands into hers. Then she took a deep breath. After a slight pause, Sharonna told the chief if he never wanted to see her after what she was about to say, she would leave immediately and not look back. The chief asked her if she was okay. She told the chief she was never better. After hesitating, Sharonna blurted out that she had fallen in love with him as soon as she saw him. She said she had gone out of her way to find out everything about him that she could. The chief held Sharonna's hand tighter and told her he was happy to hear her say that. The chief said he needed to make a confession. Then he told her he had been watching her from a distance. The chief told Sharonna he had fallen in love with her upon first sight. The two of them giggled a bit, and then the chief got serious and asked Sharonna if she would be his exclusive girlfriend. Sharonna replied that she would strive to be his everything. Then the chief drew close to her and tenderly kissed her on the lips.

Andrew was on his way into the family room to let the chief know they were ready to start the dinner hour and happened to get there just on time to see the chief kiss Sharonna. Andrew excused himself into the situation. Then the chief told Andrew he had an announcement for everyone. Andrew told the chief and Sharonna they were ready to sit at the big round table. Andrew, the chief, and Sharonna went to the private dining hall to sit at the big round table for the dinner hour.

They all greeted Sharonna and said their names as she sat at the big round table. Before sitting, the chief announced that he and Sharonna were now an exclusive item. They applauded and told the chief and Sharonna they were very delighted for them. The chief then sat down at the big round table. Melanie had the kitchen staff bring out dinner and serve everyone. They were all discussing the double wedding preparations and how they all unexpectedly finished the preparations ahead of time. That meant that the next day could be spent entirely on the brides and grooms. The dinner hour was over, but they were all having such an enjoyable time getting to know Sharonna that they stayed at the big round table talking.

Now it was close to the time to settle things down for the bedtime hour so the chief told Sharonna to return the next morning. She said she would. The chief and Sharonna kissed good night, and then she left the castle to get to her home before the street curfew came. The chief said good night to everyone and then went to his side of the castle to go to bed. The others wrapped things up and went to their quarters for the night. They were eager to see their mini-angels at the midnight hour so they all changed from their day clothes into bedclothes and wasted no time getting into bed.

The only individuals awake were the construction crew working on Michelle's and Melanie's homes so they could have them completed for their wedding day. The construction workers were using their pale one ability to work at high-speed, which made it important for all of them to know what they had to do and what the others were to do so they did not get in one another's way. It was slightly noisy for those who were sleeping in the castle, but they did not mind.

Every night, all the mini-angels went to visit Jadellya before going on to their pale one. This night was no different except now Jadellya was their queen and was responsible for letting them know what was occurring in the community and giving them work to do when the need came about. There were two mini-angels who were going to be sent out with a specific purpose. The mini-angel for the chief and the mini-angel for Sharonna were to reveal that they were soul mates. The mini-angels were also to tell Sharonna and the chief to share that information with one another. The mini-angels did not know how Jadellya knew everything. Besides being her duty, it was her secret. The mini-angels had spent their time with Jadellya so they left her to go to their pale one.

Now, the entire community was awake visiting with their mini-angels. The angels woke their pale ones with a charming wake-up song. The mini-angels spent about fifteen minutes with their pale ones unless there was something to contend with. This night was a quick night for all the mini-angels, and they returned to the Dinosaur Tail rather early compared to most nights. The next four and a half hours seemed to go by quickly. There was no mercy for the late workers who were overtired. It was now close to the five-o'clock hour, and everyone in the castle was mingling. The shift change for the construction workers was also happening, and there was not much left for them to do. They were all so energized for the events of the day that they were ready to go to the private dining hall a little early. Melanie already had her specially brewed coffee ready to serve, as she was running early also.

All those in the castle, including the chief and Deuteronomy, were at the castle's private dining hall. Deuteronomy was eating his food from a bowl on the floor next to the chief, and the pale ones were ready for some coffee. Melanie had the kitchen staff serve the coffee while she sat at the big round table with everyone else. The chief kept looking at the entrance of the castle's private dining hall, waiting for Sharonna. It was obvious he was lovesick, and Andrew told the chief not to be anxious; she would be there. As soon as Andrew said that, the butler walked into the castle's private dining hall with Sharonna. The chief stood up, walked up to her, and then gave her a big hug with a fiery kiss. The chief asked that he and Sharonna be excused for a moment. Then they walked into the castle's family room for some privacy. The chief told Sharonna that his mini-angel told him she was his soul mate. Sharonna gave a full-sized smile and told the chief her mini-angel told her he was her soul mate. They were so blissful over the revelation that they could not contain the thrill. The chief asked Sharonna if she really saw it necessary to court for a time. Sharonna asked the chief if he was going to ask her to marry him. The chief told Sharonna that the angels saw the future and had already documented them as soul mates; it did not get any better than that. Sharonna pulled the chief close and asked how soon he wanted the wedding to be. The chief asked her if she was saying yes to his near proposal, and she said yes. The chief said they needed to get through the double wedding; then they would start planning their own and hold it as soon as the arrangements were made and followed through with. Sharonna was enlivened. She told the chief that this was a dream come true. The chief proposed that they go back to the castle's private dining hall and tell everyone the lovely news.

When they got to the castle's private dining hall, they stood at the front of the room and the chief said he had an announcement to make. Everyone looked over to him in silence. Then the chief told everyone he had just asked Sharonna to marry him and she had said yes. Everyone clapped and whistled. The men got out of their seats to go shake the chief's hand and congratulate him while the women went to Sharonna and gave her hugs with a word of congratulations. Everyone sat back down at the big round table and wanted details about the upcoming wedding. The chief told everyone that Sharonna had asked when they were going to have the wedding, and he said they needed to get through the double wedding first. After that, they would start planning his and Sharonna's big day. The women spoke up together and said to let them plan and prepare the wedding for them. Sharonna said that it would be a breathtaking event once they were done with the plans. She knew the women would make it a special day all day for her and the chief. The men interrupted, telling all the women that they would help if at least one of them would tell them what to do. The women told the men they would love to have their support, and they would tell them how to help.

After the chief announced his marriage to Sharonna and there was some brief talk about it, Melanie said the breakfast hour had been upon them for twenty minutes already. They were alarmed by how fast the time was going, so they told Melanie they were ready for the breakfast meal. Melanie had the kitchen staff bring out the food and serve everyone. They ate hastily so they could move on to the double wedding preparations that were left. All that was left was to get the brides and grooms ready for the ceremony, but the brides would take some time to perfect. The decorations were done, the cakes were done, the food was almost done, and the castle occupants had placed their gifts on the second table in the castle's private dining hall. When everyone was done eating, the women and men separated so the brides did not see the grooms before the ceremony once they were dressed up in their wedding attire.

The men went to the chief's side of the castle, and the women stayed in the kids' side. They were far ahead of schedule, so the ceremony would now be done before the lunch hour. Armellya, Bridgette, and Camillia worked on Melanie and Michelle, and one hour later, the brides were ready for the ceremony. It only took the men half an hour to get Allen and Michael ready for their weddings. The chief knew they were ready, so he walked over to the other side of the castle to see if the women were ready yet. When the chief saw the women in their wedding attire with their hair done up with flowers and a bit of makeup to highlight their facial features, he got tears in his eyes. The chief could not believe how picturesque they looked. They were naturally stunning, but the makeover really brought out their beauty.

The women went up to the chief and hugged him. They told one another they loved each other. The chief pulled himself together from the sensitivity of the sentiment and announced it was time for the ceremony. Everyone needed to get to the religious hall traveling the backway, which was shorter than going through town. Andrew would transport Melanie and Michelle and get them to the back room in the religious hall. Once the women had enough time to be where they needed to be, the chief would take Allen and Michael to the religious hall by the back route also. The grooms would take their places at the altar while the brides would take their walk down the aisle upon their musical cue.

As with Armellya and Jaden's wedding, all the mini-angels would be there to line both sides of the aisle. A half of an hour after the chief went to see the brides, they were all at the religious hall and ready to start the ceremony. The piano, organ, violins, flutes, and other musical instruments started to play. With the music playing, the brides started their feminine wedding march down the aisle. The grooms both sentimentally beamed when they saw their brides coming to them. The brides met up with their grooms. Then the chief started to recite the biblical wedding vows. When the chief had completed his vows, each couple had their own special vows to recite to one another. Finally, there was the giving of the wedding rings. Upon the kissing of the brides, the entire religious hall erupted into cheers for the completion of the unions. The two sets of newlyweds walked down the aisle to leave the religious hall, going to the castle's private dining hall so the brides could change into their reception dresses. The mini-angels returned to the Dinosaur Tail, and the couples entered the kids' side of the castle. Right behind the newlyweds, the rest of the family reached the kids' side of the castle.

The brides changed from their wedding dresses into their reception dresses while everyone took their seats at the big round table in the castle's private dining hall. The new wives took their seats at the big round table next to their new husbands. The reception was to begin. The gifts were being passed to the new couples, staggering between couples so they both could engage in the gift acceptance together. It took two hours to complete the gift opening section of the reception. Bridgette kept a list of names with gift given for both couples so she could make thank-you cards for the couples to have distributed. Enough time had gone by because of the extended time for gifts to be opened that the lunch hour was upon them.

Melanie's father had made a scrumptious wedding spread with mini individual edible arrangements, hors d'oeuvres, vegetable dip trays, and many more party foods. The lunch foods were to be a party theme while dinner would be romantically prepared and served for everyone.

The family time was not for all of them to share their day; instead, it was to go around and talk to the newlyweds with love, hope, and the best of wishes. When that was done, there was still a bit of family time left and the two new couples were focusing on the chief and Sharonna's wedding planning. Sharonna tried to keep the focus on the newlyweds, trying to give their day to them, but they were too excited about the next wedding.

The reception, lunch hour, and family time were over, so the two couples went to see their new homes, and to their surprise, the homes were ready to be moved into. The head construction worker was still there and told the couples that the completion of the homes by the time they were married was the construction crew's gift to them. Everyone in the castle teamed up into two teams, one for each couple to move their belongings into their new houses. The men went with the grooms to move their belongings from where they were renting rooms to the castle. The women helped the brides move their things from the storage display room into their homes. It took the rest of the time up to the dinner hour to get the couples moved in and unpacked. All they needed to do was decorate so they would be calling on the castle's decorator that instant. Both brides spoke to the castle's decorator at the same time and told her what they wanted. Then they left it up to her to do the decorating however she chose to get it accomplished. The decorator said she was going to do both houses at the same time. She had six trained underworkers she was going to divide between the two houses, and she would preside over them with the decor job the entire time. The women did not realize the castle's decorator had become the supervisor over six workers. The women congratulated her. The castle's decorator said there were individuals needing jobs, so she trained them, right down to giving up her secrets of the profession. She asked when the women wanted to start the decor project. They both said the shops in the community were already closed for the evening so she could start first thing in the morning. The castle's decorator said she and her workers would be there right after the breakfast hour. The women thanked her and then told her they would see them bright and early.

The dinner hour was upon them, but the kitchen crew was still setting up the amorousness in the castle's private dining hall. It took a little more time to take down the party theme in the private dining hall than Melanie's father thought it would. The family stayed in the castle's family room kicking around some possibilities for the chief and Sharonna's wedding arrangements until Melanie's father sent word that the castle's private dining hall was ready to be occupied.

Melanie's mother came out of the castle's kitchen and told the family that the private dining hall was ready for them to settle in. Everyone followed Melanie's mother into the private dining room. When they got to the threshold, they were flabbergasted by the romantic ambience in the room. The room was so exquisite that the family was just standing there in a trance. Melanie's mother had to tell them to take their seats at the big round table so Melanie's father could serve them. Eventually, they were all in their places at the big round table, so Melanie's parents served the family. The chef, Melanie's father, had worked wonders with the food. It was very professionally done. The dishes were definitely gourmet greats. There was every imaginable dish possible. They all savored every bite, and it was like having a party in their mouths. In fact, there was very little conversation because everyone was focusing on the meal. The dinner hour was over, but everyone was eating so slowly that they did not fill up fast. They were going to eat for however long it took to satisfy their bellies. Eventually, everyone's belly was satisfied. By then, it was time for all of them to settle down and go to their quarters for the night. They all said good night to one another and then went their separate ways.

The chief went to his side of the castle, and Sharonna went to her home. The rest of the family had their quarters attached to the castle and went there. The chief and Sharonna were eager for the next day because that would be the day that the women were going to be planning their wedding. The two new couples were thrilled to be starting their lives together. This would be the first time they stayed together. The new couples were also motivated by receiving their reproductive healings the next day so they could have children. The whole family was impatient to see their mini-angels and share their joy with them. The day was full of nonstop activity and stimulation, so they did not realize how exhausted they were. The family finally felt how fatigued they were when they stopped long enough to put their heads on their pillows. They drifted right off to sleep in no time.

At the midnight hour, as usual, the mini-angels appeared before them and sang their lovely wake-up song. When the family was awakened, they all felt like they had just fallen asleep. They shared their joyous day with their mini-angels, and the mini-angels were contented for their pale ones' joy. None of the pale ones spent much time with their mini-angels because they were so weary and felt they needed the extra sleep. The mini-angels and their pale ones expressed their love to one another, and then the mini-angels went back to the Dinosaur Tail. They all fell back to sleep promptly and got another four hours and fifty minutes of sleep before it was time to rise. They slithered out of bed and gradually performed their morning routine to get ready for the new day. Then they went to the castle's private dining hall.

Their eyes were all at half-mast, showing their lethargy. They were all looking forward to Melanie's specially brewed coffee, which was extra strong. Since Melanie was sitting at the big round table already, her mother startled her by serving the extra-strong coffee. They all sluggishly savored their coffee and discussed some more options for making the chief and Sharonna's wedding a memorable one. In the middle of the conversation, the chief and Sharonna entered the kids' side of the castle to have coffee with them. The butler showed them into the castle's private dining hall. When they got there, everyone there delightedly welcomed them in to have coffee with them. The chief and Sharonna sat at the big round table. Then Melanie's mother served them their coffee. The discussion changed from wedding options for the chief and Sharonna to asking for their input on what they would like to see incorporated into their wedding, reception, and the dinner hour. By asking for their ideas, the women could entwine their ideas with the others' and, they hoped, make it the wedding of a lifetime. The coffee meeting over the wedding for the chief and Sharonna lasted for an hour, and then the breakfast hour had arrived. Melanie had the kitchen staff bring out breakfast, and they all ate while telling what their day held for them.

Camillia was the last to share. During her time to share, she started to stutter and seemed to forget some words she was trying to say. That attracted Jaden's attention because those actions were not normal, and Camillia had never done that before. Abruptly, Camillia's arms wrapped around her belly, and she hastily bent forward. Andrew put his arm around her and asked her if she was okay. Camillia shook her head from side to side. Jaden asked Camillia if she needed a doctor, and she nodded her head in an up and down motion. Jaden had Andrew get her to her bed so he could check her and the unborn baby. After checking Camillia, Jaden came to realize Camillia was in labor and simply got shook up, not knowing what was happening. Jaden told Andrew she would be fine, and once the baby was born, she would be able to communicate normally again. He told Andrew to have Armellya get his black bag and get there as soon as possible.

Andrew rushed from his quarters to the castle's private dining hall to get Armellya. When Andrew got to Armellya, he told her Jaden needed his black bag because they were about to have a baby. Armellya shot from her chair and ran to her quarters. She got Jaden's black bag and got to Camillia rather rapidly. Armellya assisted Jaden with the baby while Andrew talked to Camillia to help her get through the delivery.

The baby was delivered swiftly. It was a boy who was to be called Johnathan. Armellya took the baby and cleaned him up while Camillia and her bedding were being cleaned up by her personal maid. Camillia was now back to communicating normally, so Jaden asked her to describe what had happened to her. Camillia said she knew what she wanted to say, but the words just were not there. It was like she could not think. Camillia told Jaden it was like her brain's thought process shut down. She was even aware of the stuttering. Andrew felt it was a form of shock like what one did under a tremendous amount of stress or after witnessing something alarming. Armellya made it back with baby Johnathan and handed him to Camillia. Armellya told Camillia she had a fine boy. Then Andrew stepped over to admire his son. Jaden used Camillia and Andrew's bathroom to wash up and check his clothing. His clothing was still clean somehow so he did not have to change.

Armellya was still in the bedroom with Camillia and Andrew, so when he got out to them, he asked if they would be out soon. Camilla said she felt great so she would be out momentarily; besides, she had to help plan a wedding. Jaden and Armellya told Camillia and Andrew they would meet them out at the castle's private dining hall. Then they left the bedroom. Back at the castle's private dining hall, Jaden announced that Camillia was back to normal, doing well, and had just given birth to a son. Everyone was happy for Camillia and Andrew.

Before Michelle and Melanie left the big round table to assist their castle's decorators, Armellya reminded them that they and their husbands had an appointment with her and Jaden for a conception healing. The women said they could do it before the castle's decorators got there so that was what they were going to do. Michelle and Allen went to the room of relaxation first. The couple sat in chairs next to each other. Then Armellya and Jaden took their places alongside of them. Armellya put her hand on Michelle's stomach, and Jaden put his hand on Allen's stomach. Jaden's and Armellya's hands started to glow slightly. Then the light got blindingly bright and eventually dimmed until there was no more glow.

Now that Michelle and Allen were healed for conception, Jaden excused them from the room of relaxation, telling them to let Melanie and Michael know they were waiting for them. A few minutes later, Melanie and Michael were at the room of relaxation. Armellya invited them on in and told them to take their seats next to each other. Once Melanie and Michael took their seats, Armellya and Jaden took their places and did the same thing to them. As soon as the two couples finished getting their conception healing, the castle's decorator and subordinates arrived. Michelle and Melanie took their decorators into their houses and explained what style of decor they wanted and added that they wanted each room to gently transition into the next. The decorators said they needed to do some shopping for the decor they wanted, but they would be back posthaste.

While the decorators were working hard, the women, Armellya, the chief, and Sharonna were sitting in the family room having tea and cookies, discussing the chief and Sharonna's wedding arrangements. Jaden went to work at the hospital. Andrew went to the multiuse hall to meet with the construction workers for the community play hall and swimming pool, and Matthew was on patrol. Jaden was catching up on all his paperwork while Andrew was looking over some blueprints and observing toys that the multiuse hall had completed. The chief left the wedding planning up to Sharonna and the rest of the women, including Camillia, while he finished his castle's mini-reconstruction project for Deuteronomy.

Bridgette knew she had to get two different wedding thank-you cards made immediately for Michelle and Melanie so she worked on them in the family room while discussing the upcoming wedding for the chief and Sharonna. Bridgette was making a third thank-you card in preparation for Sharonna to send out after she and the chief married.

Bridgette finished the three different thank-you cards and was ready to send off Michelle's and Melanie's cards to the duplication hall, who would send them back to the castle to be personalized before they were sent to the distribution hall.

Jaden got caught up on his paperwork, and the hospital was slow, so the doctor in charge told him to go home and remain on a standby status until his eight-hour day was done so he was contentedly back at the castle with the family and his wife.

The chief finished his remodification of both sides of the castle for Deuteronomy's comfort and convenience. Jaden returned to the castle about the same moment Andrew did, so they entered through the front door together. Andrew was very satisfied with the blueprints he reviewed, and the toys made by the multiuse hall were awesome. The multiuse hall still had a lot of toys to make, but from what Andrew had seen so far, he knew they would do an awe-inspiring job. The women concluded their plans on how the wedding was going to be conducted.

Camillia took notes on what needed to be done for the chief's wedding to Sharonna. Then each one was to be delegated a task or two, except Sharonna. Bridgette even had assignments for the men and the castle's staff. She would be letting them know what they were responsible for when the wedding meeting was officially over. Upon the conclusion of the chief and Sharonna's wedding conference, the castle's decorators were just getting back with all the new decor. The castle's head decorator told Michelle and Melanie the decor would be completed in a couple of hours for them to inspect the work and, they hoped, approve of it. This day was a very productive day prior to the lunch hour and family time, and everyone was motivated by that because they got much more done than they ever expected to.

Bridgette called for one of the castle's runners, and when he got to her, she gave the runner Melanie's and Michelle's thank-you cards and told him to take them to the duplication hall and tell them to deliver them back to the castle when they were done duplicating them. The runner took the two thank-you cards, acknowledged Bridgette, and then left instantly. Once the thank-you cards were delivered to the duplication hall, he reported back to Bridgette that the job had been completed. Bridgette thanked the runner and then excused him from her presence. It was nearing the lunch hour and family time, so the family gathered in the family room to await the lunch hour to embark.

The women agreed to start giving everyone their wedding jobs to be started after the lunch hour and family time. They were hoping they could all complete their tasks prior to the dinner hour so the wedding would not be delayed any longer than necessary. The chief and Sharonna were willing to help with their wedding arrangements, but the women said no because they were the betrothed couple. After the short debate over the wedding chores and who was helping and who was not allowed to help, the lunch hour and family time had finally come. Andrew led everyone to the private dining hall, and they all sat in their places at the big round table. The kitchen staff brought out the lunch meal right away, and they served everyone promptly. As the food was being served, the family started to go around the table sharing their day so far. Jaden said he was grateful for being able to leave work early, allowing him to spend extra time with the family he so loved. Camillia and Andrew had their new bundle of joy with them and passed him around for everyone to see and say hello to. They told everyone they were blessed with their twelfth child, and he was to be called Jonathan.

Melanie and Michelle both shared that they had received their conception healing and that their homes would be perfected that day because the castle's decorators were working on them as they spoke. The chief announced that he had completed his alterations to both sides of the castle for Deuteronomy's comfort and convenience. Then he thanked them for their work in planning his and Sharonna's wedding.

Bridgette announced that they had all the plans for the next wedding on paper already and had assigned the duties to the individual best qualified for the task. Bridgette also let everyone know the thank-you cards for Michelle and Melanie were at the copy hall and would be back at the castle soon for them to personalize and send to the distribution hall. They were all content with how much had been accomplished. Now, all that was left to do that day was the job they were given for the wedding, and it was not just the family members who were getting responsibilities; it was also castle staff. The lunch hour and family time was over, but before they could get up from their chairs to leave the private dining hall, Camillia insisted they all stay in their seats at the big round table so she could tell them what their responsibility was for the chief and Sharonna's wedding. Camillia started giving orders. Bridgette would do the flower arrangements along with the bride's bouquet and the flower girl's rose petals in the basket. Melanie's father would make the romantic dinner. Melanie's mother would make the wedding cake. Melanie would make the edible arrangements. The chief and Sharonna would be responsible for their wedding rings and attire. Andrew would perform the ceremony as king of the Land of Grandeur. The castle's decorators would do the decorations in the private dining hall. Bridgette would make the thank-you cards. Jaden would transport the groom. Armellya would transport the bride. Armellya and the women would do the bride's makeover. Camillia said she was counting on holding the wedding on the next day, having the ceremony before the lunch hour and family time.

Armellya told Camillia they were going to hold the wedding in the forest with some of the animals as part of the procession. That was their wedding arrangement. Camillia agreed to having the beauty of the animals as part of the wedding ceremony. After the ceremony, they would all go back to the castle to finish the rest of their day. The lunch hour would be for the reception, and the family time would be for the cake and gifts. As Camillia finished giving her orders, there was a knock at the castle's front door. It was the duplication hall bringing the thank-you cards back to be personalized. There were two boxes, one for each new wife to personalize; then they had to get them to the distribution hall. Michelle and Melanie left the castle's private dining hall to take their boxes to their homes and start working on personalizing their thank-you cards. Melanie and Michelle planned to finish the thank-you cards in one sitting so they could get them out in an appropriate time frame. They went to their quarters to fill out their many cards with some peace and quiet. Everyone else left the castle's private dining hall to get started on their wedding tasks. It was advised to meet in the castle's family room an hour prior to the dinner hour to review what had been accomplished so far. Right then, the castle was essentially vacant because of everyone being out shopping for the things they needed for the wedding.

Melanie and Michelle finished their thank-you cards and sent them to the distribution hall by the castle's runner. Then they went to the family room to wait on the family to report their progress with the wedding preparations.

They had all finished their shopping and made it back to the castle to start with their assigned preparations. They had pretty much finished with what they could do that day, but there were some things that had to be done at the last minute, such as the food completion. Michelle and Melanie were summoned by the castle's decorators to see their home's decor and either approve or disapprove it. They both left the family room and went into their homes to see every room and observe the flow between rooms for a smooth transition. Every one of their rooms had the requested decor, and the transition between rooms was smooth. Both Michelle and Melanie approved of the jobs. They finished with the castle's decorators just in time to go back to the family room to meet with the rest of the family about the chief and Sharonna's wedding.

The whole family was now in the family room to review where everyone was in finishing their appointed tasks. Jaden and Armellya had astroprojected to the forest and spoken to the wild animals, and they agreed to be part of the ceremony.

The animals already knew where to be, how they were to be arranged, and how to be posed. Bridgette had the large flower arrangements, the bride's bouquet, and the flower girl's rose petals in the basket. Melanie's father had the romantic wedding dinner food prepped and ready to cook the next evening. He also had the reception foods ready. Melanie's mother had the wedding cake done, and the many edible arrangements, one for everyone, were made also.

The chief and Sharonna went together to get their wedding ring set and then separated to get their wedding attire. Andrew was reciting the biblical wedding vows and trying to memorize them as best he could on such short notice. Some of the castle's decorators went shopping for wedding decor and had the private dining hall elegantly decorated with an extra table for the gifts to sit on. Bridgette already had the thank-you card made, but they had to wait to see how many they would need before sending it to the duplication hall. Bridgette designated herself to keep track of who got the couple what so the thank-you cards could be personalized. Camillia was very pleased with the status of the preparations. The next day was definitely going to be the chief and Sharonna's special and unforgettable day.

Camillia thanked everyone for their arduous work and told them to relax and enjoy the dinner hour. Andrew announced that the dinner hour was upon them and asked Camillia if she was done with everyone. She said yes. Andrew led everyone into the castle's private dining hall, and they were all seated at the big round table rapidly. They had all worked so hard to complete the wedding tasks Camillia had assigned to them that they were not aware of how much of an appetite they had worked up until they started to eat the dinner placed before them by the kitchen staff. Everyone surprisingly had second helpings and hurriedly ate every bite of it. By the time they were finished eating, the food in their bellies started to give them an overfull feeling that was somewhat uncomfortable. Everyone sat at the big round table until they started to feel a bit better, and during that time, they discussed the chief and Sharonna's wedding. They knew how special the next day needed to be. After all, the wedding involved the community's only patriarch. Sharonna was quite a bit younger than the chief, so everyone was curious if they would want children. Armellya and Jaden would have to have the conception talk with Sharonna and the chief because if so, Armellya and Jaden were going to be the individuals to make it happen.

With it being an hour past the end of the dinner hour, everyone agreed to meet an hour before breakfast at the castle's private dining hall to ensure the day would go with precise organization, which they would discuss over a cup of Melanie's specially brewed coffee. With the agreement made, they all left the big round table to make their way to their quarters. Even though they had all had to work hard throughout the day and were exhausted, they were overjoyed to be a part of the wedding for the chief and Sharonna. They all ended their day by changing from their day clothes into their bedclothes and flopping onto their beds.

All the couples got into their cuddling positions and fell fast asleep. Upon the midnight hour, the mini-angels appeared to visit them. They sang their delightful wake-up song to wake up their pale ones. They shared their tiring days with their mini-angels and expressed a desire to go back to sleep. The mini-angels wished their pale ones well and then expressed their affections. Their pale ones expressed their affections back. Then the mini-angels returned to the Dinosaur Tail.

The next morning arrived and everyone was well rested and electrified for the day to progress to the wedding ceremony. As they had agreed, everyone met at the castle's private dining hall to review what was left to be done over a cup of Melanie's gourmet coffee. It was vital for everyone and the animals to work with precise unity to be able to have everything finalized for the wedding ceremony to start at the planned time. The ceremony was to start upon the bride's arrival to the spot at the forest, as they did not have rooms like the ones at the religious hall. While the women were discussing the last of the wedding preparations, the chief and Sharonna arrived at the castle's private dining hall.

As Sharonna and the chief took a seat at the big round table, they thanked the women for their vigorous work and exotic yet royal planned results. The wedding was to be out in the forest with some of the wild animals being part of the ceremony. Because Armellya and Jaden could talk to the animals and the animals were aware of their gifts, they were friends. The chief and Sharonna were not surprised by the gift that Armellya and Jaden had concerning the wild animals. Instead, the chief and Sharonna felt blessed to have such an arrangement made. It was going to be more than exotic; it was truly going to be that of royalty.

Armellya and Jaden even arranged for the mini-angels to be there, but their position in the wedding was going to be a bit different than what it was in the other weddings. A very short time after the chief and Sharonna got to the castle's private dining hall, the men of the castle arrived. They all agreed that they were in high spirits and ready to take on the day's events. The time had gone by fast since the women and everyone else arrived at the castle's private dining hall. It was now time for them to eat breakfast. Melanie had the kitchen staff bring out breakfast and serve everyone.

The breakfast hour did not last long because of everyone's eagerness to get the bride ready for her ceremony. It was also going to be a longer trip than usual to get to the site where the ceremony was to be held since it was outside the commune walls. The groom was to leave first this time to get in his place so when the bride got there she could assume her position immediately and the orchestra could start playing. There would be a carpet of red rose petals to make an aisle for the bride to walk down, and along the makeshift aisle would be the animals. The mini-angels would be fluttering about the animals. The lightning bugs that provided light for the community and forest were going to be six feet above the top of the aisle to provide an romantic ambience. The castle was starting to get the aroma of food, as Melanie's father was getting the romantic dinner prepared for the oven. As soon as the breakfast hour was over and everyone had left the private dining hall, Melanie's father would prepare the big round table's cocktail foods and beverages and then set them out.

They had only eaten half of their breakfast because they were in a hurry to get started on the bride's makeover. It would not be hard to fix Sharonna's hair, just time-consuming because her hair was so long it was dragging the ground by eight inches, much like a long veil. The women were going to line her hair with flowers like roses and baby's breath after they removed the leaves, thorns, and some of the stems. The women were going to do Sharonna's makeup to accentuate her natural beauty. All the additional steps to get her ready would be done after she had her wedding gown on. The groom had it a lot easier to dress for the wedding and would be ready much sooner than the bride.

They all headed for their temporary dressing rooms. The chief went to his side of the castle with the men and used his own bedroom for his dressing room. Sharonna and the women went to Armellya's home and used her family room as a dressing room. As the chief was dressing, he called for his and Andrew's runners to go to Sharonna's house, pack her things, and then bring them to his side of the castle. After the wedding and other processions involved in the traditional wedding affair, the chief and Sharonna could unpack her belongings and then call the castle's decorators to decorate their side of the castle how she wanted it to be done.

Armellya and Jaden discussed the possibility of a conceptual healing for the chief and Sharonna and then decided to talk to the chief and Sharonna together on the day after the wedding. The castle's runners got to the chief without delay. Then the chief told them what he wanted them to do, and they got on it right away. Sharonna felt blessed to be able to become a part of the royal family and reside in the castle. It was like a dream come true. Because of the need for precision between the humans and animals, there had to be a slight change of plans in the preparation of the bride and groom. Armellya and Jaden had to go to the forest to make sure the animals were in their places and the mini-angels were there. There were lions lining the aisle backed by elephants with large birds on their backs. The bride would walk up the aisle with a unicorn on either side of her. They were there waiting for Sharonna. Any other animals that wanted to be there were to be around the main event, and from what Armellya and Jaden understood, there were going to be many extra animals to bless the couple's union.

The chief was now leaving his side of the castle with all the men to meet up with Armellya and Jaden. Fifteen minutes later, Sharonna and the women left to meet up with the wedding party. Once everyone was there, the ceremony began and flowed smoothly. The whole thing went as envisioned. Once the bride and groom kissed at the end of the ceremony, the new couple got into the chief's buggy and drove back to the kids' side of the castle. Everyone else followed the bride and groom back to the castle. As the pale ones left, the animals went back to their routines, and the mini-angels went back to the Dinosaur Tail. Everything was going as planned and right on schedule. Now at the castle, everyone went inside to the castle's private dining hall except for the bride. Sharonna went to Armellya's family room to change from her wedding dress into a party gown. When Sharonna returned, she sat at the big round table and everyone indulged in party foods and beverages while the wedded couple opened their gifts. Bridgette kept note of who gave what for the sake of the thank-you cards. With the completion of opening the wedding gifts, the castle's runners reported to the chief that Sharonna's belongings were in his side of the castle.

The guests heard and volunteered to help them unpack her things. Sharonna thanked everyone for the offer and said she would take them up on it. When things settled down a bit, the chief stood up and said he had an announcement. The chief announced that they planned to get a conception healing so they could have children. Then he sat back down. Everyone supported the new couple and congratulated them.

Armellya and Jaden told the chief to just let them know when they were ready, and they would be at their service. Sharonna told Armellya and Jaden she would like the healing before the bed hour that same day, and Armellya said to pull them aside, and they would go to the room of relaxation and do it.

The family said they were ready to go to help put Sharonna's things away since they had just had a large snack, and there was some time before the dinner hour, so why not do the healing now and then meet the family at the chief's side of the castle?

The chief and Sharonna agreed, so they along with Armellya and Jaden went to the room of relaxation and shut the door behind them. Armellya had the chief and Sharonna sit in the chairs that were side by side. Then they took their places on either side of the newlyweds. Armellya explained the process to Sharonna so she was not alarmed by the touch and glowing. The chief already knew what to expect. Jaden put one hand on the chief's stomach, and Armellya put one hand on Sharonna's stomach. Armellya and Jaden's hands started to glow. Then the glow became a bright, blinding light that dimmed back down after a few seconds. Armellya and Jaden removed their hands from the chief and Sharonna and said that was all there was to it. Sharonna and the chief thanked them. Then Armellya and Jaden wished the chief and Sharonna good luck. They left the room of relaxation and joined everyone else on the chief's side of the castle to get Sharonna moved into the castle. They decided to have Sharonna and the chief do nothing but say where things belonged, and with everyone putting things where they said, they finished in a flash. There was still quite a bit of time before the dinner hour, so the chief summoned the castle's decorators to work on the decor under Sharonna's supervision.

When the castle's decorators arrived, Sharonna told them what she wanted in each room with a flowing transition between the rooms. The head decorator had her six subordinates separate and do one room a piece. They had to leave the castle to shop for the things they needed, but they wasted no time out in the community and were back without delay. The decorators worked efficiently and got the decor done before the dinner hour arrived. The head decorator took Sharonna through the castle to have the work approved. Sharonna was pleased with the work and told the head decorator so. The chief's side of the castle had been lifeless and drab before the decorators intervened. Now, it was positive and full of life. It made the chief feel perky. He was beginning to see that bachelorhood had been making him older fast.

Sharonna invited the family to her and the chief's side of the castle to get their opinion of the decor. Between the changes the chief made for Deuteronomy's comfort and the overhaul by the decorating team, the castle did not even look like the same structure. The family told Sharonna she had worked wonders on their side of the castle, and they were glad she did it. It was nearing the dinner hour, and so much had occurred that day, it completely astonished the chief, Sharonna, and the rest of the family. Everyone felt thankful to be around one another, and the castle now felt alive. They all congregated in the kids' family room, waiting for one of Melanie's parents to let them know it was time to enter the private dining room. Melanie's mother came out to the family and told them dinner was ready and then led them into the private dining hall.

The men seated their wives and then were seated themselves. Then the kitchen staff brought out the most amazingly romantic dishes there were and served everyone. The wedding cake was the table's centerpiece. It was colossal and picturesque. The family began to eat, and the food was so exquisite that they had to compliment the chef. Melanie's father had definitely gone out of his way to prepare the meal. After the meal ended, it was time for cake and homemade ice cream. The family found it difficult to save room for the extraordinary dessert because the dinner was so complimentary to the palate, but each of them had done so. Melanie's mother cut the cake while her father scooped the ice cream and served it. The family savored the dessert just as they had the dinner, and the top of the cake was set aside to be kept for the chief and Sharonna's one-year anniversary just as Melanie's mother had done for the rest of the couples in the family.

Once they finished their dessert, their bellies were comfortably full. They all retired to the family room to spend two hours of quality time together before the hour of sleep. The time went by expeditiously, especially since they were enjoying themselves and one another. Sharonna was delighted to be a part of such a close and large family. She had never fathomed she would be so fortunate. Before becoming a pale one, she never knew families could be so close and loving. Sharonna was still used to the ways of life as a human, how they were segregated, warlike, sad, and unimaginable. Becoming a pale one, she had learned of peace, joy, and unity, but she had never imagined having a lifelong mate and children of her own. The time for them to go to their own quarters for the night was upon the community.

They all said their good nights then. As the chief and Sharonna were headed for their side of the castle, the chief turned to them and told them they had made that day a special and memorable one. Then he thanked them. Everyone welcomed Sharonna to the family. Then they all verbally expressed their love toward one another and went their own ways.

When the chief and Sharonna got into their bedroom, they had planned to consummate their union, and they did. Then they went to sleep.

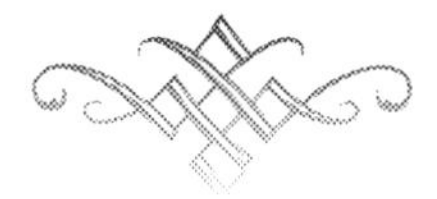

CHAPTER 6

THE ONLY TWO INDIVIDUALS AWAKE IN THE ENTIRE castle were Santuvious and his nanny. The nanny was having a grim time getting him to stop crying, so he took Santuvious to Armellya's front door and knocked on it. Jaden got out of bed to answer the front door, unsure of who it could be. When Jaden saw the nanny with Santuvious, he called for Armellya to come to the front door. When Armellya got there and saw it was the nanny with Santuvious, she asked what the problem was. The nanny told Armellya and Jaden he could not soothe Santuvious, and he did not know what was wrong with him. Jaden took his son and tried to soothe him, but it did not quiet him, so he handed Santuvious over to Armellya, and the baby immediately stopped crying. Apparently, he wanted his mother, so Armellya told the nanny she would keep Santuvious overnight. The nanny went back to the nursery, and Jaden shut the front door. Armellya and Jaden went to their family room so Armellya could sit in the rocking chair and rock Santuvious to sleep. While she was holding Santuvious in her arms, he turned his head toward her arm. He bit her and then sucked on her arm. Although the bite was intense, she did not drop him. It took a few minutes for Armellya to realize what he was doing; he was suckling the blood out of her arm. Armellya shifted so Santuvious could not reach her wounded arm. Then she realized how serious the bite was.

Armellya and Jaden were a bit fearful of Santuvious. Could he still have a dark side to him? Armellya's arm was still freely bleeding, and she needed to get the bleeding stopped, so she handed Santuvious over to Jaden. The child was content for the time being. Jaden asked to see her arm, and when she showed it to him, he said she needed stitches. Armellya and Jaden were both amazed at the severity of the bite. Jaden took Santuvious to his bedroom and put him in his crib. Then he went to take care of Armellya. Jaden got into his black bag to get everything he needed to sew up her arm. Jaden had just enough time to numb Armellya's arm, sew it up, and properly discard everything before Santuvious started screaming again.

Jaden went to the bedroom to pick up Santuvious, but before Jaden picked him up, he stopped crying immediately. Then Jaden noticed he had a bizarre look on his face. It frightened him. Jaden picked Santuvious up and took him out to the family room to be with him and Armellya. Santuvious started sucking on his own hand like a lot of babies did. Then he bit his wrist open. Jaden and Armellya could not believe what they were seeing. Santuvious was essentially drinking his own blood, and his wrist was bleeding heavily enough that he could not drink fast enough to keep it from flowing down his arm and onto Jaden. Jaden told Armellya about the bizarre look Santuvious had on his face prior to him picking him up, but it was difficult to describe. The only way Jaden could describe Santuvious's expression was to tell Armellya it was a look of evil.

Because of the extent of the wound on Santuvious's arm, Armellya was going to have to hold him down on the couch so Jaden could sew up his arm to stop the bleeding. Jaden laid Santuvious on the couch, and Armellya kept an eye on him while Jaden got his supplies out of his black bag. When Jaden was ready to suture Santuvious's wrist, Armellya held him down with his wrist out. Jaden numbed his wrist and then sutured the wound. Santuvious screamed the entire time. He did not like being held down. Jaden put Santuvious back into his crib, and he started to scream again. Jaden ignored the child's tantrum and went back to the family room to discuss any practical options for dealing with Santuvious's thirst for blood.

The couple did not know what to do about their child's biting problem. It was obvious that Santuvious was purposely biting to draw blood for drinking. Armellya and Jaden came up with no answers on how to handle his actions. Jaden said he would stay with Santuvious and told Armellya to astroproject to the Dinosaur Tail. They needed their mini-angels to visit early. Armellya got to the Dinosaur Tail and instantly found their mini-angels. Then she told them what had transpired with Santuvious. Their mini-angels told Armellya to get back to her body, and they would be there momentarily. Because of the urgency in the mini-angels' voices, Armellya said nothing more and promptly returned to her body.

Before Jaden could ask any questions, the mini-angels appeared. The mini-angels tried to get into Santuvious's mind through telepathy, but he was stopping them from perceiving anything, and that was suspicious. It suggested a lurking evil. When the mini-angels tried to get close to Santuvious, he used the power of his mind to thrust them across the room. That was also a malevolent sign. Evil could not handle the presence of good. Armellya told her mini-angel they had vanquished the fallen angel, the angel of death, and a dark soul from Santuvious. Then Armellya asked her mini-angel what could possibly be behind her child's behavior.

The mini-angel reminded Armellya that they had told her there may be a part of his brain responsible for the judgment of good and evil that may have been triggered to malfunction and produce pure evil. There was no telling what triggered Santuvious, but it was obvious his brain was triggered and all he could produce would be negative behavior. The mini-angel told the couple that the child would only get worse. Armellya asked the mini-angel what they were to do in the situation. They could not allow him to hurt himself or anyone else. The mini-angel told the couple they had mentioned medicating him and keeping him in seclusion, but that was for when he got older; they could not do that with a toddler. The mini-angel said the other option was euthanasia.

Armellya and Jaden were grief-stricken. Jaden asked the mini-angels if there might be anything Jadellya could do with Santuvious. The mini-angel told the couple it would be a lifelong fight between siblings for good versus evil. The mini-angel told the couple that was no life for Jadellya. Armellya and Jaden asked the mini-angels what would be the best way to handle the child. The mini-angel apologized and then told them to euthanize him before he got strong enough to murder through mind control. The mini-angel told Armellya and Jaden he was already strong enough to go into others' dreams and kill the individuals through extreme terror, and he would know exactly what he would be doing.

Armellya knew his first target would be herself, and she feared he would try to target Jadellya after her. Jaden told Armellya they did not have a choice; they were responsible for the child and had to do what was best for the community. Armellya started to cry and agreed with Jaden. Then she said she would not be able to be a part of the euthanasia. The mini-angels told Armellya and Jaden to physically bring the child to the Dinosaur Tail, and they could do the euthanasia painlessly. They would use a certain sweet plant that would put him into a permanent sleep. Then all that would be left to do was to put his body to rest in his own crypt and have it sealed. Jaden asked what could happen if someone broke the seal to his crypt. The mini-angel told Armellya and Jaden he could awaken and become more dangerous than ever.

It was appearing to Armellya and Jaden that the only solution was to euthanize their son instead of putting him into a deep sleep. The mini-angels told the couple they could explain his death away by telling others it was a crib death. The couple knew what they had to do, but that did not make it any easier to accept. Jaden asked the mini-angels if they could be with them while they euthanized their son. The mini-angels said they could do it for them if it would make it easier to mentally deal with the loss. The couple agreed that it would be easier if the mini-angels did it and that it needed to be done as soon as possible. The mini-angels said they could do it right then, and the couple agreed to allow it. The couple sat on the couch in the family room while the mini-angels went to the nursery where Santuvious was.

The child started screaming louder. Then, after two

minutes, he stopped screaming altogether. The mini-angels came out of the nursery. They told Armellya and Jaden the job was done; he had been euthanized, not put into a deep sleep. Armellya started to grieve hard, and Jaden was trying to hold himself together so he could support his wife. The mini-angels told Jaden it was time to take the deceased child to his crypt. Jaden said he would do it and wanted a mini-angel to stay with Armellya while another mini-angel guided him to the place of rest. The mini-angels agreed to Jaden's condition.

Jaden went into the nursery and picked up Santuvious. Then he covered him with a receiving blanket. When Jaden walked through the family room, Armellya grabbed his arm so he stopped walking. Then Armellya kissed her deceased baby on the head. She sat back down on the couch while Jaden walked out the front door with the mini-angel.

Jaden took the baby to the crypt the mini-angel had told them about and placed his body in it. When Jaden walked out, the mini-angel sealed the crypt. Then Jaden started to cry. Jaden and the mini-angel went back to the castle to be with Armellya. The couple was very saddened to have lost their beloved son. The mini-angels went back to the Dinosaur Tail, leaving Armellya and Jaden to address the grief between the two of them. The couple had known this day would come, but even though they had tried to prepare for it, there was just no way to do that. Armellya and Jaden were still awake at the midnight hour, and their mini-angels returned to check on them and make sure they were going to go through the grieving process so they could come to terms with their loss.

The couple's mini-angels told them it would be a promising idea if they had another baby, not to replace

Santuvious but to have their family complete. Armellya was not sure she could have any more babies because it might remind her of Santuvious. The mini-angel advised them to have another baby and then went back to the Dinosaur Tail. Armellya and Jaden lay in their bed but could not fall asleep. By the time the morning hour had arrived, the couple was still awake, and now it was time to start the new day.

Armellya and Jaden changed out of their previous day's clothes into clean day clothes and did their morning routine to prepare for the new day. Armellya and Jaden sadly joined the rest of the family for early coffee even though they wanted to isolate. The couple knew what they needed was support from the family, and they would finish the grieving process eventually.

When Armellya and Jaden got to the castle's private dining hall, the chief looked up at the couple and told them they looked like Hades. After they took their seats at the big round table, Jaden announced that Santuvious had passed away from crib death during the night.

The family somberly told the couple they were sorry for their loss. They offered to be there for anything the couple may need them for, and Armellya and Jaden tearfully thanked them. Though there was a tragedy in the castle, everyone, including Armellya and Jaden, needed to keep a schedule for their responsibilities. Melanie called for the kitchen staff to bring out breakfast and serve everyone. Armellya and Jaden did not eat much; they mainly picked at their food. There was no talk during the breakfast hour, but Jaden did telepathically tell the chief to meet with him at his house after the breakfast hour ended. The chief subtly nodded his head at Jaden. The chief had the idea that Jaden wanted to see him about Santuvious's death.

The breakfast hour ended rather early, so Andrew went to check in with the multiuse hall to see how the community's play hall was coming along. Jaden and Armellya went to their house, and the chief followed them there after telling Sharonna he would see her after checking on Armellya and Jaden. Jaden had the chief take a seat in their family room. Armellya went to Santuvious's nursery, picked up a receiving blanket, held the blanket to her face, and began to cry. Jaden and the chief heard Armellya crying as she questioned why the child could not have been saved. The chief walked into the nursery, took Armellya around the shoulders, and then led her out of the nursery. Once the chief brought Armellya out to the family room, he sat her on the couch next to himself. He kept an arm around her and told her she would probably always wonder if things could have been different, but time would ease the pain. Jaden started to tell the chief that Santuvious did not pass from crib death; that was just what they were telling the family under advisement of their mini-angels. Jaden revealed that Santuvious had been euthanized by the mini-angels because he was still evil. Jaden told the chief in detail how the child had attacked Armellya and then himself. The chief told Armellya she should spend some time with Jadellya because she would be able to take the pain away, as she was a very gifted child.

Jaden had not thought of that idea, but it sounded like a promising one so he sent for Jadellya's nanny to bring her to them. Jaden also told the chief how the mini-angels had advised them to have another baby. The chief felt that having another baby was a beneficial idea also. The chief told

Armellya that having another baby was not to try to replace or make her forget Santuvious, but it would contribute to her recovery by helping her to see that she was still a successful mother. Armellya said she understood what having another child could do for her, and she fully intended on trying the suggestion, but she was concerned about being able to love another child like she should.

Jaden told Armellya he knew she would love their next child as she should; she had the gift of a never-ending love for herself and others, and that was what had attracted his attention and love for her. Armellya pulled herself together and then told the chief and Jaden that she wanted the house nursery redone immediately and finished that day. The chief told Armellya it would be done and then asked if there were any requests for the new nursery. Armellya said to make the nursery for another girl. Right after Armellya made her request for the new nursery, there was a knock on the front door. The chief got up to answer it, and it was Jadellya's nanny bringing her to them. Armellya took Jadellya and hugged her. Then she started to cry again.

Jadellya started to babble in baby talk. Then she put one of her tiny little hands on her mother's face and began to glow. Jadellya's glow spread all over Armellya. Then the glow turned to a blinding, bright light. Some of the bright light shot over to Jaden and made his midsection begin to brightly glow. After the light reached its brightest, it began to dim and then disappeared. The chief felt he understood what had just happened and figured Armellya and Jaden would become pregnant with a girl by the next day. Armellya said she could feel herself ovulating. Jaden asked Armellya if she was ready to have another baby, and she said yes.

Armellya told the chief and Jaden that Jadellya had healed her grief and set things up so they could conceive another child immediately. The chief told Armellya he would take Jadellya back to her nanny, and the couple could spend the day together in private. Jaden thanked the chief as Armellya was thanking Jadellya. Jadellya reached for the chief so he took her and said goodbye to the couple. He left to take Jadellya back to her nursery to be with her nanny. Jaden put a "Do Not Disturb" sign on the outside of the front door and then shut and locked it behind the chief.

Jaden walked over to where Armellya was standing, took her into his arms, and hugged her affectionately. Armellya hugged Jaden back and told him she loved him. Jaden said he loved her also. Then she kissed him passionately. Jaden asked Armellya if she was truly ready to spend some intimate time together, and she told Jaden that was what she was feeling so yes. Jaden took Armellya by the hand and led her to their bedroom, where they undressed and then lay on the bed together.

The couple cuddled for a short while, and it led into foreplay. Soon the foreplay turned into fiery lovemaking. When the lovemaking was over, Armellya and Jaden lay together for half an hour and then decided it was time to address the house nursery makeover. Before getting out of bed, Armellya told Jaden she knew she had conceived. Jaden told Armellya he knew he had given her another girl. Finally, they both seemed to be at peace with what occurred with Santuvious. He would never be forgotten or loved any less, but they did what was necessary for him and the community. Santuvious could be at peace also.

Jaden and Armellya were out of bed and redressed, so

Jaden took down the "Do Not Disturb" sign from their front door and summoned the castle's decorators. They arrived in an abbreviated time, and Armellya instructed them on what she wanted for the house nursery that was to be redesigned. The head designer understood and gave each of her subordinate designers tasks. Then they all went to do what they were told. The head designer told Armellya it would be done before the lunch hour and family time. Armellya thanked her.

While the chief was with Armellya and Jaden, Bridgette had the wedding thank-you cards made for their wedding gifts. Sharonna had been working on personalizing them so she could get them sent to the distribution hall that day. By the time Armellya and Jaden had come out of their house, Andrew had just returned from the multiuse hall. Jaden told Armellya and Jaden how wonderful the building was. It was the largest building they had in the commune. The only thing left was to fill the swimming pool with water and get the last of the large toys into the building and bolted down. The community was getting excited about the new community play hall. The parents could not wait for the time they would be able to spend together socializing while watching their children have fun.

Moving on to the next task, Andrew had a proposition for Michael and Allen so he sent for them. Once Allen and Michael were standing in front of Andrew, he told them to sit down, so the three of them sat in the castle's family room. Andrew told the two men he needed a couple of paramedics to be on site at the community play hall just to be safe, especially with there being a swimming pool. Both men were delighted that they were asked and thought it was important to have someone there also. Michael and Allen told Andrew they would do it and to just let them know when it was to open and make sure they would have anything that may be needed on site if anyone got hurt. Andrew told the two men to write up a list of supplies with the amounts of each supply and propose a uniform so they could be easily spotted. Both men said okay and got together to write the list and agree on a uniform style.

While Allen and Michael were taking care of some new work-related business, the others were wrapping up their duties that held the deadline of the lunch and family time hours. Sharonna finished with her thank-you cards and turned them over to a runner to take to the distribution hall. All Sharonna's cards would be delivered before the dinner hour, and she was contented to have them done. Michael and Allen had finished their list of supplies and amounts along with their work uniform details. Andrew was in the castle's family room waiting for the entire family to arrive so he could lead everyone to the private dining hall.

With nobody else in the family room, Allen and Michael went ahead and showed their list to Andrew. When Andrew saw their idea for a work uniform, he was really impressed. The uniforms were simple, easy to make, comfortable to wear, and water-resistant and would definitely stand out in a crowd. Andrew was more than delighted with the men's ability to work together with such precision. He believed he had done well teaming up the two paramedics. They had worked out in the community since they became pale ones and had encountered each other many times. They were a remarkable team out there. Before becoming pale ones and having telepathy, they had a way of communicating without words so they did not alarm a patient who was experiencing a significant issue. Now having telepathy, they would be at the top of their game for sure. Andrew told Allen and Michael he would have the dressmakers get with them after the lunch hour and family time to get their measurements and get started on their uniforms. Andrew asked how many uniforms were needed for each of them, and they said three each would suffice for a seven-day-a-week job. Andrew said it would be done, and just as he was putting the list in his satchel for reference after the lunch hour and family time, the family started to drop in for the lunch. It was a brief amount of time before the entire family was in the family room, but once they were all there, Andrew led everyone into the castle's private dining hall.

They all gleefully sat in their places at the big round table and then greeted Melanie. Melanie sat next to her husband at the big round table and called for the kitchen staff to bring out lunch. Melanie had the kitchen staff working hard that afternoon. She had them make individual lunches for all of them so they could get their favorite lunch foods. Everyone was surprised and grateful. They all thanked the kitchen staff and Melanie. Melanie did this occasionally for the breakfast meal, and doing it this day for the lunch meal was her effort to get the day to continue to be a terrific one. There had been enough tragedy lately, and she hoped the negative streak was over. While eating lunch, they went around the table to share what their days held for them.

Armellya and Jaden went first to share their expected rest of the day. Armellya announced that they were pregnant with a girl and that Jaden was going to be her obstetrician. She was hoping to have the baby at home among the family. Armellya said that Jadellya blessed them with another girl. All she needed to do was get her confirmation blood test, and she was going to do that in the afternoon. Armellya said she would let the family know what the blood test revealed at the dinner hour. Andrew announced the opening of the community play hall to be sooner than expected and that Allen and Michael would be working there as paramedics. Melanie and Michelle were surprised by the announcement. They did not know their husbands would be working there; they had not had a chance to tell them. Melanie and Michelle were delighted to know their husbands liked children enough to work around them all day and then come home to their own children, when they would have them. They were happy for the two couples but asked when they planned to get pregnant. Michelle and Melanie both said they were ready. Michael and Allen cut into the conversation and told everyone they were ready for children also. Armellya and Jaden told the two couples that pregnancy, delivery, and child rearing were a real blessing; experiencing the child's stages of maturity was a real learning experience for the parents.

Sharonna told everyone that she suspected she and the chief were pregnant also, but she had originally wanted a blood test before announcing it. Jaden told Sharonna he could perform the blood test and have the results twenty minutes after taking her blood to the laboratory. Sharonna asked Jaden if he could be her doctor also, and he said family always came first so certainly. Sharonna asked Camillia how different it was to have the baby in the hospital versus at home. Camillia told Sharonna she would rather have her babies at home, where it was a personal setting and a family-oriented event. Camillia said that the hospital setting was so professional that it seemed impersonal and cold. Sharonna asked Jaden if they could plan the delivery of her baby to occur at home, and he responded affirmatively.

Michelle and Melanie said they could not wait to conceive so they could have children and an old-fashioned doctor who made house calls. They too wanted to have their children at home. Jaden told Michelle and Melanie that he would be honored to be their doctor and birth their children in the comfort of their homes. Armellya told everyone he was serious when he said the family came first. She told them if they needed any medical care, he would be right there. Everyone managed to eat while talking so the lunch hour and family time had come to an end. Jaden told Michelle and Melanie to work on conception. Then he told Armellya and Sharonna to meet him in the castle's family room for their blood work.

They all expressed their love for one another and told each other to have a great rest of the day and they would see each other at the dinner hour. Then they went to where they needed to be. Armellya and Sharonna went to the family room so Jaden could draw their blood. Michael and Allen went to their homes to wait for the seamstresses to get their measurements for their uniforms. Melanie and Michelle went to their homes with their husbands so they could have some personal time with them after the seamstresses were finished with them.

After getting her blood drawn, Armellya went to get Jadellya from her nanny to take home and spend some time with her. Andrew took Camillia to the community play hall for her to see how breathtaking it was so far. Melanie's father and mother were secretly working on a congratulatory dinner for the women of the castle.

Jaden got six tubes of blood from Armellya and Sharonna and then took the blood samples to the hospital himself. When Jaden got to the laboratory, he asked the technicians to run the tests immediately, so they put what they were doing on hold and ran the tests for both women.

Twenty minutes later, the results were ready so the technician gave the paper results to Jaden. After looking over the test results, he went straight back to the castle. When Jaden got back to the castle, he rounded up Armellya with Jadellya, Sharonna, and the chief to tell everyone they were in fact pregnant. The chief picked Sharonna up by the waist and twirled her around, saying he loved her and their baby. Then he set Sharonna back on the floor and rubbed her tummy. Armellya told Jaden she loved him. Then they hugged adoringly and gave each other a tender kiss. When Armellya and Jaden looked at Jadellya to thank her for her baby sister, she had an enormous smile on her face. Armellya and Jaden thanked Jadellya. Then Jadellya giggled and waved her tiny little hands about.

The seamstresses entered Allan's and Michael's homes to take their uniform measurements. It did not take them long to measure the men so they could get back to their dressmaker's shop. The dressmakers told Allen and Michael they would have their uniforms ready for them the next day. The men thanked the dressmakers, and then they headed for their dress shop. Once the dressmakers were gone, Melanie and Michael spent some passionate time together while Michelle and Allen spent some sexual time together also. Both women and their husbands were hoping to conceive.

It was time for Jadellya's evening routine to start, which included her dinner, so Armellya took Jadellya back to her nanny for the night. Before turning Jadellya over to her nanny, Armellya gave her lots of affection and told her Mommy would see her the next day. As Armellya left Jadellya's castle nursery, she turned toward Jadellya and blew kisses at her.

When Armellya left the nursery, she went looking for Jaden in their home, and he was there. Armellya told Jaden she was feeling terrific about the current pregnancy and wanted the house nursery redecorated from a neutral look to be made up for a girl. When Armellya told Jaden what she wanted, he instantly called for the castle's decorators. The castle's head decorator was standing before Armellya within ten minutes, and her six subordinates were on their way. Armellya told her that she wanted the extra house nursery redecorated. She said that there was nothing wrong with what they had already done; it was that they knew the next baby was going to be a girl so she wanted the room made up for a girl. Armellya also told the head decorator that she wanted some alterations to Jadellya's home nursery. Armellya wanted Jadellya's nursery upgraded from an infant's room to a toddler's room. The castle's head decorator said she had it under control, and then when the subordinate decorators arrived, she told them what to do, and everyone moved right on it. She said she could have both nurseries finished by the end of the dinner hour.

Armellya told her not to work through her dinner hour. Even though the castle's head decorator was willing to start working that evening, Armellya told her to wait until after the breakfast hour the next morning. The castle's head decorator said she and her subordinates would report to her first thing after the breakfast hour. Then she and her subordinates left Armellya's home.

Melanie and Michael and Michelle and Allen concluded their personal time and left their homes to spend time with the rest of the family since the dinner hour was close. Melanie, Michael, Michelle, Allen, Armellya, and Jaden were in the castle's family room visiting and talking about pregnancy when Melanie and Michelle asked Jaden and Armellya if they had a way to know when they were ovulating. Armellya told the women she could feel herself ovulating, but she could not tell when another woman was ovulating. Armellya told Melanie and Michelle that they could tell when other women were pregnant. Melanie and Michelle asked how early in the pregnancy they could tell there was a baby in the womb, and Jaden told the women they knew right away. They could communicate with the babies intrauterine. They always knew what the sex of their children were because they would talk to them and ask them. Michael and Allen asked Armellya and Jaden to help them get pregnant. Then Jaden told them they were already pregnant.

The two couples asked if he was sure, and Jaden told them he could take a blood sample and run it to the hospital to let them be sure, but he and Armellya already saw the babies and knew the sex of both. Melanie and Michelle confessed that they had had intimate time with their husbands that day so the pregnancies were only hours along. Jaden said he was aware of that and said a blood test would still show the presence of the pregnancy hormone, but a urinalysis would not show their pregnancy that early. Michelle and Melanie asked Jaden if he would take their blood and test it for their pregnancies, and he said absolutely. Armellya went to her and Jaden's home to get his black bag for him so he could get what he needed from it for the blood work. Armellya returned to the castle's family room with Jaden's black bag, and Andrew had just walked in when Armellya arrived.

Andrew saw Jaden's black bag in Armellya's hand so he asked if everyone was okay. Armellya told Andrew everything was fine and that Jaden was doing a pregnancy confirmation blood draw on Michelle and Melanie. Andrew was ecstatic about Michelle and Melanie being pregnant. He said nearly all the women in the castle could be pregnant together and support one another. Andrew jokingly said it would be ironic if they all went into labor in the same hour on the same day. Armellya said that would be ironic all right, and she was not sure how Jaden would be able to handle that. She hoped they would not have to find out in real time. Jaden took out the things he needed for a blood draw from his black bag. He drew six tubes of Michelle's blood first and labeled them. Jaden got back into his black bag and got more supplies out for Melanie's blood draw. He drew six tubes of blood from her also and then labeled them. Jaden gave the blood samples to the castle's runner to take to the hospital to be analyzed. The hospital's runner would bring the paper results to Jaden at the castle.

Right after Jaden finished with the blood draws, family started turning up in the family room to gather for the dinner hour. Jaden hurriedly ran his black bag to their house and then returned to the family room to gather for the dinner hour.

Once the whole family was present, Andrew led them to the private dining hall. They all took their seats at the big round table and waited for the kitchen staff to bring dinner out to them. The entire kitchen staff came out of the kitchen, holding plates for those at the big round table. The kitchen staff members organized themselves to be standing behind an individual so they could set everyone's plate down at the same time. When the kitchen staff set the dinner plates down in front of everyone at the big round table, the family noticed the pregnancy theme on their plates of dinner and their desserts. The idea of the theme lightened the hearts of everyone; it was certainly a cute surprise. The dinner conversation was wrapped around all the mothers-to-be. In the middle of the dinner hour, the butler escorted the hospital's runner into the castle's private dining hall so he could give the blood test results on paper to Jaden. Jaden took the results, thanked the runner, excused the runner from his presence, and then read the results. Jaden then told Michelle and Melanie congratulations, and everyone else congratulated them also. Camillia was starting to feel a bit left out. She was the only woman in the castle who was not pregnant. It had not been very long since Camillia gave birth to Johnathan.

Armellya noticed that Camillia's body language portrayed discomfort so she read Camillia's thoughts with her telepathy. Armellya realized Camillia was feeling out of place by being the only woman in the castle not with child. However, Armellya knew Camillia was pregnant, but she had no symptoms so she had not suspected she was. Armellya asked Camillia to come to her house after the dinner hour so she could show her something. Camillia agreed to come and bring Andrew.

The dinner hour came to an end so Camillia, Andrew, Jaden, and Armellya went to Armellya's house, and then Armellya told Camillia not to feel out of place by believing she was the only woman in the castle not with child. Camillia tried to pass the situation off by telling Armellya she had misread her thoughts. Armellya told Camillia that her thoughts were not true because she had conceived right after birthing Johnathan. Camillia and Andrew asked Armellya if she was saying Camillia was pregnant again, and Armellya told them yes. Armellya asked Camillia if she wanted a blood test, and Camillia said yes, so Armellya called for Jaden.

When Jaden got to Armellya, Andrew, and Camillia, Armellya told Jaden Camillia wanted a blood test to prove she was with child because she would not just take her word for it. Jaden told Armellya, Andrew, and Camillia there would be no problem drawing her blood for a pregnancy test. Jaden got into his black bag to get the supplies he needed to draw Camillia's blood. He took six tubes of blood from her, labeled them, and sent them to the hospital with the castle's runner for analysis.

Camillia and Andrew stayed at Armellya and Jaden's house conversing while they waited for the hospital's runner to bring the blood test results. Thirty minutes later, the hospital's runner returned. Jaden looked over the paper blood test results and told Camillia and Andrew congratulations they were definitely pregnant.

It was now time for them to settle down and go to their houses for the night, so Andrew and Camillia said good evening to Armellya and Jaden and then left to go to their own house. Fifteen minutes after the family all got to their homes, the help was settled down and headed for their quarters. They got to sleep early. The men wanted their wives to get optimum sleep to keep their pregnancies healthy. They all wanted to get their house nurseries and castle nurseries ready for their new babies, so they were going to talk to the castle's head decorator the next day. Everyone slept well until the midnight hour. The mini-angels appeared and sang their special wake-up song and woke their pale ones. All those in the castle shared their news of being with child with their mini-angel and had a pleasing discussion with them. The mini-angels spent their time with their pale ones and then returned to the Dinosaur Tail. Everyone got five more hours of sleep and then had to wake for the new day.

They got out of bed, did their morning getting-ready-for-the-day routine, and then went out of their houses, heading for the castle's private dining hall. Once everyone sat at the big round table, they enjoyed some of Melanie's specially brewed coffee and discussed motherhood. Camillia was so eager about getting the official news of her pregnancy that she announced it during the morning gathering. Everyone was on cloud nine for Camillia and Andrew. The breakfast hour had come, so Melanie had the kitchen staff bring out the breakfast food for everyone. The women had said they wanted their house and castle nurseries decorated and stocked for when their babies arrived. They agreed to talk to the castle's head decorator together and let her handle the tall job her way. There were still seven months at least for the decor to be appropriately done in the nurseries so the women knew it would be finished on time, but they wanted their rooms done sooner than later.

Everyone was so electrified that the whole castle was expecting that they felt it might be fun to have a baby club. The men were as enlivened for their wives and about becoming fathers as their wives were about becoming mothers, but they were not interested in joining a baby club. That was a woman thing. Breakfast was not quite over when all the castle's decorators embarked and so did the seamstresses. The decorators waited in the family room for the women. The seamstresses dropped off Allen and Michael's uniforms and then left. Once the breakfast hour had ended, the women of the castle went to the head decorator to tell her what they wanted done in the nurseries. As each woman explained what she wanted, the head decorator assigned her subordinates to the jobs and made sure they understood what to do. The head decorator would be overseeing all the subordinate decorators.

They all got started on the house nurseries to allow time for the nannies to awaken and get their morning routine finished before being imposed upon. The community shops were just opening so the decorators went to the shops to purchase what they needed for both the house and castle nurseries they were appointed to decorate.

Allan and Michael got their uniforms for their new jobs at the community play hall and took them home to try them on. The uniforms fit perfectly.

All six of the castle's decorators were working hard to complete the six house nurseries as the five women wanted them done. All five of the women in the castle wanted their new babies' nurseries done differently, and Armellya wanted Jadellya's house and castle nurseries changed from an infant theme to a toddler one. All the men were staying out of the way of the women and their nursery projects.

Jaden left for his eight-hour shift at the hospital so Andrew took Allen, the chief, and Michael to the community's play hall so they could start to get familiar with the layout and Andrew could check on the workers' progress. All they had to do when Andrew was there last was fill the swimming pool with water, put the last of the large toys into the building, and bolt them down.

When the men got to the community's play hall, the workers had the swimming pool filled up and had just bolted the last of the large toys down. Andrew was very gratified with how the play hall had turned out. He thought the turf grass on the floor inside the building was a fantastic addition. The turf would greatly soften any falls that the children may have. Andrew spoke to the construction workers and the multiuse hall's workers and thanked them, telling them he never expected the play hall to turn out so brilliantly. The workers all said they felt privileged to be a part of the construction of such a powerful addition to the community. The workers got the last of their gear put away and then left the play hall after one last look at their masterpiece.

Andrew took Allen, the chief, and Michael into the play hall to walk about and see what was where. There was every toy imaginable in there, including water spouts to run under. The swimming pool was stunning and large enough to fit over half of the community in at one time. There was plenty of plush seating for the adults to comfortably sit and watch their children play. There were a couple of large lockers for extra medical supplies, and inside the lockers were hooks for the fanny packs that Allen and Michael would wear while on duty. They would contain basic medical supplies for the booboos that were common on a playground. Michael and Allen were energized for the play hall to open so they could experience the thrill that the children would have there. They were looking forward to getting to know the parents as well. Andrew, Allen, the chief, and Michael left the community's play hall to go back to the castle and spread the news of the play hall being completed and ready for opening. The men were also wanting to see how far the castle's decorators had gotten with the new nurseries.

When Andrew, the chief, Allen, and Michael got back to the castle, they found all the women in the castle's family room discussing pregnancy and childbirth, so they let them be and went on to their houses to check on the progress of the house nurseries. The castle's decorators had nearly concluded their first project, and the rooms were stunning and elegant. After checking on the nurseries, Andrew caught up with Allen and Michael again to see if they had gotten their uniforms checked out for a good fit. They both told Andrew they had tried the uniforms on to ensure they fit like they should, and both men told Andrew they were impeccable. Andrew asked to see one of the uniforms because when they told him what they wanted, he only had a vague idea of what they would look like and he wanted to see exactly what they looked like. Allen went to get one of his uniforms, and when he came out with it, Andrew looked it over. After Andrew inspected Allen's uniform, he said it was well designed. Then he asked them who came up with the design. Allen and Michael told Andrew the design was a combined effort.

After finishing with Allen and Michael, Andrew went to see the women in the castle's family room. He needed to have announcements made to let the community know the play hall was going to be open for use and to invite all parents to take their children to play. Bridgette was usually the one who did cards and the like, but Andrew figured it would be a talented group project among the women, since there were so many invitations to be produced and he wanted them to appeal to every parent. When Andrew asked the women about making the announcements, they all wanted to contribute their talents. Bridgette said she would head the project, and the other women could each have a diverse contribution to the invitations. All they had to make was one masterpiece. Then the duplication hall would copy enough to send to all the households in the community.

Once the copy hall had done their job, the distribution hall would get the invitations out to all the homes in the community. Bridgette estimated they could have the invitations out to all the homes by the dinner hour. The women started on the invitation right away by offering ideas of what type of picture to have on it. The women finally agreed on a picture, so Bridgette drew it on the paper designated for the invitation. Next, the women had to come up with a way to word the invitation so it was direct yet friendly. They were easily able to agree upon how to word the invitation. Armellya wrote the words because she knew how to do calligraphy. Sharonna did the shadowing on the picture, and then Melanie did the colored outline. The invitation was very alluring, as the women wanted it to be. Michelle called for the castle's runner to get the single invitation to the duplication hall with instructions to send the duplications to the distribution hall for every house to receive one. The community play hall was to open on the next day and would be available from right after the breakfast hour until half an hour before the community's curfew time.

Allan and Michael could hardly wait for the next day to come so they could watch all the children have a fantastic time at the community play hall. The two men were also looking forward to mingling with all the parents and getting to know the citizens of the community. The women were conversing about the play hall and wanted to go see it themselves. From what they had been hearing, it was a masterpiece. The women decided to get with Andrew to go see the play hall before the day's lunch hour so they could get a good look at it before the children and their parents occupied it.

Camillia told the women she would find Andrew and talk him into taking them to the play hall. Then she left the family room in search of Andrew. She checked her house to see if Andrew was there, and he was so she asked him if he would take her and the women to get a glimpse of the play hall. Andrew told Camillia to gather the women in the castle's family room, and he would be there to take them to the community's play hall. Camillia gave Andrew a peck on the cheek and then dashed for her front door saying thank you.

When Camillia got back to the family room, the women were all still there waiting on her to let them know if Andrew was going to show off the play hall. Camilla told them that Andrew was on his way to take them to the play hall, and they all got keyed up to go. Andrew flowed into the family room to get the women. Then they all left the castle for the community play hall.

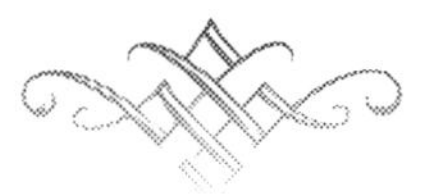

CHAPTER 7

While the women and Andrew were at the community play hall, Jaden was at the hospital finishing his day, the chief was in his side of the castle working on training Deuteronomy, and Allen was with Michael getting their fanny packs set up for work the next day. Right as Andrew and the women got back to the castle, Allen and Michael were over and done with setting up. The women and Andrew met Allen and Michael in the castle's family room, where they would stay and socialize until the chief and Jaden got there for the lunch hour and family time. The socialization was interrupted by a knock on the castle's front door, so the butler answered it. It was one of the flower pickers. The butler let her inside. As she entered, she pulled a cartful of flowers behind her. The flower picker asked if she could leave a bouquet of flowers in every room of the castle. She said when the flower girls were outside the wall picking flowers, they came across some flowers they had never seen before so they picked a lot of them to leave some at every house, hall, and hospital room to allow the community to enjoy them. The flower girls also wanted to spread the flowers about so when individuals ordered flowers, they would know of the newfound flowers as an option. All the women in the castle stopped their conversation and got up to go to the flower cart so they could admire the splendor of the unfamiliar flowers. Each woman of the castle got a bouquet from the flower picker and commented on how lovely they smelled. The flowers were completely atypical, different from any other flower they had seen before. They were colored like a very vibrant rainbow.

As the women were appreciating the bouquets, the chief and Jaden arrived for the lunch hour and family time. The flower picker asked if she could go from room to room, placing some bouquets in each room. No one saw any harm in receiving flowers, so the women told her they would be grateful for having the flowers. After placing flowers in each room on the kids' side of the castle, the flower picker asked the chief if he wanted some of the bouquets in his side of the castle. Sharonna said she would love to have some of those marvelous flowers on her side of the castle. After the flower picker finished placing bouquets in each room on both sides of the castle, she left to go home for her lunch hour. Everyone was present and in the family room when the flower picker left, so Andrew led the way to the private dining hall.

After everyone was seated at the big round table, the kitchen staff brought lunch. As they ate, they went around the big round table sharing their day. Michael and Allen expressed their anticipation for starting their new job the next day. Not only were they pleased about holding a position in the community they felt useful at, but they really wanted to spend time fraternizing with the public. The chief proudly shared the major progress in Deuteronomy's training. Andrew shared how scenic the community play hall had turned out and that he was energized for the children to take pleasure in it. The women shared their appreciation for their conception healing and their delight in being pregnant. The men were elated that their wives were sharing their pregnancies with all the other women in the castle. They felt the women had a great support circle. Jaden jokingly spoke up and told the women not to plan their deliveries on the same day. They all relished their food and concluded the sharing of their day. That was the end of the lunch hour and family time.

When the women left the big round table, they went to go inspect the house nurseries and find out where the castle's decorators were on completing them. Each woman was captivated by her house nursery. The decorators even stocked the nurseries with baby supplies. After approving what the decorators had done with the house nurseries, the women went to investigate how the castle's nurseries looked. The decorators were adding the concluding touches and would be out of the castle within ten minutes. Once the decorators finished stocking the nurseries, they said they had accomplished their tasks and were ready to leave after their work was approved.

The women thought the castle's nurseries were as alluring as their house nurseries. The women thanked the decorators, and then the decorators departed. Armellya was pleased with the new baby's nurseries, but she was especially impressed with what the decorator did with Jadellya's nurseries in making them relate to a toddler. Armellya decided to go shopping and purchase some toddler toys for Jadellya and give her current toys to the new baby.

Before leaving the castle, Armellya asked the other women if they wanted to go shopping with her. All the women wanted to go so they could also purchase some baby toys for their unborn children. Armellya asked the stable boy to hitch two horses to her large buggy, and he straightaway went to the barn to follow her instructions. In a short amount of time, the stable boy had the horses and buggy ready for the women. Everyone loaded up on the buggy, and Armellya drove them on to Jaden's parents' shop. When the women got to the shop, they were taken aback by the new selection they had. Jaden's parents told Armellya they had been the main shop for so long so to stay that way, they needed to get the latest things available that the public was looking to purchase.

The women walked through the shop and found so many items to purchase that they just could not leave without, so they ended up getting everything the babies would ever need and then some. When they got back into the buggy, there was barely enough room for their purchases, but they somehow managed to get everyone and everything back to the castle. When the women got into the castle, they went to their own homes to place their items about their house nurseries. Then they stepped back and observed the rooms for a continued efficiency. The addition of toys did not interrupt the flow of efficiency at all. All of the women were so thrilled with the house nurseries that they went for their husbands to have them come inspect them. The women did find their husbands and took them to their house nurseries, and the men were beside themselves when they saw the outstanding job the castle's decorators and their wives had done. As the couples were walking out of their house nurseries, the women started to stagger as if they were drunk on alcohol. They were not feeling well, and when they tried to verbally communicate that to their husbands, their speech was slurred with incomplete sentences. Jaden and the rest of the men put their wives into their beds. The rest of the men went in search of Jaden. They figured Armellya had taken Jaden to their house nursery just as their wives had done with them, so they went directly to Jaden and Armellya's house. The men found him right away and discovered that their wives were not the only ones displaying the odd behaviors. Jaden was not sure what was causing the women's symptoms but believed it was due to something they all had been recently exposed to. Jaden told the men that whatever the exposure was due to, it had to be something new. There were a lot of new things surrounding them, but it had suddenly occurred to Jaden that the strange epidemic was only affecting the pregnant women, not the men or women who were not pregnant. Jaden suspected there could possibly be pregnant women in the community who might come down with whatever was ailing their wives. He suggested they get their wives to the hospital immediately and have them in rooms next to each other for easier access to all of them. The men got two of the large buggies ready, and they placed the women in the back and then pushed the horses hard to get to the hospital without any unnecessary delay.

When they all got to the hospital, Jaden called for help from the hospital's porters to get the women into a room and on the beds. When the men got their wives into hospital beds, they were barely conscious. Things were getting injurious rapidly.

Jaden appealed to the retired doctor to help solve the mystery illnesses that the women seemed to be suffering from. He felt more comfortable talking in the privacy of his office because he did not want anyone misunderstanding and thinking there was an epidemic. The retired doctor felt that if someone thought there was an epidemic, word would spread throughout the hospital and leak out to the community. Then there would be a serious, uncontrollable panic throughout the community. The retired doctor had been a doctor most of his human life and all his pale one life so his expertise was unmatchable. He checked all five of the castle's women and then told Jaden they were all in the same state so that suggested to him that they had all been exposed at the same time. He asked Jaden if he had any idea of what could have been brought into the castle that was new or unusual. Jaden told the retired doctor that all the nurseries had been redone for the babies on the way and Jadellya. Then later, they received some unusual unblemished flowers. The retired doctor asked if there was a reaction when the nurseries were originally done, and Jaden told him none of the women were pregnant at the time the nurseries were originally fixed up generically. Then once the babies were born, the nurseries would be slightly altered.

Jaden and the retired doctor were disrupted by the charge nurse saying there was a nurse in each room keeping watch over the women, but they had better get to them promptly, as they were in a state of anaphylaxis. The retired doctor and Jaden darted through the hospital's halls to get to the women as quickly as possible before their status crashed. The retired doctor and Jaden agreed that the women needed to be on life support or their lives and definitely the lives of the unborn children would be at risk. The retired doctor and Jaden got an experienced trauma nurse to help them intubate the women.

Those nurses were instructed to put an extra intravenous line in the women and set them up with fetal monitors. Jaden and the retired doctor gave the women medicine to combat their anaphylactic symptoms, but it did not change things. Because the medicine did not help at all, the retired doctor and Jaden suspected whatever was causing the allergic type reaction was still nearby. The retired doctor and Jaden searched the women's rooms to see what was in each room that was not a fixture for a hospital room. There was only one item the retired doctor and Jaden agreed that was not part of the hospital's fixtures, and that was the bouquet of extraordinary flowers. Though those flowers were all over the forest and had always been there, they were unfamiliar to the pale ones.

Thinking back into the evening, Jaden could say the women's symptoms started shortly after they had received the bouquets. Without delay, the retired doctor and Jaden had the bouquets of flowers removed from their hospital rooms.

Jaden thought the mini-angels might be familiar with the flowers since they knew everything about the forest. After all, that was their home. Jaden did not recall seeing those flowers near the Dinosaur Tail, but their effect on pale ones who were with child could be part of the reason. Jaden told the retired doctor he might be able to get some answers about the new unfamiliar flowers, but he would have to use his office. The retired doctor was more than willing to allow Jaden access to his office, but he told Jaden he had no information on botanicals. Then he questioned Jaden on his request for the use of his office.

Jaden revealed that he could astroproject to where the mini-angels were, and they may know of the specific flowers they had received. The retired doctor was stunned that Jaden had the ability to astroproject and to have access to the mini-angels whenever he needed them.

Jaden told the retired doctor he needed a safe place to leave his body. Then the retired doctor said he would stand guard outside of his office. Jaden went into the retired doctor's office and relaxed in the chair behind the desk. Then he astroprojected to the Dinosaur Tail. Jaden looked for his mini-angel. After several seconds, his mini-angel caught sight of him. The mini-angel asked Jaden how she could be of help, and Jaden described the new flower to her and then asked if she knew of them. Jaden's mini-angel told him she and the other mini-angels were experienced with the flower he spoke of. It was called the rainbow flower. The mini-angel told Jaden that while the flower was very pleasing to the senses, it was deadly to anything of purity. The rainbow flower was created by malevolent spirits that lived underground before the pale ones took the land over. The rainbow flower was produced to kill mythological creatures that were of purity and take the new souls about to enter this world. The malicious souls that produced the flowers were the very souls that human priests exorcised from their fellow humans. The mini-angel told Jaden the pregnant women of the castle were in danger of losing the children they carried because those were innocent souls preparing to enter the world. Jaden asked his mini-angel how to protect the women and children. The mini-angel said the rainbow flowers must be destroyed. Jaden knew the rainbow flowers would not die easily so he asked what needed to be done to destroy the rainbow flowers. The mini-angel told Jaden the rainbow flower could only be destroyed by the touch of an innocent soul. Jaden asked his mini-angel where he was to find an innocent soul who would be willing to kill. The mini-angel laughed and told Jaden Jadellya was an innocent, and she would know what to do. The mini-angel reminded Jaden that Jadellya's body may be that of a young one, but her spirit was old and wise. Jaden asked his mini-angel if the rainbow flowers in the forest needed to be destroyed also, and the mini-angel told Jaden eventually yes, because they would take over the forest and then the community if not stopped. Jaden said he would consult with Jadellya and get back with her. The mini-angel thanked Jaden and then told him to work briskly.

Jaden went back into his body and then went to tell the chief, Allen, Andrew, and Michael what he knew so far. The retired doctor followed Jaden to the waiting room and heard what Jaden had said to the men. He asked what he could do to help. Jaden told the retired doctor to stay with the women and try to keep them and the babies stable, and he would go get Jadellya for her to work her magic so to speak.

Jaden raced to the castle, heading directly to Jadellya's nursery when he got there. He snatched Jadellya out of her crib and ran to the buggy with her, going straight back to the hospital. When Jaden walked into the hospital with Jadellya, the retired doctor quickly asked him why he had brought a healthy toddler to a place full of sickness. Jaden told the retired doctor to follow him and he would explain while he and Jadellya were fixing the problem. Jaden took Jadellya to the nurses' break room where the floral bouquets were. Then he asked her if she knew what they were. Jadellya nodded her head up and down. She reached her body and hands as if she were trying to touch the flowers, so Jaden moved toward the counter they were on so she could reach them. Jadellya caressed the flowers, and they wilted and then died. It looked like something out of a human movie shown in slow motion.

The retired doctor would not have believed it if someone had told him of that event, but seeing what happened with his own eyes, he could not deny that Jadellya exterminated the rainbow flowers with a simple gentle touch. Jaden explained to the retired doctor that the flowers were created after the nuclear war below ground by dark souls to rid the earth of human life, pale one life, angelic life, mythological life, and any other purity that existed. Those dark souls had the ability to see into the future to know humans would inhabit the underground as pale ones. Jaden told the doctor that the mini-angels, Jadellya, Armellya, and he could also see into the future. Although Jadellya was young, she had an antiquated, wholesome soul and could therefore combat immorality easily. Jaden said he found these things out from their mini-angels, and there was more: there were other gifts within the royal family that were beyond those of a regular pale one.

The retired doctor told Jaden he knew that Andrew and Camillia were the blessed ones when they could conceive because the legend told of only two humans who would go through the change and not be barren, but seeing the extraordinary gifts that the royal family had had just authenticated his beliefs in them. The retired doctor asked Jaden how they were going to eradicate all the rainbow flowers in the forest before they took over the underground foliage and food products.

Jaden told the retired doctor that Jadellya already knew how, and he was not worried about it because she had defeated worse things, such as the angel of death and the fallen angel. The retired doctor said he would keep vigil over the women and their babies and for him to go do what was necessary to liberate the underground from the rainbow plant. Jaden hugged the retired doctor, and Jadellya blew him kisses. Then Jaden and Jadellya left the hospital to take on their journey to the outside of the commune walls alone.

When Jaden got to the enormous opaque wall, the guards did not want to let him pass because it was not allowed for a commoner to go out. Only pickers and hunters were allowed out and during certain hours as well. It was allowed for the king and queen to go out but only with the security of several hunters each. Jaden told the guards they did not have time to squabble. The queen's life was in jeopardy, and the errand he was trying to fulfill would save her life. He told the guards that if they did not let him and Jadellya out, after the queen died, he would make sure it was their heads that got hung in the center of town. The guards distrustfully opened the commune door and let Jaden and Jadellya out. Jaden did not know where to go, but he knew Jadellya did and she could communicate with animals, so he let the reins rest on the saddle horn so the horse could liberally go where Jadellya guided it.

The ride from the great wall to the area Jadellya wanted to be in took half an hour so when the horse stopped walking, Jaden got off and walked to the edge of the foliage. Jaden had an atypical inkling to set Jadellya on the ground, so he did. Jadellya crawled about fifty feet into the forest. Then she started to glow. As Jadellya glowed brighter, the ground started to glow also. With the onset of the glow, there was a noise that arose, and as the glow spread, the noise got louder. The noise was like a screech of pain. Jaden surveyed his daughter closely and could see how she was working relentlessly as the glow on the ground was spreading farther and farther. Eventually, the ground was glowing for as far as he could see; it even went up all the trees. Jadellya was sitting on her buttocks with her hands held up to what would be the sky if they had one below ground. Jadellya giggled the whole time the ground and trees were glowing, and she held her physical pose for close to half an hour. Finally, the glow receded until it disappeared. When the glowing stopped, so did the sound of screeching in pain. Upon the conclusion of Jadellya's ridding of the rainbow flowers in the wild, abruptly from out of nowhere, a lion came out to the edge of the forest and approached Jadellya. She reached one of her hands up to the lion, and he moved close to her, flopped down, and rolled onto his side. Jadellya was petting the lion on his belly, so Jaden tried to gradually approach the lion. The lion let Jaden pet him on the belly also. It was a pleasing encounter.

After a fleeting time, the lion stood up and ran back into the forest. Then it let out a colossal roar as if to say farewell. Jadellya held her hands up to Jaden for him to pick her up and head back to the commune. The eradicating of the rainbow flowers seemed to be too easy to Jaden because sin did not perish without a good fight. Jaden looked Jadellya right in the eyes and asked her if all the rainbow flowers were dead. Jadellya shook her head from side to side, a negative answer. This concerned Jaden. Jadellya put one hand on Jaden's forehead to show him the live flowers and how she was going to attend to them. The flowers that had been picked and spread around the commune were still alive, but just before the midnight hour, Jadellya was going to perform the same technique to the whole commune that she had done to the entire forest. She could convey to her father that she was aware there were still some live rainbow flowers, and she was going to take care of the situation. Jaden was relieved that he and the community had Jadellya. Jaden got back onto his horse with Jadellya and headed back to the commune.

Once inside, Jaden was going to drop Jadellya back off at the castle's nursery with her nanny and then go directly to the hospital. Jaden was hoping there had been some improvement in the women's conditions. He got to the great wall, and the guards let him in with no mistrust. Jaden continued to get to the castle without delay. Once there, he was greeted by Deuteronomy so he played with the wolf for a few minutes and then took Jadellya back to her nanny. Before leaving his daughter, Jaden gave her a snuggly hug and then kissed her forehead and told her she had done well. Jaden left the nursery and went out of the castle. Then he mounted his horse and rode hard to get back to the hospital at once.

When Jaden got to the hospital, he left his horse with the hospital's stable boy and rushed through the hospital doors. Jaden continued to scamper. Then when he finally got to Armellya's hospital room, he slowed down as he entered and approached her bedside. The retired doctor realized Jaden had returned, so he pulled him aside and told him the women were no worse, but they were no better either. Jaden told the retired doctor that there were still some of the rainbow flowers alive but that Jadellya was going to destroy them during the night. Jaden let the retired doctor know that there were no more rainbow flowers in the wild; the live ones were in the compound. The retired doctor asked if there was anything he could do to help extinguish the rest of the rainbow flowers, and Jaden told him Jadellya had it all under control. Jaden asked the retired doctor if there was anything else that could be done for the women and their unborn babies, and he told Jaden he wished they could help, but it seemed to him it was up to Jadellya to get the rest of the live flowers and depended on how hard the women fought to come back to them. Jaden went to the waiting room to find the men, but they were not there, so he checked the other women's rooms, thinking they were with their wives. They were not there either. Jaden sent runners to the castle to see if they were at their homes, and while he was waiting for the runners to get back with him, he went into the hospital room with Armellya. Jaden had barely sat in the chair next to Armellya's head when she unpredictably started to seize.

Jaden called out for the retired doctor to come promptly, and he got to Armellya's bedside swiftly. Then noticed she was having a violent seizure. The retired doctor instantly checked on the other women, and they too were seizing. The retired doctor got five syringes and drew up some antiseizure medicine in each syringe. Then he went room to room, giving all five of the women the medicine, and it stopped the seizures rather rapidly. The runners returned to Jaden with the men, and they told Jaden they were gone to partake in the dinner hour at home. Jaden said he did not realize the dinner hour was upon them so soon. He told the men about the women having seizures, and the men became worried about their wives. They only left to go home and get some nutrition. Then they were going to return to their wives' hospital rooms promptly. Jaden had planned to spend the dinner hour in his wife's hospital room eating food from the hospital's cafeteria. The rest of the men decided to do the same. All the men went to the hospital's cafeteria together to get their nutritional choices for the dinner hour, and then they returned to the hospital rooms that their wives were in.

When Jaden started to eat his dinner, Armellya began to violently twitch. It appeared to be a less severe seizure than what she'd had earlier. Jaden called out for the retired doctor.

The retired doctor emerged just in time to see Armellya twitching. He agreed with Jaden that Armellya's movements were caused by a seizure. Armellya started to fight the respirator, and her pulse shot up dangerously high. When the twitching stopped, Jaden took Armellya's vital signs, and her blood pressure was high enough to prompt a stroke. The retired doctor went to check on the other women, and they had done the same as Armellya, according to the men. The retired doctor went to the medicine room and drew up ten syringes of antiseizure medicine to keep in his lab coat pocket. If the seizures got too severe, he would not have to waste any time administering the medication.

Upon finishing his meal, Jaden, out of the blue, remembered that when the flower picker was at the castle's family room with the many bouquets of rainbow flowers, Armellya and the other women not only studied the unfamiliar flowers, but they handled them and then positioned their faces on them to smell the tender aroma they put out. Jaden went in search of the retired doctor to tell him of the women's contact with the rainbow flowers. He found the retired doctor in the nurses' break room eating his dinner. The retired doctor was surprised to see Jaden away from Armellya's bedside. He asked Jaden if something was wrong, and he said yes. He told the retired doctor that if someone was allergic to something, they would have to remove the allergen entirely to stop the anaphylaxis, and he agreed. Jaden then told the retired doctor that it would be wise to have the women washed down immediately. He explained that the women would not get any better without a thorough sponge bath with the water being changed after every dunk of the sponge.

Jaden told the retired doctor that when the flower picker had entered their home, the women marveled at the rainbow flower, and in doing so, they came into contact with the flowers with their hands and faces. The retired doctor now understood why the women were not getting any better. The pollen from the rainbow flowers was on their hands and faces. He left his dinner and went to the nurses' break room to get a group of nurses to wash the women thoroughly. The retired doctor gathered five nurses and five certified nursing assistants and gave them precise orders on what to do, step by step. Then he forewarned them that the women's lives depended on how good of a job they did in washing them up. The workers acknowledged the retired doctor and then without delay went to get the supplies they would need and headed for their affected individual.

The nurses also took the initiative to get the bed linens changed in case there was any pollen on them. Each nurse and certified nursing assistant took over an hour washing the patient and changing the linens. They all wanted perfection. What they were doing might not have seemed very important, but in their case, it was a matter of living versus dying for the women and their unborn babies. The nurses checked back with the retired doctor to let him know they were done with cleaning their charges and changing their linens. The retired doctor thanked the nurses and certified nursing assistants for doing such an exceptional job.

He got all the men together to talk to them about their wives' condition and the changes he expected to see. After speaking to all the husbands, he suggested they go home and get a good night's sleep so they could return the next morning and stay all day if they wanted to. The men agreed to go home and wind down for bed. Besides, the community's curfew was very close. Before leaving the hospital, Jaden asked the retired doctor to notify him if there were any changes with Armellya's condition, good or bad. The retired doctor told all the men he would let them know if there were any changes either way with their wives.

The men traveled together going back to the castle and were discussing how awful it was that such a flower existed the whole time they lived there and they had just found out. Jaden told the guys that even though their wives were the only ones affected by the flower, it was fortunate that they had found out quickly what the culprit was that made their wives so ill. The men asked Jaden if he thought the women would pull through the tragedy that had stricken them. Jaden told the men that their wives were strong and would not let anything or anyone hurt their babies. The men finally rode up on the castle so they took care of their horses and then went into the castle to go to bed.

All the men had a troublesome time lying still in their beds because they were used to having their wives next to them. Finally, everyone was asleep except Jadellya. Jadellya sat up in her crib. She raised her hands high above her head and started to glow. As the glow got brighter, it started to spread throughout the nursery and into the Land of Grandeur. After fifteen minutes of glowing brighter than the sun on the earth's surface, she started to dim until her glow was gone. Jadellya lay back down, got comfortable, and then went back to sleep. A couple of hours later, the mini-angels appeared before them to see how they were doing. The men told their mini-angels about their wives and asked if there was anything they could do to help, but they said no. The mini-angels told the men they had to stay away from the rainbow flowers because they would slowly eradicate them. The mini-angels told the men that Jadellya had already expunged the community and forest of the rainbow flowers so the women should make a full recovery in due time. The mini-angels had spent their time with their pale ones so they expressed their love for their individuals, and their pale ones expressed their love back. Then the mini-angels vanished to return to the Dinosaur Tail.

It was an hour before the time to awaken when there was someone pounding on the front door of the castle. The butler got up to answer the door in his pajamas, and it was the hospital's runner. The butler let the runner inside and asked whom he needed. The hospital runner told the butler he needed all the men. The butler told the runner to sit in the family room and he would retrieve all the men. Then he said it was good news, he hoped. The runner told the butler it was good news; the women were conscious. The butler was elated and ran through the hallway hollering for the men instead off knocking on single doors. That way, he would wake all the men at once instead of one at a time. All the men were awakened by the butler's hollering and went out to the hallway to investigate why he was being so boisterous in the early-morning hours. The butler's actions were abnormal so the men knew it must be something important that affected the entire castle.

Once every man was in the hallway at the butler's side, he told them that the hospital's runner was there for them, and it was terrific news. The men sprinted for the castle's family room to find out what the runner had to say to them. The hospital's runner told the men that their wives were conscious and ready to come off the life support. The runner said the retired doctor wanted the men at their wives' side when he removed the life support. The men told the runner to let them get some day clothes on, and they would be back in a flash. The men all sped off like the speed of light to get some day clothes on and get to the hospital as hurriedly as possible.

Although the men got their day clothes on in a frenzy and they were disheveled, they were ready to get their horses and get to the hospital as briskly as possible. The men and the runner pushed their horses to get to the hospital on the double. When everyone got to the hospital, they flooded the hallway to get to their wives' rooms. The retired doctor saw the men enter their wives' rooms, so he knew it was time to remove the lifesaving machines from the women since they no longer needed them. The women came out of a state of unconsciousness to right away being awake and alert. The retired doctor had never seen anyone recover so expeditiously in his entire time of practicing medicine. Usually after being on life support, patients would be somewhat confused and take a few days to get their wits about them.

All the men except Jaden were in talking to their wives. Jaden was talking to the retired doctor just inside Armellya's room. Armellya heard everything the two doctors were saying and was trying to get their attention. Finally, she used her foot to hit the bedrails, and that got the doctor's attention. Jaden dashed over to Armellya and asked if she was okay. She shook her head in an up and down motion to say yes. Jaden used telepathy to tell Armellya to talk to him. Armellya responded telepathically saying she wanted the tubes removed from her lungs. Jaden asked the retired doctor if he could remove the life support, and he said yes. Then he told Jaden he was going to the next room to remove Camillia's life support and move from room to room removing the rest of the women's life support. Jaden asked if he wanted help removing the others' life support. The retired doctor told Jaden to stay with his wife, and he would get the rest of the women taken care of. Jaden thanked the retired doctor for his selfless assistance with his wife and the rest of the women. Just before Jaden was going to take the life support off Armellya, he told her it may make her gag a bit, but she needed to take a deep breath and he would pull the tubes from her lungs as she was breathing out. Armellya nodded her head slightly in a yes motion.

Jaden said, "Now!" as he pulled the tubing out.

Armellya got tears in her eyes, but she did not gag. Jaden told her she did a superb job working with the uncomfortable process. He set the tube down and then turned off the machine and turned back to Armellya. Armellya was trying to sit up so she could give Jaden a hug and kiss, but she had lost a little of her strength. Jaden told Armellya to take it easy and give it some time and she would regain her strength. Then he gave her a snug hug and affectionate kiss. Armellya started to talk and instantly realized her throat was very sensitive and scratchy feeling. Jaden told her that too would pass and to talk in little bits at a time. Armellya was asking for Jadellya because even though she was in a comatose state, she was still able to hear everything around her, and she knew it was Jadellya who had exterminated all the deadly rainbow flowers. Armellya told Jaden that she was aware of her mini-angel visiting her. Also, the mini-angel spoke warmhearted words and left her with a kiss on the forehead. Armellya said she tried to let her mini-angel know she heard what she was saying, but she was not sure the mini-angel knew. Jaden told Armellya she could let her mini-angel know during the next evening, but he did not feel it was a safe idea for her to astroproject until she got her strength back.

Armellya agreed not to astroproject until her strength was up to par. Jaden told Armellya that he wanted to go check on the rest of the women and tell them how blessed he felt that they were okay. Armellya said that was fine and to hustle back; she missed him already.

Jaden went to the other women's hospital rooms and spoke with them and their husbands to make sure there was nothing they needed and that they were still doing remarkably well without the life support. Everyone was doing well and wanted to go home. Jaden told them the women needed to stay overnight to be monitored for prenatal safety reasons, but they could have anything else they wanted within reason. The women were thankful to Jaden, and he told them it was Jadellya who knew what the cause of the crisis was and took care of it.

Jaden told them that he and the retired doctor only helped Jadellya by using medical technology to help everyone hold on until she could perform her mission with the matter. They all wanted to see Jadellya to thank her and give her their love, and Jaden told everyone that Armellya had already requested Jadellya be brought to the hospital so after she saw her mommy, he would bring her to everyone else. Upon returning to Armellya's room, Jaden got ahold of the hospital's runner to send for Jadellya and her nanny. The runner acknowledged Jaden and then hurried off. Twenty-five minutes later, the runner returned with Jadellya and her nanny and showed them to Armellya's room. Jaden thanked him and then excused him from the room. The nanny handed Jadellya to Jaden and then said she would wait in the waiting room until they concluded their visit. It was practically the breakfast hour, so Jaden gave the nanny a good amount of money and told her to go to the hospital's cafeteria and get herself some nutrition on him and Armellya. The nanny gratefully thanked Armellya and Jaden as she took the money. Then she asked them if they wanted something from the cafeteria. Jaden said he did not want anything, and Armellya said she would eat what the hospital kitchen served her at the breakfast hour.

As soon as the nanny left, Armellya gave Jadellya lots of kisses on her cheek and told her she loved her. Jadellya made some cheerful noises. Then Armellya told Jadellya how thankful she was that she purged of all the rainbow flowers and saved everyone's life. Armellya played with Jadellya for a good hour before Jaden said it was time to take her to see the rest of the family. Armellya gave Jadellya another kiss and hug, and then she handed Jadellya over to Jaden. Jaden said it would be a while before he got back with the baby, and Armellya acknowledged him and then lay back in her bed. Jaden took Jadellya to see Camillia and Andrew first.

Camillia was delighted to see her granddaughter. She gave her hugs and kisses and thanked her for saving her and her baby's life. After Camillia and Andrew played with Jadellya for a short time, Jaden said they needed to move on to the next room. Andrew and Camillia said their goodbyes. Then Jaden took Jadellya to see Sharonna and the chief.

Sharonna and the chief gave their love to Jadellya and played with her as they thanked her for the lives of mother and child. The next stop with Jadellya was with Melanie and Michael. They did like everyone else; they thanked Jadellya, gave her love, and played with her for a brief time. Next, Jaden took Jadellya to see Michelle and Allen. They gave Jadellya love, played with her, and thanked her for saving everyone's life.

Jaden took Jadellya and was on his way back to Armellya's room when he noticed Bridgette and Matthew walking up the hospital's hallway toward him. Jaden waved at them and continued toward Armellya's room. He figured they were there to see the women. Before Jaden got into Armellya's room, Bridgette called out to him. Jaden turned in her direction and asked her what he could do for her. Bridgette waited until she got close to Jaden before telling him what she wanted from him. Matthew had a full-sized smile on his face as Bridgette told Jaden she believed she had just conceived and wanted him to run a pregnancy blood test for her and Matthew. Jaden told Bridgette to sit in the chair in Armellya's room, and he would draw her blood right away. He just had to go get the things he needed and would be back in a jiffy. Bridgette sat in the chair next to the head of Armellya's bed and told her Jaden was on his way back and that she had to borrow his medical skills. Armellya asked Bridgette if she was okay, and Bridgette said she was more than okay; she believed she had conceived that day. Armellya told Bridgette it was advantageous timing because she had missed the flower alert and would be able to share her pregnancy with the rest of the women in the castle. Bridgette said she was excited to be able to be part of the pregnancy club. The support of other women in her condition was immeasurable.

Jaden walked into Armellya's room at that moment and asked Bridgette if she was ready to give blood, and she said, "Absolutely." Jaden got everything set up, and then did the blood draw. It was over more rapidly than Bridgette thought it would be. Jaden took the usual six tubes of blood and got them to the laboratory himself. The technicians were not doing anything, so they said the test results would be ready in twenty minutes. Jaden told the technician he would be somewhere in the hospital and to just send the results to the nurses' desk. Jaden said he would make sure the charge nurse always knew where he was until he got the results. The laboratory technician acknowledged Jaden and then got to work instantly. Jaden left the laboratory to go to the nurses' desk. When Jaden got to the nurses' desk, he told the charge nurse he was waiting on some laboratory results and the technicians were told to leave them with her. Jaden told the charge nurse he would be in Armellya's room, but if that were to change, he would make sure to let her know where he could be found. She said okay, and then Jaden walked off.

Jaden got back to Armellya, Jadellya, Bridgette, and Matthew. Jadellya's nanny walked into Armellya's room right after Jaden and told everyone it was time for Jadellya to go back home, because she needed to be kept on a schedule. Armellya and Jaden kissed Jadellya, and then the nanny took her from Jaden and left to go back to the castle's nursery.

For Bridgette, time was going by slowly while waiting on the pregnancy test to come back, but it had been fifteen minutes since the test was started. Matthew was pacing the floor while Bridgette was bouncing her legs as she sat in the chair at the head of Armellya's bed. Jaden finally broke the silence when he said he was going to the nurses' desk for the blood results. Jaden got to the nurses' desk at the same time the laboratory's runner got there, so he gave the paper results to Jaden. Jaden thanked the runner and then looked over the test results and gave a gigantic smile. He walked at high speed to get to Armellya's room so he could tell Bridgette and Matthew the good news.

Jaden entered Armellya's room. Bridgette got off the chair and walked up to Jaden, and Matthew stopped his pacing next to Jaden. They both looked at him with a look of interest. Jaden reached around both, pulled them into himself, hugged them tightly, and said, "Congratulations! You are pregnant." Bridgette told Jaden she knew he had a lot of patients. Then she asked him if he would be able to take one more. Jaden told Bridgette that he had told them many times that family came before the community, so of course he would be her doctor. Bridgette told Matthew she was going to go visit with the other moms-to-be so she could tell them the good news. Matthew said he would go with her to see the men and find out how the women were doing.

When Matthew and Bridgette got into the hospital's hallway to go to Camillia's room, they noticed the nursing aides going around giving patients their breakfast nutrition. Matthew and Bridgette did not realize the breakfast hour was upon them, so they elected to go to the hospital's cafeteria to get their breakfast nutrition before visiting the women and their husbands. Matthew wanted to make sure everything was done with exactness for Bridgette and the support of her pregnancy. When they got into the cafeteria, they could not believe all the wide variety of dishes that were offered. The cafeteria had a little bit of everything. Bridgette got all her favorite breakfast foods, and Matthew just got a breakfast sandwich. Bridgette ate in a leisurely way, and the breakfast hour was over before she had completed her meal so she and Matthew sat in the cafeteria for another fifteen minutes for her to conclude her nutrition. Now that the couple was done receiving their breakfast nutrition, they instantly headed for the women's rooms.

Armellya had already heard the good news of Bridgette being pregnant, so Bridgette went on to the other women's rooms to tell them of the good news. Camillia, Melanie, and Michelle were very thrilled that Bridgette was pregnant. They had previously felt dreadful that she seemed to be left out of the pregnancy club. As a woman and friend, Bridgette was with them during the pregnancy club gatherings, but now she could fully benefit from the meetings. The women knew they would be having their babies within a week of one another, and that was exhilarating to them. They could not wait to go on outings together with their babies. They were not sure how Jaden would handle things if two or more of them went into labor on the same day close to time, but they had faith in him; he was an exceptional doctor. Armellya, Camillia, Michelle, and Melanie wanted to take a nap so Bridgette and Matthew left the hospital to go home and spend some time with each other.

When Bridgette and Matthew got inside the castle's front door, they were greeted by Deuteronomy. Deuteronomy jumped up on Matthew's chest. He was taller than Matthew, but he just wanted to say hello and get some affection. When Deuteronomy finished greeting Matthew, he sat at Bridgette's feet, waiting for her to show him some tenderness too. Deuteronomy was a majestic friend to the occupants of the castle and an uncompromising guard dog. He checked out everyone who entered the castle. Because of Deuteronomy, the chief knew someone was home, and he figured it might be Bridgette and Matthew, so he went to check. The chief ran into them in the castle's hallway. He asked them how the women were doing. Bridgette told the chief that the women had to stay over that night, but then they could come home. It was only for fetal observation. The chief became concerned and asked Bridgette if the babies were okay, and she said yes, that it was just precautionary after the women had been on life support and the babies had been slightly affected by the rainbow flowers' pollen. Bridgette told the chief the women were napping, but in an hour or so, he should go visit them. The chief said he would. Bridgette and Matthew went into their house, and the chief went back to his side of the castle.

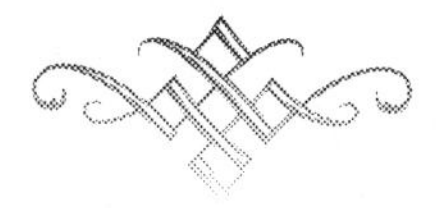

CHAPTER 8

AT THE HOSPITAL, THE WOMEN WERE WAKING from their naps. They were pleased to see that their husbands were still there. The women really wanted to go home that day, so they all wanted to see Jaden or the retired doctor to try to talk them into letting them go. Armellya spoke to Jaden about going home, and he told her it was important to ensure the baby was not going to have any complications from the trauma that she had just recovered from. Armellya pleaded to go home, telling Jaden that if anything were to occur she had him there to attend to the dilemma. Jaden told Armellya that if he let her go home, he would have to let the other women go home also, and if anything did happen, he would have to try to figure out how to take care of all of them at the same time. Jaden cautioned Armellya that taking care of five traumas was practically impossible for one doctor to do in a home setting. He pointed out that being in the hospital, he would have the retired doctor and the many nurses to help if something were to go amiss. Armellya suggested having a home health nurse for each one come home with them. Then Jaden told Armellya to let him confer with the retired doctor about the circumstances and he would get back with her on the affairs.

Jaden went out to the nurses' desk to see if the charge nurse knew where the retired doctor was, and she told Jaden he was in his office. Jaden went down the hall and around the corner and found the retired doctor right where the charge nurse said he was, in his office. Jaden interrupted the retired doctor at the doorway and asked if he could speak to him for a moment. The retired doctor invited Jaden inside, asking him what was on his mind. Jaden entered the office and sat in the chair in front of the retired doctor's desk. The retired doctor was in the process of documenting the rainbow flowers' history and effect on pregnant women versus the rest of the community. He stopped writing to speak with Jaden, and Jaden told him he was there to review the women's health status. He told Jaden the women were all trying to debate going home. Jaden told the retired doctor that was exactly what was going on, and he wanted a second opinion on how safe it would be for the women and babies to go home if they sent a home nurse with them. The retired doctor said there had been no abnormalities found with the fetal monitor readings, and the women were back to being themselves, so he did not see any reason to keep them in the hospital any longer. Jaden then asked the retired doctor if he felt the need for home health nursing, and he said for the next twenty-four hours, it would not hurt anything. He said the nurses would be there to monitor the women for any postintubation complications.

The retired doctor had said just what Jaden had thought, but he wanted to get his view on the current circumstances.

The retired doctor told Jaden to let the women and their husbands know they could go home as soon as the nurses completed their discharge duties, and he was going to go tell the nurses to start the discharge process. Jaden acknowledged the retired doctor and then left his office to go see the women.

When Jaden got back to Armellya's room, she knew by the expression on his face she was approved to go home. Armellya asked Jaden what the retired doctor had said, and he told her she could go home but she had to have a home nurse to ensure there would be no complications arising from being intubated, but the nurse would only be there for twenty-four hours.

Armellya was eager to leave the hospital. She wanted the comforts of home. Jaden told Armellya he needed to go let the women know they too were going home with a home health nurse and why.

Jaden went room to room, telling each woman individually that she was going home that day but was going to have a home health nurse just like Armellya. Jaden explained the home health nurse was a precaution in the event they should have some sort of difficulty from being intubated, and it would only be for twenty-four hours. The women were elated to be going home and to be able to spend time with one another and their husbands in the privacy of their homes.

As the charge nurse was working on the discharge process for the women, the men went back to the castle to hitch their horses to buggies so they could get the nurses and women all home in one trip. By the time the men returned to the hospital, the charge nurse was winding up the discharges. Their timing was impeccable. The women were already changed out of their hospital attire and into their day clothes.

The men went into their wives' hospital rooms to take them out to the buggies. Each home health nurse went into her individual's room to help her walk to the buggies. The home health nurses knew the women had gotten changed on their own, but they were not sure their legs had maximum strength to allow them to walk very far. The home health nurses gave orders to the men to be on one side of their wives. They would be on the other side. They had to be prepared for their legs to unexpectedly give out. The men walked with their wives and held on to them so if their legs did give out, they would not strike the floor brutally. The women had grappled with their legs and had to stop a couple of times to rest, but they had made it to the buggies. The men helped their wives get up on the buggies, and then the home health nurses got up onto the buggies and sat with them.

After getting their wives and home health nurses up on the back of the buggies, the men got up in the front and drove the team of horses to the castle. The men and home health nurses got off the buggies and helped the women off. The women were incapable of standing without their husbands holding them up, so they carried their wives into the castle and put them in their beds. The home health nurses were going to be helping the women do leg exercises in their beds to help strengthen their legs.

The brief amount of time the women had been in the hospital should not have been enough time for their leg muscles to atrophy to the point that they were at, and Jaden did not understand it. He told Armellya he was going back to the hospital to converse with the retired doctor about the effects of the rainbow flower because it was baffling him why she and the other women were so physically inadequate.

Jaden left for the hospital that moment. When he got to the hospital, the retired doctor was outside the emergency doors getting ready to leave for home.

Jaden called out to the retired doctor to get his attention before he rode away, and it worked. The retired doctor walked toward Jaden while he was dismounting. He told Jaden he must have had a relapse with the women to be back so soon. Jaden told the retired doctor that the women were very physically weak, and they were only on life support for two days. The retired doctor acknowledged Jaden. Then Jaden told the retired doctor that he did not understand the degree of atrophy the women were suffering from. The retired doctor told Jaden that the rainbow flower primarily targeted the muscular system, which was why they had to be on life support. The muscles responsible for the respiratory system had stopped contracting, disallowing them to breathe on their own. Jaden told the retired doctor he would be interested to read his documentation of the rainbow flowers' effect on pale ones when he completed it.

The retired doctor told Jaden he had concluded. Then he told Jaden to follow him and he would get it for him to take home to study. Jaden thanked him as he took the paper file and promised to have it back to him soon. The two doctors walked out of the hospital together and then said their farewells and headed for home. When Jaden got back to the castle, he went to check on Armellya and to tell her he was about to find out just how the rainbow flower affected her and the women so he would know what to expect in their recovery. Jaden told Armellya he wanted to delve into the retired doctor's document right away, but he wanted to make sure she did not need anything first. Armellya said she was fine and for him to do as he wished. If she needed him, she would let him know. Jaden said he was going to stay at her side while reading, he just needed to find out how much damage the rainbow flower inflicted on them. Armellya told Jaden she loved him very much, and he was an exceptional doctor and perfect husband and father.

Jaden gently hugged Armellya and then gave her a passionate kiss and told her she was so accepting of his shortcomings. The two of them softly laughed. Then Jaden sat back down and started to read the retired doctor's report on the rainbow flowers' effects on pale ones. Jaden was interested to know why it only affected pregnant pale ones and their fetuses. The flower did not affect children or the elderly, and their health scans were very much like those of the pregnant individuals apart from the specific pregnancy hormone, of course. In reading, Jaden found that the retired doctor did a variety of bodily fluid tests between the healthy nonpregnant women and the women, and he found there were sizeable changes that occurred in the pregnant pale ones. Not only did the women have the pregnancy hormone and slightly different blood values than a healthy nonpregnant human would, but their other bodily fluids had changed considerably also. It appeared that the women were a sort of breeding ground for the rainbow plant to develop spores that hibernated in their bodily fluids and with proper exposure to anything living would grow. That meant the flowers could not directly affect anyone or anything except the pregnant women, but in them, they would affect anything living. At that point, Jaden realized that getting the women healed by Jadellya as promptly as they did put a stop to a possible mass casualty from occurring. Jadellya did not have the ability to heal individuals with spores, so it was a blessing that things turned out the way they did.

The mini-angels were a colossal help in getting the women to Jadellya quickly. As Jaden went on reading the retired doctor's report, he noticed he had written notes that reflected on Jadellya's help and the mini-angels' advice and knowledge of the deadly flower. Finally, Jaden had reached the part of the report he was anxious to see: what the flower was doing to the women's body systems. As the retired doctor said, it was primarily breaking down their muscle tissue quickly. The flower was causing the alveoli in their lungs to collapse, which meant if Jadellya had not intervened, the women would have only survived on the life support for another hour or so. They would have died of respiratory failure. Jaden finished reading the retired doctor's report and had a perplexed look on his face.

Armellya noticed the look on Jaden's face so she asked him what he had found out. Jaden explained to Armellya what was happening to her and the other women's bodies from the rainbow flower and how he was concerned there may be some permanent damage done to them. Armellya asked Jaden what kind of damage he thought she and the women may have, and he told her he was primarily concerned with their lung capacities and overall muscle function. Before Armellya could say anything else, Jaden told her he was going to take her back to the hospital to run some tests, and if anything came back abnormal, he would decipher if there was a way to reverse the damage.

Armellya became concerned about her and her unborn baby's survival, but Jaden convinced her to let him do the worrying. She just needed to function as best as she could.

Jaden told Armellya not to tell anyone about the concern or running the tests. He wanted to check her only, and her results would reveal the same as the other women's would. There was no reason to alarm everyone. Armellya understood and agreed with what Jaden had said, so she said she would be ready to go to the hospital whenever he wanted to take her. Jaden told Armellya they were going right away so they could slip out of the castle and back in before anyone missed them.

Armellya was still in day clothes, so Jaden picked up Armellya and carried her outside. Once outside, Jaden told the new stable boy to hitch the small buggy at once. The new stable boy hitched a horse to the small buggy and brought it out posthaste. Jaden laid Armellya in the back of the buggy and then climbed up front. He drove the horse hard to get to the hospital in a dash. He was concerned that with enough exertion by the women, they would suffer breathing difficulties much like what a normal human would suffer from asthma or even chronic obstructive pulmonary disease. Now at the hospital, Jaden called for the hospital's stable boy to hold the horse steady while he lifted Armellya out of the back of the buggy. The stable boy went on with the horse and buggy, while Jaden carried Armellya on into the hospital. The charge nurse saw Jaden coming and rushed to his side to check on Armellya and get her to a hospital room.

Jaden told the charge nurse Armellya was okay now, but he needed to get her into a hospital bed at once. The charge nurse took Jaden to her usual room. Then he placed Armellya into the bed. Jaden asked the charge nurse to stay with Armellya while he beckoned the retired doctor for his assistance. He went to the retired doctor's office, and he was not there, so Jaden requested the hospital's runner search him out and bring him to Armellya's hospital room.

The hospital's runner left without delay and called back that he would check at the retired doctor's home. Thirty-five minutes later, the hospital's runner delivered the retired doctor to Armellya's room. The runner said the retired doctor was at home, and he apologized for taking so long. Jaden told the runner he had done a suitable job and not to worry about the time. Then he excused the runner to go on with his own business.

The retired doctor asked what was going on with Armellya, and Jaden explained his alarm for the pregnant women. Jaden told the retired doctor that he worried the women could have lifelong respiratory issues from the damage that the rainbow flower had caused, and he wanted to test Armellya for confirmation of healthy lungs or serious respiratory disease. The retired doctor concurred that was a good precaution and then asked Jaden why he did not want to test the other women. Jaden told the retired doctor that all the women had the exposure at the same time and had symptoms at the same time, and then their negative responses to the exposure followed the same pattern at the exact same time. He went on to tell the retired doctor that he did not want to cause a castle-wide panic unnecessarily.

The retired doctor agreed with Jaden. Jaden told him he wanted to test Armellya and whatever her results were would give him a promising idea of what the other women's results would be. Jaden told the retired doctor that if Armellya's results were normal, he would not fret about the other women, but if her results were abnormal, he would test all the other women individually to compare their results to their baseline and see how serious it really was. The retired doctor told Jaden he was at his service and would work as his assistant. Jaden told him he appreciated his selflessness and would prefer him to work as his equal and to offer his many years of experience as well. Jaden then remembered he had the retired doctor's file on the effects of the rainbow flower on pale ones so he returned it right away. The retired doctor thanked Jaden and then asked if there was anything he felt should be added. Jaden told the retired doctor he had done a very thorough job on his documentation and even had a few details that he was not aware of.

The lunch hour had sneaked up on them, and because Armellya had just arrived, there was no lunch nutrition ordered for her, so the charge nurse came into her room and offered to get her some nutrition from the hospital's cafeteria on the house. Armellya said she was feeling the need for nutrition, so she told the charge nurse what she would like to have, and before she was able to leave the room, Jaden gave her a modest hug and thanked her for watching out for Armellya. The charge nurse told Jaden that he and Armellya meant a lot to her personally and not just because she would be her queen someday. She had had many talks with her. Even when Armellya could not talk with her voice, they had spoken telepathically and had formed a close friendship. The charge nurse said there was nothing she would not do for Armellya. The charge nurse asked Jaden if she could be of service to him and the retired doctor with Armellya's care this time, and Jaden said absolutely. They were going to ask for her assistance anyway. Then the charge nurse left the room to get Armellya's nutrition. She returned promptly from the hospital's cafeteria and told Armellya they had just what she wanted. Then she placed her nutrition in front of her on a bed table. Armellya thanked the charge nurse and gave her a friendly hug.

Before the charge nurse could leave the room, Jaden called her to walk over to the head of the bed where he was. She speedily walked over to Jaden and asked how she could be of service. Jaden told her to make someone else in charge out at the nurses' desk because he was taking her off the floor to be a part of Armellya's project. The charge nurse told Jaden she would be back momentarily. Then she rushed out of the room, going to the nurses' desk. The charge nurse pulled a nurse out of the pack of nurses and told her she was in charge until further notice. Then she let the other nurses know that nurse was acting charge nurse, and if there were any questions or concerns, she would still be available.

The charge nurse left rapidly and returned to Armellya's room to report for duty to Jaden and the retired doctor. Jaden asked the charge nurse how much she knew about the rainbow flower and what it had done to the women. She told Jaden she was not aware of the deadly flower doing anything other than nearly shutting down their lungs, but she had an inkling that it had also affected their muscular systems. Jaden told her she was correct. Then he went on to tell her the exact details of how the women's lungs were medically affected. The charge nurse was verbal about her concern that there may be some permanent damage with their lungs and muscle tissue. Jaden told the charge nurse she was right on, and that was why he had brought Armellya back in. The charge nurse asked how Armellya was doing, and Jaden told her she was stable for the time being, but he wanted to run some tests to check on her pulmonary function. The charge nurse said she would stand by in the event Armellya needed to be reintubated due to pulmonary exacerbation. Jaden told her that was a wise decision.

Armellya heard Jaden talking to the charge nurse and became apprehensive about the testing. Jaden told her she was in good hands, and they would do everything possible to keep her from having a crisis, but it was vital to do the testing. Armellya said she understood the importance of the testing and that she would comply, but it did not take away the reservations she had. Jaden told Armellya to finish with her lunch nutrition, and they would start the testing then. Armellya positively acknowledged Jaden and went back to eating what was left of her meal. The charge nurse left the room to gather the tools that would be needed in the event of respiratory failure and was back without delay. Jaden told the charge nurse they would have to transport Armellya to the room where they tested cardiac function so they could put her in a holster on the treadmill to get her walking briskly enough that she would have to breathe harder to evoke the need for more room oxygen. The retired doctor added that if Armellya were to physically give out, the holster would prevent her from falling to the floor, but they would have to act hastily to get her to the bed in there so they could do whatever was necessary.

The charge nurse was sensing Armellya's fear and hesitation, so she caressed her head and assured her that she would be safe in their hands and they would not allow anything to happen to her. Armellya asked the charge nurse for a hug so the charge nurse bent down over her and gave her a sympathetic hug. Then she told her she would do just fine; she was young and strong. Armellya was finished eating so the charge nurse took the bed table away. Jaden told Armellya it was time to start the testing, so he and the charge nurse wheeled her in her bed to the cardiac care portion of the hospital. Once there, Jaden got Armellya over to the treadmill and holstered up. The retired doctor told Armellya to commence walking at a comfortable pace so she did. After five minutes, the retired doctor turned the speed up on the treadmill, and Armellya kept up easily. After another five minutes, he turned the treadmill up faster, and she was having some difficulty keeping up. The retired doctor left the treadmill at the pace it was at for fifteen minutes and monitored Armellya's oxygen saturation. So far, she could breathe well enough to keep her oxygen saturation at a normal level. The retired doctor asked Armellya if she could handle it if he turned the treadmill up a bit, and she said she would try. The retired doctor turned the treadmill up a little more, and Armellya kept up but was struggling slightly. Although she was practically running, she appeared to be keeping up with the treadmill, and her oxygen saturation was bountiful. The retired doctor left Armellya on the treadmill at a jogging speed for twenty minutes to ensure that she had the endurance to continue to move briskly and keep her oxygen saturation at a normal level or above. After twenty minutes, he lowered the speed of the treadmill, and every five minutes after that, he would lower the speed again until the treadmill was at a stop. Jaden asked Armellya how she felt overall, and she said her legs hurt, but her lungs felt fine. Jaden and the retired doctor were not sure if the muscle tissue in Armellya's legs and other large groups of muscles would be able to get back to the strength they were previously at, but they discussed having some physical therapy done with her. The retired doctor knew an excellent physical therapist who would push Armellya to her limit but no more and was remarkable with encouraging the patient. The retired doctor even said if he were to need a physical therapist, he would hope to get that specific therapist. Jaden asked the retired doctor to see if that physical therapist had the time to take on Armellya as a patient. The retired doctor sent for a runner that moment to track down the physical therapist and bring him to them.

While the retired doctor, Jaden, and the charge nurse were waiting on the physical therapist to arrive, they got Armellya back into her bed and wheeled her back to her room. The physical therapist was waiting for them in her room. Once they got Armellya's bed in place and locked the wheels, the retired doctor greeted the physical therapist and thanked him for getting there so promptly.

The retired doctor had told the physical therapist a condensed version of what Armellya had been through recently and asked him if he had room in his schedule to take her on as a patient. The physical therapist told the retired doctor that his workload was full, but he would be more than willing to work with Armellya on his personal time. Jaden asked how much he got paid per hour for his services, and the physical therapist told him. Jaden told him he would pay double, and they could do the therapy at the castle. The physical therapist told Jaden he would do the therapy for free, but Jaden told him he would not hear of it. He told the physical therapist to give him a detailed list of the equipment he would need, and he would have it in the castle within twenty-four hours. The physical therapist told Jaden he did not need much equipment but what he did need was expensive, and Jaden told him money was no problem. The physical therapist took a notepad out of his back pocket and wrote down the things he would need. Then he gave the paper to Jaden. Jaden called for the hospital's runner to take the paper to the hospital supply room to get the equipment they needed moved to the castle and a bill of how much he would owe. The runner got there without delay. Then Jaden told him what to do, and the runner left speedily. Within fifteen minutes, the runner returned to Armellya's room with a bill for the therapy equipment. Jaden reached into his pouch and took out the money necessary to pay the bill and sent the runner to the supply room to pay. The hospital runner returned to Jaden to tell him the equipment would be at the castle by the end of one hour. Jaden thanked the runner and then excused him to go.

Once the equipment issue was taken care of, Jaden turned to the physical therapist to explain what was going on with Armellya so he had a concise picture of what he was up against and how best to address it. The physical therapist told Jaden the retired doctor had told him a substantial amount of information, but he was free to tell him anything that would help the therapy. Jaden asked the physical therapist what he knew so he would not repeat anything. After the physical therapist told Jaden what he knew, Jaden told him he knew all there was to know. The physical therapist agreed to start working with Armellya the next day since she had the test that day, which gave her a hefty workout. Jaden asked the physical therapist with the information he had about the damage from the rainbow flower, if he thought he could get Armellya strong again. The physical therapist told Jaden he could help her strengthen healthy muscle, but if there was dead muscle tissue there, he could not fix it. The physical therapist asked Jaden since he was a doctor and a prodigy if he could find a way to know the condition of the muscle tissue. Jaden told the physical therapist he was just a trauma doctor not a specialist but to let him confer with the retired doctor and find out what the options were to determine the status of Armellya's muscles. The physical therapist told Jaden he would report for work the next day and if there was any additional information to let him know, but he had to go to work with a patient.

Jaden and the physical therapist said their farewells to each other and then went on to do what they had to do. Jaden turned to the retired doctor and asked him if he knew a good musculoskeletal doctor who could help with finding out the condition of Armellya's muscles. The retired doctor told Jaden he did not know a doctor personally, but there was a musculoskeletal doctor in the hospital they could meet with. He told Jaden to stay with Armellya, and he would get the other doctor, Jaden thanked the retired doctor and said he would be right there. The retired doctor left immediately to go fetch the specialist.

Armellya was exhausted and just wanted to rest so Jaden gave her a compassionate kiss and told her to go to sleep. Armellya nestled down in the bed, shut her eyes, and swiftly fell asleep.

The charge nurse and Jaden were having a casual talk to pass some time while waiting on the retired doctor and—they hoped—the specialist when abruptly Armellya sat straight up in her bed crying about something. Neither the charge nurse nor Jaden could decipher what Armellya was bawling about. They rushed to her bedside, and they both tried to calm her.

They finally calmed Armellya down as the retired doctor and the specialist walked into the room. The retired doctor and specialist stood back while Jaden and the charge nurse spoke with Armellya about what was troubling her. Armellya told them there was something wrong with the baby, and she needed their help. Jaden asked Armellya what was wrong with the baby, and she said the baby was suffocating. She could feel the baby fighting for her life. That instant, Jaden got the handheld ultrasound machine and checked on the baby. He could tell the baby was in distress. The umbilical cord looked normal and was not around the baby's neck so Jaden got the impression he needed to check Armellya's oxygen saturation. Armellya's oxygen saturation was so low that he could not understand why she was not in respiratory failure. Abruptly, Armellya went apneic and immobilized in her position, and after thirty seconds, she still had not moved or started to breathe. Straightforwardly, Jaden called out to the charge nurse to put two lines in Armellya. Then he called out to the retired doctor to draw up the intubation drugs. Both the retired doctor and charge nurse sprang into action doing just what they were told to do. After the charge nurse got the two intravenous lines into Armellya, Jaden told the retired doctor to push the drugs. At the same time as the retired doctor gave Armellya the intubation medicine, Jaden hastily shoved Armellya from a sitting up position to a lying position. Immediately, Armellya's lungs were temporarily paralyzed, and she was unconscious.

Jaden took a stance at Armellya's head, and the charge nurse assisted Jaden in intubating her. The retired doctor got Armellya hooked up to a respirator and set the respirator's settings for what was appropriate for her. Armellya's oxygen saturation went up right away, and the retired doctor got her hands restrained so she could not pull the tube out of her lungs, as that was an autonomic response. Jaden did another ultrasound to check on the baby, and she was moving comfortably again.

The charge nurse told Jaden she was not questioning his decision to intubate Armellya, but she did not understand what his decision to intubate was based on. Before Jaden could respond to the charge nurse, the retired doctor started to explain. He said that Armellya's lungs were not getting enough oxygen from room air, and it affected the fetus before affecting Armellya. Because Armellya was sleeping, she did not recognize her lack of oxygen, but when the fetus started to struggle, she noticed a problem with the fetus and awoke. Jaden said if Armellya was not intubated that instant, she would have gone into respiratory failure, and her body would have started shutting down organs and possibly the fetus.

The charge nurse told Jaden it was a good thing Armellya was so aware of her baby and that the baby was moving about abnormally. Jaden told the charge nurse that unlike other pale ones, Armellya had a telepathic link with her unborn children. Because Armellya had an abrupt onset of prolonged apnea following her boisterous episode and her body was not profusing properly, Jaden wondered how the others were doing. The retired doctor told the charge nurse to go with Jaden and they would take five other nurses to go check on the other five women. Jaden told the charge nurse that if their services were needed at the castle, she would oversee the other five nurses. Each nurse would handle one of the women, and their husbands could get them into the buggy and ride in on their horses and then carry their wives to a bed.

The retired doctor said he would stay behind, set things up for four intubations, and keep an eye on Armellya. Jaden and the charge nurse got ready to leave, and by the time they got to the emergency exit, they noticed a large buggy pulling up wildly. It was the other women being brought in by their husbands. They were panic-stricken. Jaden told the charge nurse to get five beds out there right away and call the retired doctor to let him know that he had five patients on the way. She said okay and then darted back into the hospital.

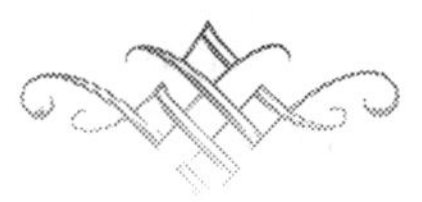

CHAPTER 9

THE RETIRED DOCTOR HEARD THE COMMOTION and already knew he was getting the five women. The retired doctor started roaring for five porters to get themselves outside with gurneys. At that point, the charge nurse knew the retired doctor was aware of the women's admittance. He told the charge nurse to get five nurses and have them ready to put two lines in each woman. She got five nurses and had them in the rooms they were going to be working in. All the nurses were trauma nurses, so they were composed and ready to work. The porters got outside to the women on the double. Then their husbands laid them on the gurneys. Once they were on the gurneys, the porters rushed them into their appointed rooms, and the trauma nurses started to get two intravenous lines in each one.

Jaden and the retired doctor were intubating two of them while three of the trauma nurses were using oxygen supplementation with a bag valve and mask to oxygenate the other three. The retired doctor and Jaden were working rapidly and had their first one intubated and were on the way to their second within six minutes. The retired doctor and Jaden had their second patient intubated, and then the retired doctor had the last one intubated. Now, the doctors had to focus on finding the cause of the extensive apnea the women were suffering from. Jaden and the retired doctor called the men out of their wives' rooms and wanted to take them to the retired doctor's office to discuss their wives' episode and current prognosis. None of the men wanted to leave their wife's bedside. Jaden had tried to ask them politely, but they insisted on staying where they were. Finally, Jaden put his foot down and told the men if they did not have the discussion he and the retired doctor needed to have with them, they could be the cause of their wives dying. The men were already upset about their wives' conditions, but now that Jaden had told them of the importance of the discussion they needed to have directly, the men were feeling hopeless.

All five of the men went to the retired doctor's office and took a seat. They were anxious to find out what the discussion was to be about. The retired doctor told the men he needed to know about the onset of the respiratory distress. They all said practically the same thing: it was unexpected, and they did not notice right away until they checked on their wives and could not get them to wake up. The men said they were spending man time together and had checked on their wives in intervals, which they did in conjunction with one another because of the man time. Jaden asked the men where their wives were, and they told Jaden the women were in their beds relaxing. They had had their lunch nutrition and then took naps and never woke up. The retired doctor asked the men if they had any idea of how long the women were unconscious, and the men told the retired doctor maybe fifteen minutes.

Jaden was concerned for the five fetuses because of the fifteen minutes of inadequate oxygenation and suggested they check the babies thoroughly. The retired doctor concurred. The men wanted to know if their wives and babies were going to be okay. The retired doctor told the men they did not know the cause of the respiratory distress, but they would get to the bottom of it. The doctors knew the current condition of the women was related to the previous exposure to the rainbow flowers.

The retired doctor and Jaden excused the men to go back to their wives' rooms after letting them know there may be some questions for them to answer later. The men told the retired doctor and Jaden they would help any way possible if they could. The retired doctor and Jaden stayed in the office to debate the women's circumstances in detail from the beginning to where they were currently. They figured there had to be more to the situation than what they had seen. The two doctors did not believe their illnesses were like human disorders of asthma or chronic obstructive pulmonary disease because their ailments did not present anything like them. The two doctors were sort of at a loss after looking at documented human sicknesses as a probable diagnosis, and what made their ailments more perplexing was that pale ones did not get ill, so why were the women ailing?

The retired doctor and Jaden established that they needed to take lung biopsies to get an idea of what kind of shape their lungs were in and to possibly ascertain how to fix the issue if it was a fixable scenario. For the time being, the women were doing satisfactorily on the life support.

The dinner hour was upon the community, so the doctors agreed to get their dinner nutrition before doing the lung biopsies on each of the women. Jaden and the retired doctor went to the hospital's cafeteria to sit down for their lunch nutrition and reviewed their suspicions of the problem with the women's lungs. Both doctors knew that pale ones had the ability of accelerated healing and regeneration with some things, but they were not sure what the extent of those things were for their condition. The lunch hour was not a relaxing time as it should have been since both doctors were still trying to verbally evaluate the women's circumstances. The lunch hour came to a hasty end so the doctors went back to the retired doctor's office. Together, the two doctors went through what they knew from the retired doctor's report on the effects of the rainbow flower to pale ones and what they knew of pale one anatomy and medicine to enable them to justify the lung biopsies. They again came up with the need to do biopsies. The retired doctor and Jaden agreed they would each take two of the women and perform the biopsies, and whoever finished first would take the fifth, so they left the office to go do that. The two doctors got their biopsies and made sure they were labeled in the event there were differences that showed a positive solution or even an accelerated negative concern.

The doctors expected to see the same thing in all the biopsies, but they had to treat the samples individually since the women were all individuals and might have differences in their tissues. Because Armellya had more gifts and one being the gift of healing, the doctor's half expected to find her sample in better condition than the others. They went directly to the forensic lab with their tissue samples and started to observe their first tissue sample under the microscope. They immediately noticed the alveoli were abruptly collapsing. However, some of the alveoli that were already collapsed when the doctors looked into the microscopes were attempting to regenerate, but it was a more sluggish process than normal. The doctors decided to keep the first samples to observe longer and find out if they could completely regenerate and approximately how long it would take. The biopsy regeneration would give the doctors an idea of how long to leave the women on life support. The retired doctor and Jaden felt it was necessary to leave the women on life support until their lungs were completely healed or they may have the same crisis again with respiratory exacerbation. If the biopsied alveoli could fully regenerate, they knew that the women's lungs would fully regenerate, so the doctors felt some hope.

Next, the doctors looked at their second biopsies under the microscope and saw the same scenario. This time, the retired doctor was observing Armellya's lung tissue and did see a difference from the other women's tissue samples. The alveoli were not collapsing; they were obstructed by a mucous-type fluid. What they saw was indicative of a deadly case of human pneumonia. To get a second opinion, the retired doctor asked Jaden to examine Armellya's tissue sample. Jaden analyzed the microscope slide and got the same impression that the retired doctor had gotten. The two doctors knew how to treat Armellya, but they would have to have the medicine room make more of the medicine they needed than what they ordinarily carried, which only Jaden could approve, and he fully intended to do just that.

Now that the doctors had an idea of what was going on with the women, Jaden left the forensics room to go to the medical medicine-making room while the retired doctor made his rounds among the women. Jaden got to the medical medicine-making room and found they only had two vials of each of the three antibiotics Jaden needed for Armellya. Jaden told the employees of the medical medicine-making room how much of each antibiotic he needed per day and they had better get a move on it. Jaden explained that Armellya was at death's door, and she needed the antibiotic medicines the instant they were ready to administer. Every minute counted. The medical medicine-making room workers said they would get right on it and get the antibiotic medicines to her room as soon as they were ready. Jaden thanked the employees for being on top of it and for their understanding of his slight attitude. He speedily left the medical medicine-making room to go back to see how the women were doing. When Jaden got back in the hallway that led into the women's rooms, he could hear one of the respirator alarms going off. Then he saw several nurses and the retired doctor rushing for Armellya's room.

When Jaden recognized that there was a potential emergency with Armellya, he broke out into a full sprint. Jaden got into Armellya's room right after the alarms were shut off and witnessed the retired doctor suctioning Armellya's airway. Jaden asked what was going on, and the retired doctor told Jaden there were copious amounts of mucous in Armellya's airway, which congested the respirator, keeping it from being able to pump her lungs with oxygen. The retired doctor said he was going to keep two nurses in her room always to make sure her airway stayed clear. The retired doctor said he wanted the safety of two nurses. In the event one needed to go for help in a crisis, the other could stay and try to intervene.

The retired doctor told Jaden he felt Armellya was in worse shape than the other five women. The other women just needed the respirators to assist the healthy alveoli in getting enough oxygen throughout their entire bodies until the damaged alveoli completed the regeneration process. The retired doctor told Jaden he theorized that Armellya may have gotten too close to the rainbow flowers to smell them and possibly gotten pollen into her lungs, and at the current time, her lungs were trying to purge the pollen by creating the mucous to bind to the pollen. Jaden told the retired doctor that was a sound theory and then questioned the need for antibiotics. The retired doctor told Jaden if he remembered correctly, Armellya's white blood cell count was phenomenally high, so he suggested Jaden go ahead with the antibiotics.

Now that the emergency with Armellya was over and there were two nurses appointed to her, the retired doctor and Jaden went to check on the other five women. The women's husbands were in their wives' room's, trying to be supportive, but they found it difficult to see them in a medically induced coma. The men were petrified for their wives' recovery. It was hard to see the women surrounded by tubes and machines. Jaden tried to assure the men that their wives would pull through and that he and the retired doctor were doing everything possible to help them.

The men asked for a simplified explanation of what was happening to their wives. Jaden explained that there was an internal microscopic part of their lungs that was collapsing so their lungs had a decreased ability to obtain enough oxygen to send throughout their bodies. Jaden told the men that the reduced oxygen availability would have caused their bodies to shut down parts that were not vital to maintaining life, which meant primarily the pregnancies followed by the limbs and so on.

As the men's eyes welled with tears, Jaden told them there was a vast promise in the women's favor that he and the retired doctor had discovered. He told the men the microscopic part of the women' lungs that were collapsing were undergoing a regeneration process. That meant the women needed to stay on life support until the regeneration process was complete. Then they would essentially have new lungs and be healthier than their husbands were. The men were stimulated to hear such a positive prognosis, and their tears of fear turned into tears of relief. The men's next question was how long their wives would need to be on the machines and in a comatose state. Jaden told the men it would be better for the women to remain in a medical coma while they needed to be on the machines, and they would stay on the machines until their lungs were fully repaired. He could not give a time line; one woman may heal faster than another. It was hard to tell, so he would not make any promises of an approximation to time. The men did not understand why it was so important to keep the women unconscious, so Jaden told them that their bodies would do more efficient healing if they did not need to fight for oxygen or against the machines. Also, it was far less traumatic for the women to do it that way. The body did its best recovery during a state of sleep, and that was why it was important for everyone to get adequate sleep on a regular basis. He told the men that once he and the retired doctor got confirmation the women's lungs were completely healed, they would wean them off the medicines responsible for keeping them comatose. Jaden concluded by telling the men once the women were fully alert, he or the retired doctor would take the esophageal tubes out of their airways.

The men had one more question: Did their wives know they were there? Jaden apologetically told the men their wives most likely had no knowledge of their surroundings, and he would be surprised if they even dreamed. He said the women might start being aware of their surroundings and dreaming once they started to come around. Then he added that they might even hallucinate as they came off the medicine. The men asked if they could stay at the hospital around the clock while their wives were there, and Jaden said he would get some hospital porters to bring some sleeping cots and linens for them.

Jaden understood their desire to stay at their wives' sides because he had the same need. He decided to have a sleeping cot put into Armellya's room for himself. One of the nurses walking past Jaden heard the request for six sleeping cots so she said for him to deal with Armellya, and she would get the porters to get things settled for him and the other men. Jaden thanked her and then headed for Armellya's room.

When Jaden got to Armellya's room, he saw the retired doctor checking her out so he asked him how she was doing. The retired doctor told Jaden she sounded less congested since the nurses had been deep-suctioning her airway. Before Jaden could say anything, the retired doctor told him the baby was doing magnificently.

The hospital porter had just shown up with a sleeping cot for Jaden and asked permission to enter the room. Both doctors told the porter it was okay to go in. The porter said he did not want to intrude on a private conversation, and Jaden told the porter he was fine and thanked him for the sleeping cot and linens. The porter placed everything where it needed to go and then told the doctors to have a delightful day. Then he promptly left to go get the other men's cots in their rooms.

Right as the retired doctor and Jaden got ready to check the other women and got to the threshold of Armellya's door, an alarm sounded, then another, and then another. All Armellya's alarms were sounding, and that meant there was a life-threatening situation. Armellya's heart had unexpectedly stopped, and before Jaden could finish turning to exit the doorway to get the crash cart, a nurse came rushing in with it. She nearly scampered over Jaden. The retired doctor grabbed the edge of the crash cart and shoved it next to Armellya's bed. Then, he began to cut her hospital clothing off. Jaden jumped into action and took Armellya as another patient instead of viewing her as his wife. The dissociation allowed him to do his job as a doctor instead of being like an onlooker and falling apart at the thought of experiencing the possible death of his wife. In the brief amount of time it took Jaden to dissociate, the retired doctor was administering the first shock to Armellya's heart. The two doctors paused for a few seconds to give the monitor a chance to show some cardiac activity. Armellya's heart was still flatlined, so the retired doctor ordered Jaden to turn up the joules and prepare to shock again. The retired doctor hollered, "Clear!"

Then Jaden said, "Clear!" and the retired doctor administered a second shock. He and Jaden watched the cardiac monitor for a few seconds, and finally, it showed a normal cardiac rhythm. The assisting nurse laid a sheet over Armellya. She was not going to redress Armellya in the event she crashed again.

The porter minded his own business and stayed out of

the way of any emergency traffic that might bleed into the hallway, but he did get the other five sleeping cots and linens into the other women's rooms. Knowing that Armellya had had a major incident, the other men were concerned that their wives may have one also. Jaden and the retired doctor did not understand why Armellya flatlined. Out of the blue, Jaden had a theory of what made her heart stop. Jaden told the retired doctor that according to his report on the rainbow flower, it not only attacked the respiratory system but broke down the muscular system. The retired doctor concurred and then asked Jaden what he was thinking. Jaden told the retired doctor that the pollen in Armellya's lungs might be active because the flowers affected the muscular system as well. Then Jaden pointed out that the heart was the largest muscle in the body, and the flower did prove to affect the women's leg and arm muscles. The women's breathing was affected because the muscles responsible for moving the diaphragm so the lungs would increase in size and then decrease in size to move air were weakened also. Jaden solicited the retired doctor's thoughts about whether while the pollen was being consumed by mucous and traveling up the airway, it could be producing spores that might be able to burrow through soft and cartilaginous tissue on into nearby organs, such as going from the trachea into soft tissue and then the heart.

When Jaden told the retired doctor his thoughts, he put them into simple terms, but he knew the retired doctor could follow the simplicity, making it complex enough to get the visual that Jaden had. The retired doctor was not sure about Jaden's theory because no one knew much about the rainbow flower except the mini-angels, and their knowledge was even somewhat limited. Jaden and the retired doctor left Armellya's room to go to the retired doctor's office so they could sit comfortably and discuss the issues in private. When the two doctors got into the retired doctor's office, Jaden said he could astroproject to the Dinosaur Tail and see what the mini-angels could do to help with the situation. The retired doctor agreed that it was a great idea, so he stood outside of his office, and Jaden astroprojected to the Dinosaur Tail.

Jaden found his mini-angel instantly and asked her for help. The mini-angel said she would help any way she could. Then she asked what was going on. Jaden explained what was happening to Armellya and to the other women. Jaden told his mini-angel his medical theories and then admitted he was unsure of what to do for the women to rid their bodies of the flowers' pollen and possibly spores. The mini-angel told Jaden the flowers' pollen could not produce spores once the pollen entered the body, but it was important to make sure all the pollen was removed somehow. The mini-angel told Jaden Armellya's body was purging the pollen. It would take some time, but she would pull through, and her lungs would be like new. Jaden asked the mini-angel why Armellya went into heart failure, and the mini-angel suggested he check Armellya's cardiac enzymes because she was sure her cardiac enzymes were abnormal and that was a reasonably easy fix. The mini-angel told Jaden to watch all the women's laboratory results closely because they would fluctuate and keeping them regulated would accelerate their recovery. The mini-angel concluded by telling Jaden they were on the right path with Armellya, antibiotics, stable laboratory results, and constant suctioning. Jaden thanked his mini-angel and then went back to his body.

Once Jaden was back in his body, he rushed to the office door and whipped it open. Then he instructed the retired doctor to enter. The retired doctor went into his office and sat down. Jaden sat in the other seat and began to advise the retired doctor all about what the mini-angel had said. Jaden enlightened the retired doctor. They were doing well with Armellya, administering antibiotics, deep suctioning, and monitoring and stabilizing her cardiac enzymes and other laboratory results was just what she needed. Jaden notified the retired doctor that the mini-angel recommended that they monitor the other five women's general laboratory results and keep them stable because they would fluctuate. Jaden informed the retired doctor if the women's blood results were kept within a normal range, they would heal faster. Jaden stated to the retired doctor that the best thing the mini-angel informed him of was that the pollen in Armellya's lungs would not produce spores. The retired doctor expressed to Jaden that the news was magnificent.

The retired doctor had nurses go into the women's rooms and draw blood samples for testing anything and everything so the doctors could see if there was anything to correct. While the nurses were drawing the women's blood, the men stepped out into the hallway to see if Jaden or the retired doctor was near. They each had some questions for them. Neither doctor was in sight, so the men asked the nurses who drew the women's blood if they could call upon the doctors for them, and the nurses assured the men that at least one of the doctors would be there for them soon.

At that point, Andrew commanded the nurse who drew Camillia's blood to retrieve one of the doctors for them to speak to. The nurse got an obstinate expression on her face, but before she could respond, Andrew swiftly apologized for his insolence. The nurse told Andrew and the other three men that the doctors were in the retired doctor's office and would be out momentarily. The nurse also told the men she could relate to the stress that their concern for their wives' well-being placed them under, but they needed to keep in mind that the situation the women were in had never been heard of or dealt with before. Andrew said he was speaking for all the men when he said they were learning about their conditions as they were being treated, and the doctors were doing everything possible, but they were petrified for them and just needed a little encouragement every so often. The nurses all told the men they were there for support as well. They could not replace their wives, but they could be a friend and offer an ear, a shoulder, hugs, and anything else within reason.

All four men thanked the nurses and told them they meant no disrespect; they just were not being themselves because of the circumstances, but they would try to tone down their attitudes. The nurses told the men not to worry; they were used to deviant responses from patients, and it was normal for someone in their position to act atypically. The nurses gave the men sociable hugs and informed them they would be there for them and to let them know if they needed anything. The men acknowledged the nurses. Then the nurses took the women's blood samples to the laboratory.

The men went into their wives' rooms and sat on the chairs next to the heads of their beds to patiently await the doctor's return.

Jaden and the retired doctor become conscious that it was the dinner hour, so they went to the women's rooms to get the other men to sit down to eat and deliberate on their wives' circumstances. Jaden went to two of the rooms while the retired doctor went to the other three rooms, and they all seven walked toward the hospital's cafeteria together. The seven men were headed off by one of the employees of the medical medicine-making room. He instantly notified Jaden they had the three antibiotics for Armellya. Jaden asked the employee how much they had, and he told Jaden enough for three days. The employee alleged they would continue to make the three antibiotics regularly until they were told it was not necessary anymore.

Jaden told the employee that was a wise way of handling the situation, and he would keep them apprised. The employee handed Jaden the first dose of each antibiotic and then went to go have his lunch nutrition. The seven men continued to the hospital's cafeteria. Then they got their food and sat at a table together. The retired doctor told the men their wives were in a more advantageous shape than Armellya, so they did not have to be apprehensive about what happened to her happening to them. Andrew spoke for all the men when he asked how Armellya was doing and what had happened to her. Jaden told the men that Armellya's heart had stopped, but it was due to abnormal levels of natural bodily chemicals responsible for keeping the heart working correctly. Jaden said he had a nurse draw her blood so they could see what was abnormal, and they were able to give Armellya the proper supplements to keep her heart healthy. Jaden told the men that they would periodically draw blood from all the women so they could keep track of their heart and other bodily functions.

Jaden revealed that he had astroprojected to the Dinosaur Tail to find out what the mini-angels knew about getting the women healthy again. The men asked if their wives would ever get back to the state of health they were previously in. The retired doctor told the men that the women would get more wholesome than what they were before. Jaden explained to the men that Armellya had gotten pollen in her lungs by getting extremely close to the rainbow flowers to smell them. The other women had not. The retired doctor told the men that their wives were affected by the deadly flower from a distance so all they needed was to keep their bodies' overall chemistry stable and give them time to regenerate their lung tissue. Armellya needed to rid her lungs of the pollen, have her body chemistry kept stable, and regenerate her lungs.

Jaden told the men their wives would be off the life support quite a bit before Armellya. The retired doctor told the men that if the women were kept stable, the babies would be just fine and the women should be off the life support before the babies were due to be born, but it might be a close call.

Andrew questioned what the retired doctor meant by a close call. He disclosed that at the rate the women were healing, they would be off the life support before delivering the babies if the babies were full term. The retired doctor warned the men that if the babies were not full term, they may have to deliver them while the mothers were on life support, especially if their healing were to slow down. They were all eating their dinner supplement sluggishly because of the conversation, and the dinner hour was nearly complete, but the men still had close to a full plate of food and many more questions for the doctors. The doctors recognized the men still had a lot of concerns and wanted answers, but they requested they save the rest of the conversation until after the dinner hour. The doctors told the men they would meet later but for now to finish their dinner supplementation so they could keep their strength up. The men agreed to eat silently if the doctors would spend some time with them after the dinner hour was completed. The doctors agreed. Ten minutes of eating without a sound marked the conclusion of the dinner hour. The seven men left the hospital's cafeteria and convened in the retired doctor's office.

When the men got near the retired doctor's office, the retired doctor noticed a nurse waiting for him and Jaden. The nurse had a small stack of papers in her hand, and when the group got close to the nurse, she told the doctors she had the five women's laboratory reports. The retired doctor took the papers from the nurse and thanked her for getting the reports to him and Jaden so punctually. After giving the blood results to the doctors, the nurse went back to her station to get her nursing reports over and done with before going home and having a new nurse take over her watch.

Jaden was looking over Armellya's laboratory results and found some results were out of the normal range, which meant he would have to give her more supplemental support. The retired doctor looked over three of the women's laboratory results and found they were borderline normal. Jaden looked at the last two laboratory results for the fourth and fifth women, and they were also borderline normal.

While reviewing the laboratory results, both doctors tried to keep stoic facial expressions, but the men were still on edge to know what the laboratory reports indicated for their wives. All the men watched the doctors with looks of suspense on their faces, and when the doctors did not verbalize what the laboratory results indicated fast enough to give them an idea of how their wives were doing, again, Andrew spoke up for all of them and asked what their wives' blood values gave them the impression of. The retired doctor notified the men whose laboratory values he saw and that they needed mild supplementation, but they were doing fine. Jaden told the other men that their wives were the same; they needed some minor amounts of supplementation, but otherwise, they were doing fine. The men then wanted to know how Armellya was doing, so Jaden told them her blood values showed she needed more supplementation, but if she got it within a reasonable amount of time, she would be fine.

The men wished Armellya good health and then went to the rooms where their wives were and sat in the chairs by the heads of their beds. The retired doctor and Jaden went room to room conveying to the nurses who were posted for each woman what the women needed and to get the supplementation in them the second they got it.

Before one of Armellya's two nurses could leave the room to get her supplementation, Jaden gave them the three antibiotics that were to be administered, with detailed instructions. Both doctors went to the retired doctor's office to write in the women's files and catch up on their notes. Both doctors had to write in each chart. One of the nurses from Armellya's room and the only nurses in the other women's rooms left the rooms to hurriedly get what the women needed so they could get back and get the supplementation infused at once. All the nurses reentered the rooms, and when Armellya's second nurse stepped up to the side of her bed to hang the antibiotics and infuse the nutrition supplements, Armellya started to seize again. One of the nurses stayed with Armellya to ensure she did not accidentally hurt herself or the unborn child while the other nurse went after Jaden and the retired doctor. Armellya's second nurse got near the retired doctor's office rapidly, calling for the doctors as she was approaching. The retired doctor and Jaden stepped out of the office, and when they did, they both noticed the nurse was one of Armellya's. Both doctors took off toward Armellya's room, and as the doctors got to the nurse, she changed direction, heading back to Armellya's room, and was conveying to the doctors that Armellya was actively seizing again.

The nurse, the retired doctor, and Jaden got to Armellya's room, and the nurse who stayed behind with Armellya advised the doctors that she had just discontinued seizing. The retired doctor left the room to go to the medicine cart to draw up two syringes of antiseizure medicine to keep in Armellya's room so if she were to seize again, the nurse could administer one of the syringes.

While the retired doctor was retrieving the medicine, Jaden was checking Armellya's vital signs. They were normal for someone who had just had a seizure, but he noticed Armellya was sweating profusely. Jaden told the nurses to get a cool, wet cloth to wipe Armellya's brow. While one of the nurses was getting a cloth, Jaden took Armellya's temperature and found it was 101 degrees Fahrenheit. The normal temperature for a pale one was only 65 degrees Fahrenheit. Jaden straightaway left Armellya's room to go to the equipment room to get a cooling blanket to put over her. Jaden speculated that she had had a febrile seizure and would have more of them if her body temperature was not brought down rapidly.

While Jaden was getting the cooling blanket, the retired doctor went to go check on the other five women. All five were still getting their supplementation, but they were nearly finished so the retired doctor told the nurses to take another blood sample a couple of hours after the supplementation ended. The nurses acknowledged the retired doctor. While they were keeping an eye on their appointed women and their husbands were keeping vigil, the retired doctor went back to his office to try to complete his notes in the women's charts.

Meanwhile, Jaden returned to Armellya's room with the cooling blanket and draped it over her. Jaden felt that the cooling blanket could keep Armellya's temperature down, but he was not sure how rapidly it would drop her temperature. He was concerned about Armellya having another febrile seizure, so to try to avoid that, he instructed the nurses to go make some ice bags so they could place them in strategic places on her body.

Jaden said he would stay with her and for the nurses to work with haste. They left Armellya's room together, and on the way to the ice room, they grabbed two other nurses who did not appear to be doing anything to go with them. At first, all four nurses were packing bags of ice, and then halfway through the packing, one nurse ran as many ice bags as she could carry to Armellya's room. After giving Jaden the ice bags she had, she went back to the ice room. As she was headed back to the ice room, she passed one of the other nurses who was packing ice headed for Armellya's room. Armellya's two nurses had their arms full of ice bags and headed for Armellya's room. They excused the other two nurses and thanked them for their help. The extra two nurses told Armellya's two nurses to let them know if they needed anything and they would be prepared to help. Armellya's nurses thanked the extra two nurses again and replied they would keep their offer in mind.

Armellya's two nurses made it back into her room and placed the ice bags they had in the strategic spots used in medicine to abruptly drop an individual's body temperature. Jaden made sure there were enough ice bags and that they were all in the correct places and then covered Armellya with the cooling blanket. Jaden told Armellya's two nurses that he appreciated their brisk response with the ice bags. Then the two nurses told Jaden they had drafted two other nurses to assist in bagging and running the ice bags. Jaden told them that the situation with Armellya had taught him how important nurses were, and he had not always treated the nurses as they ought to be treated, but from then on out, he would treasure what the nursing staff did for the doctors.

Jaden advised the nurses that he had some paperwork he really needed to get done so he was going to the retired doctor's office and to come there if they needed him for anything. The nurses reassured Jaden they would keep a close eye on Armellya and her temperature and told him to just go do what he needed to do. Jaden left Armellya's room and went to the retired doctor's office. He found the retired doctor was nearly finished with his portion of the reports.

Jaden took the charts that the retired doctor had done already and started his part. The retired doctor had organized all his reports shortly after Jaden started, so he laid his head on his desk and proceeded to nap. It took quite some time, but Jaden achieved his portion of the reports in every chart so he decided to go to Armellya's room and nap on the sleeping cot. It had been two hours since all five of the women had finished receiving their supplemental infusions, so it was time for the nurses to draw laboratory blood work as the doctors had instructed them to do.

One of Armellya's nurses left the room to get the things she needed to do the blood draw. While the one nurse was retrieving the blood draw items, the other was taking Armellya's temperature and found it was sixty-eight degrees Fahrenheit, which was only three degrees off, and that was good timing, because the ice bags were melted and needed to be removed. The other nurse returned. She got Armellya's arm ready to place the needle into it, but Armellya awoke and started to flail about and yelp. This was not supposed to happen. Armellya had been getting regular doses of medicine to keep her in a medical coma. The commotion woke Jaden, and when he realized Armellya was awake but not completely alert, he scurried to the medicine cart and collected the medicines necessary to put Armellya back under.

Once the medicine was injected into Armellya's intravenous line, it took fifteen seconds to put her back under. The nurse finally got her blood samples and took the tubes to the laboratory for testing. Because Armellya woke up, Jaden wanted to examine the other five women to make sure they would not awaken. The other women were not awake, but they were moving about a great deal, and this was indicative of them starting to awaken from their medically induced comas.

Jaden gave the other women some more medicine to make certain they would not wake up; then their nurses took their blood samples. Armellya's screaming woke the retired doctor up so he went to evaluate the situation with all five women, and Jaden filled him in on what had occurred. Then he stayed in the room with Armellya. The men did not understand why their wives needed extra medicine or how Armellya woke up when none of that was supposed to happen. The retired doctor informed the men the women were getting the minimum amount of medicine to keep them in a comatose state, and they may have acclimated to the amount of medicine they were getting, which meant they would have to have a minute amount more to keep them under. The retired doctor advised the men they were trying to give the women as little medicine as possible because anything they got the babies would get also.

The men were concerned for the babies being in a medically induced coma also, and the retired doctor assured the men their babies were okay. The retired doctor told the men there was a fetal monitor on all the women to allow them to know how the babies were doing. It tracked the babies' heart rates and movement. The fetal monitors currently used were much more sophisticated than what the humans had used.

The retired doctor told the men they would be doing another ultrasound on the women soon, as that was a regular thing he and Jaden had been doing. Then the retired doctor offered to let the men watch and study their babies intrauterine. The men were inspired to get to observe their unborn babies, and they told the retired doctor that it would be breathtaking to watch. The retired doctor would perform Armellya's ultrasound while Jaden observed. For the time being, the retired doctor called Jaden out of Armellya's room to do the ultrasound on two of the women while he did the ultrasound on the other three. Jaden did not mind accommodating the retired doctor's orders, as this was one of the few heartwarming parts of being a doctor.

Jaden did the ultrasounds on Camillia and Melanie. Andrew, the chief, and Michael were stunned to see their unborn babies. Jaden did an extra-long ultrasound for Andrew and Michael to watch the babies move about. During the ultrasounds, Andrew and Michael put their hands on their wives' bellies, and the babies gravitated toward their hands as if they knew the touch was their father's. When Jaden finished the ultrasounds, the men thanked him for letting them bond with their children. Jaden told Andrew and Michael he was pleased to see them interact with their children, and the expressions on their faces were indescribable. Jaden hugged Andrew and Michael and then went to Armellya's room to watch the retired doctor do her ultrasound.

The retired doctor did Bridgette's, Sharonna's, and Michelle's ultrasounds so Matthew, the chief, and Allen could watch their children move about. They too touched their wives' bellies during the ultrasounds, and those babies gravitated toward their father's hands also. The men were all feeling sentimental and were content seeing their children. Each man stayed in the room their wives were in and decided to settle down on their sleeping cots. The retired doctor entered Armellya's room and then prepared to do Armellya's ultrasound so Jaden went around to the other side of her bed from where the retired doctor was. When the retired doctor got the ultrasound machine on Armellya's belly, the baby was not moving, but there was a sufficient heartbeat. The retired doctor pushed on Armellya's belly to try to wake the baby, but that did not work. Jaden laid his hand on Armellya's belly and talked to the baby. Then she woke up and moved to Jaden's hand. The retired doctor and Jaden saw great movement at that point, and they both assumed the child was just sleeping. Jaden became emotional while watching the baby; the whole situation with the women was finally starting to wear on him.

The retired doctor was aware of Jaden's state of mind because of telepathy, so the retired doctor told him he was there for him. Jaden confessed that he was aware his wife would pull through the horrible floral attack, but it still seemed hopeless because of the long amount of time she had already been sick. The retired doctor told Jaden he needed to keep hope, and he would help him do that. Jaden told the retired doctor he was appreciative of his offer of support, but what he really needed was to see some improvement in Armellya's condition. The retired doctor told Jaden there was some improvement. She had less mucous to suction, and there was still some wheezing in her lungs, but she did have clearer lung sounds than she had at the beginning of her treatment. Jaden was sure the retired doctor was truthful with him, but he wanted full testing done on Armellya to see what her condition was now compared to what it had been when she was originally brought in. The retired doctor told Jaden that was in fact a valuable idea, and it would be good to do the same with the other women.

The retired doctor called second nurses to assist the nurses with the other women, who only had one nurse watching over them, to transport them to other parts of the hospital. When all the nurses were with the women who were supposed to be there, the retired doctor told them what tests were to be done, so they knew where to take the women.

It was very near the hour of sleep for the evening, so

the retired doctor advised Jaden to get some rest while the women were getting their tests done because it was going to take a considerable amount of time before they were returned to their rooms. Jaden knew it would take a little more time after the women were returned to their rooms before the test results would be prepared for reading. Jaden informed the retired doctor he would lie down on the sleeping cot and try to get some rest, but he was not sure how much rest he was going to get because his mind was tremendously active still. The retired doctor reminded Jaden of what he had told the men about requiring adequate and regular sleep for the body to heal and recover from the day.

Jaden admitted he needed some sleep, but he wanted to check on the women's biopsies before the reports came back from their current testing so he would have an idea of what the reports would reveal. The retired doctor knew Jaden would not take a break until he knew how the women were doing now. The retired doctor accompanied Jaden to the forensics room to view the lung biopsies. While Jaden was primarily interested in Armellya's biopsy, the retired doctor started to view the other women's. Jaden examined Armellya's biopsy for two minutes and was startled as he observed the lung tissue regenerate. Jaden detected that there had already been some phenomenal amounts of regeneration. The fact that the lung tissue was still alive was a marvel, and Jaden wanted the retired doctor to inspect the microscope slide to verify he was seeing what he thought he was seeing. Jaden's hopes were so high that he was not sure if his eyes were playing tricks on him. The retired doctor checked the lung tissue through the microscope lens and was also astonished at what he saw. The lung tissue had come close to a fully regenerated state and was still showing signs of regeneration. The retired doctor confirmed to Jaden that he saw what he thought he saw. The two doctors knew that if Armellya's lung tissue was doing so well, that the other women's lung tissue must be fully healed.

The two doctors got the other women's lung samples and started studying them through the microscope. They found they were fully healed, as they had thought they would be. The doctors knew that the lung samples they viewed under the microscope were just pieces of the lungs; the women each had a whole lung, so the rational thought would be that there would still be some regeneration going on in their lungs. The retired doctor and Jaden considered the women's need for the ventilators to be set so high. The two doctors felt it was time for the women's ventilators to be turned down some. The retired doctor expressed to Jaden that it was best for the women's lungs to gradually be given the opportunity to take over their function rather than doing it all at once and possibly setting them up for failure. Both doctors went back to the women's rooms so they could recalculate the ventilators right away when they were returned to their rooms.

When Jaden crossed the threshold of Armellya's room and the retired doctor checked in the rooms of the other women, they were startled to see they were back already. The doctors recognized they were in the forensics room longer than they had originally thought, but they felt it was for the best. The doctors had some tremendously pleasing news for the men. They reduced the settings on the women's ventilators and then told the nurses in their rooms to keep a cautious watch over them. The doctors informed the nurses that they had decreased the ventilator settings, and the nurses reported to the doctors that they would guard the women attentively. The men were all sleeping well, so the doctors debated whether to wake the men for the splendid news or wait until morning. They decided to wait for morning and let the men get a good night's sleep.

Jaden finally lay down on his sleeping cot to get some quality sleep while the retired doctor went back to his office. The retired doctor sat in his desk chair and tilted it against the back wall; then he went to sleep.

The charge nurse with Armellya perceived that there was less and less mucous to suction, and she was not sure if the mucous production was diminishing or if it was not being expelled, which would mean it was essentially drowning Armellya. The charge nurse was apprehensive to wake Jaden, but it was better to be safe than sorry, so she did. Once Jaden was fully alert and sitting up on the sleeping cot, he asked if there was something wrong with Armellya, and the charge nurse told Jaden she was not sure. Jaden asked the charge nurse to clarify her suspicious findings, so she told him about the scarcity of mucous that day compared to what they had been getting out of her the previous day. The charge nurse said it was too radical of a change for the brief amount of time that had passed, and she was concerned about the mucous building up in Armellya's lungs. Jaden told the charge nurse that Armellya was most likely producing a reduced amount of mucous, but if the change was as extraordinary as she said, he would check her test results from earlier.

Jaden and the retired doctor had gone to sleep without looking over the women's test results and had made the decision to lower their ventilators based on the vivid positive change in their tissue samples. Jaden told the charge nurse he was going to check the test results on Armellya and the rest of the women right away. Then he left the room on the double. Jaden went unswervingly to the retired doctor's office to get the reports.

When Jaden entered the retired doctor's office, he found him sleeping, so he tried to find the reports noiselessly. Jaden was unable to find the reports, so he felt he needed to wake the retired doctor because he thought it critical that he review Armellya's report just in case her lungs were filling up with mucous instead of expelling it. Armellya's condition was much like that of a deadly case of human pneumonia, and there had been documented cases where some humans' lungs had filled with fluid and some of those humans died from it. Armellya's case was not truly pneumonia, however; it was a reaction to the pollen of the rainbow flower. The retired doctor finally awakened enough to respond to Jaden's request for the test results, so he elected to review them with him.

Armellya's results were miraculous. Her lungs were nearly regenerated and had truly stopped producing the copious amounts of mucous. Jaden went on to review some of the other women's test results and found them to be in more of a restored shape than Armellya's, but both doctors had expected that. It became even more obvious than before that the other women would be off their ventilators before Armellya was off hers. Both doctors were very pleased with the test results. They were healthier than they had expected. At first, the women's immune systems were lethargic, but over time, they became resilient and were now accelerated as a pale one's immune system should be.

The doctors were going to go back to sleep but heard

the hospital's hallways getting busy. That was an indication of the morning hour being upon them. The retired doctor checked his desk clock, and it confirmed it was the waking hour, which meant the breakfast hour would be there soon. He recommended to Jaden that they get breakfast nutrition with the men and deliver the wholesome news about their wives at that time so they could start their day off pleasantly. Jaden agreed with the retired doctor and then said he was going to the hospital's washroom to clean up for the new day, and he would be back momentarily. The retired doctor nodded, and then Jaden left the office.

On his way to the hospital's washroom, Jaden spotted the men waking up, so he figured on his way back to the retired doctor's office he would let the men know they needed to get breakfast nutrition with him and the retired doctor.

Jaden had washed up and was on the way back to the retired doctor's office when he saw the retired doctor telling the men to join them for the breakfast hour. The men agreed even though they did not know there was an encouraging update for them.

The men were finally ready for the day, and the breakfast hour was close enough to head on down to the hospital's cafeteria. The retired doctor and Jaden went to the women's rooms to gather all the men, and then they all headed for the cafeteria. They got their meals, sat at one of the tables, and then started to eat in silence. The retired doctor and Jaden were looking at each other. Then Jaden nodded at the retired doctor. He was going to tell the men the latest news about their wives. The men picked up on something going on between the retired doctor and Jaden, but they did not know what it was. The chief broke the silence by asking what was going on. The retired doctor told the men he and Jaden had some fabulous news for them. The men stopped eating and gave the retired doctor their undivided attention. He told the men he and Jaden had taken another look at the women's lung tissue samples, and they surprisingly found them still living. The retired doctor went on to tell the men that the samples were not just alive but had practically regenerated. Jaden told the men that the women would be off the ventilators within the week and that he and the retired doctor had turned their ventilators down the previous evening and the women had tolerated it very well. The retired doctor said he and Jaden would be turning the ventilators down again after the breakfast hour.

The chief noticed that the doctors were referring to their wives and excluding Armellya, so he inquired about her. Jaden said Armellya was making some great progress but had more healing to do than the other women, so she would be on the ventilator longer. The men asked when the doctors would start to let the women wake up from their medically induced comas. The retired doctor told the men not until their lungs were ready to function without the ventilator, but it would not be very much longer. All the men thanked the doctors for their vigilance because the men knew neither doctor had slept the whole time the women had been in the hospital. The doctors had gotten a few naps in, but it was in shifts. The men thanked the doctors for giving them such hope and starting their day out with good news.

The doctors planned to make their first rounds right after the breakfast hour, and during that time, the doctors would give each man the specifics of how his wife was doing and a detailed prognosis.

The breakfast hour had another ten minutes, but the men excused themselves from the table and then left the cafeteria. The men convened in the hallway to discuss getting a home-cooked meal delivered to the hospital for them and the doctors. The men would send for Melanie's father to put something together. The men suddenly realized they had not been sending word home to their wives' parents, and they must be worried sick about their daughters. The men decided to send word with Melanie's father to the other parents about their daughters and let them know they could stop by. An important thing to let the women's parents know was that there were a lot of machines and tubes around them, and it looked scary, but they should not let that stop them from visiting unless they could not handle the fright of the life-support setup.

The chief went to the nurses' desk before going into Sharonna's room to have the hospital's runner retrieve Melanie's father. The acting charge nurse summoned the runner and said she would send him into Sharonna's room when he got to the desk. The chief thanked her and then went to Sharonna's room. Right after the chief sat on the chair at the head of Sharonna's bed, the runner made an entrance in the room and declared he was reporting for duty.

The chief asked the runner to go to the castle and fetch Melanie's father and have him present himself at the hospital. The runner said he would depart at once and then did just that. Twenty-five minutes later, the runner revisited the chief and had Melanie's father with him, so the chief stepped out into the hallway to chat with him. Before communicating with Melanie's father, the chief thanked the runner and excused him to go. The chief requested that Melanie's father wait while he got the rest of the men, and he agreed to do so.

The chief went room to room getting the men out to the hallway. Now that all the men were in front of Melanie's father, they asked him about making a lunch to be brought to the hospital for them and the doctors. Melanie's father thought that was a splendid idea and said to consider it done. Now that the next meal was taken care of, the chief told Melanie's father he could pay a visit to her. He warned him it appeared grim, but she was doing great. Melanie's father did go in to visit her and talk sentimentally to her. Then he gave her kisses on the forehead.

Before Melanie's father left, the men told him to let the other parents know their daughters were doing terrifically well. Melanie's father said he would urge the parents to show up and chat with the doctors about their daughters and then go to see their daughters. The men thanked Melanie's father for the lunch he was going to bring and for relaying their messages. He told them it was his pleasure and then left.

The men noticed the doctors strolling up the hallway toward them and were relieved they did not see Melanie's father because they wanted the home-cooked meal to be a surprise for the doctors. The retired doctor went into the first woman's room to make clear to her husband her exact status while Jaden went into the second woman's room to do the same. The retired doctor went into the third room, Jaden went into the fourth room, and then retired doctor went into the fifth room, and soon all the husbands were clear on their wives' specific conditions. While the doctors were consulting with the husbands, they were turning the women's ventilators down some more, and that was a satisfying sight to the men.

A couple of hours had passed by, and it was time to medicate the women so they did not awaken, but the doctors were hesitant because they felt it was about time to let them become alert so their ventilators could be removed. The doctors still wondered if it was a couple of days too early, so they decided to give the women half the dose of medicine instead so they would stay relaxed but not comatose. Armellya was the exception; she had longer to stay on the ventilator because of her direct exposure to the rainbow flower. It was remarkably fortunate that the other women did not get the direct exposure also. As the doctors went to the women's rooms to administer their medicine, they told the men that the women would start to become somewhat aware of their surroundings within a couple of hours, but they would not be fully alert. The men were motivated to hear that their wives were closer to being off the ventilators. The doctors had told the men that the women were close to being off the ventilators, but now it was just becoming a reality for them. Armellya had completed her series of antibiotic treatments but still had to have her white count monitored closely.

The doctors did not think Armellya's white count would rise again because of her stage of recovery, but they were having her blood drawn every six hours because as rapidly as she healed, she could regress. Time had gone by swiftly this day because of all the additional information and changes with the women. The lunch hour sneaked up on everybody. The doctors were being called to the nurses' desk, and they could not imagine why, so they hurriedly went in case it was something to do with one of the women. When they got to the nurses' desk, the men were gathered there, and right in the middle of the men were Melanie's parents.

At first, the doctors thought they were there to get the latest news on Melanie, and then they noticed all the food. The men called out, "Surprise!" Then Melanie's parents told the doctors the men felt it was time for some gourmet food. The doctors thanked Melanie's parents, and they were very surprised. They had definitely missed the first-class food. The hospital's cafeteria food was okay, but because it was made for everyone, they made it bland so everyone could eat it.

Printed in the United States
By Bookmasters